Inhab

A Story Like No Other

NIGEL JOSLIN

To Laura,

Hope you enjoy it!

Nigel x

Copyright © 2025 Nigel Joslin

All rights reserved.

ISBN: 9798305662764

Android—a robot that has been designed to look like a human being and programmed to behave like one.

CONTENTS

Author's Notes

Prologue i

Title Pg 1
About the Author Pg 339

AUTHOR'S NOTES

Disclaimer

This book is a work of fiction. As such, if any person mentioned within it bears any resemblance to anyone living, it is entirely coincidental.

An agency that actually exists in real life is mentioned in this story. However, any incidents involving them or methods of operation used in this story are purely the product of my imagination.

Acknowledgements

I would like to thank my dear wife, Sue, for her invaluable advice when I reviewed the book. And also extend a heartfelt thanks to my proofreader.

In addition, I am indebted to Amazon KDP for making the production and marketing of this book possible.

PROLOGUE

'Ambulance! As soon as possible!!'

Sergei gripped his phone clammily as he snapped out the request. Shooting frantic glances all around the busy scene.

A beep.

Followed by two clicks.

'Hello?' he urged the sounds, his ears straining for something more enlightening.

'Ambulance service,' announced a sudden, crisp voice. 'What's the address of the emergency?'

The Russian hissed an expletive in his native tongue. Following up with a faltering 'erm...' and another eye-dart around the busy street.

'I don't know,' he confessed, his heart now racing. 'It's a car accident. And the woman is hurt. Badly.'

'Right. Can you see a street name or anything like that?'

'One minute...' Turning to the gathering crowd, he bellowed, 'Please! Can anyone tell me where we are, the street name?'

Time froze aggressively, trapping Sergei in a void of

muzzy and helpless non-action. Until a confident, competent voice brought instant focus to the dithery air.

'This is Shaftsbury Avenue, mate. And that there's Curzon Street.'

Shaftsbury.

Curzon.

Urgently but calmly, Sergei addressed the phone again. His eyes fixed rigidly on the tangle of limbs lying below him.

'We are near meeting of Shaftsbury Avenue and Curzon Street.' He suddenly raised his eyes and frowned across the street. 'And there's a building on the other side of the road, a cinema, I think.'

'Right, good.'

'Please, she has been hit by a car and is hurt very bad.'

'Right, sir, an ambulance is already on its way. Is she responsive and breathing normally?'

'Concussed, maybe. Breathing, er…difficult.'

A timely gurgle seized his attention as she started to unfold. Distracting him from the telephone-voice that was asking for the woman's approximate age.

'Fifties, I would say. Tell the ambulance to hurry.'

A strained and awful cry escaped the dry lips down below. Followed by a stare that seemed to recede in despair from Sergei yet cling to his soul like a limpet.

'Help me,' came a moan.

'The ambulance is nearly here,' soothed Sergei gently, dropping down onto his knees beside her and reaching for her hand.

'It should be with you in under five minutes now,' declared the voice in the phone.

'Not long now,' he assured the victim.

The desperate eyes fell shut again and Sergei closed his own. The road beneath his shins digging in with renewed hardness.

Suddenly feeling very, very foreign.

1

'Hello?'

Only the deep, black silence replied. By seeming to gulp away the question.

Something...

She didn't know what, but it was definitely there. Sharing the darkness with her. Violating her air.

Up came her hand. Furtive, fearing being seen as it groped in vain along the wall.

Where the hell had that damn light cord gone?

She gave up, instead raising a slow, fearful head from the pillow. But all that could be made out was the feeble, grey glow that was trying its best to oblige her by squeezing past the edges of the heavy old curtains. The final act of a late May twilight hanging on by its finger tips.

Ugh!

A prickly realisation skittered through her.

It was starting.

Down there.

That was where it was going to happen. Just beyond the end of the bed. Just like it used to. Just like...

A sudden, sharp crack rang out. Making her contract with fear.

But then...

So sweet was the wave of relief that she expelled a little laugh.

She'd amplified a red herring into a red whale. All it had been was the stirring of centuries-old timber that had yet to bed down fully for the night. Something perfectly natural.

Unlike what was going on down *there*.

She tightened again.

The dilemma...part of her needing to face it whilst the other, larger part yearned for the sanctuary of a tug on the unfindable light cord.

What to do.

All of a sudden, the decision had been made. And she had rolled onto her front and buried her face into the pillow. Screwing it up, her eyes tightly closed as she willed the intrusion to go away.

Alas, she should have known better. It was even more intense now. Swelling with purpose.

Screwing her face up even more, she squeaked into the polyester depths. And then acquiesced, resigned to the inevitable.

This was how it was going to be again.

Clearly, she was very much back.

She knew the score. First would be the actual encounter. To be followed a few hours later by the worst bit.

The dreams.

'Dreams,' she rasped huskily as she rolled back onto her back.

The tension within her was on a mission now. Heaving her chest in great big, stressed huffs. Threatening to give panic a free reign.

But, no.

No, no!

She set her jaw resolutely.

Remember who you are – Shona McShane! It may have been a few years, but you've dealt with this before. Many times.

Slowly, pluckily, she raised her head. Opening her eyes to their widest.

To let it all in.

Despite her preparedness, she flinched. At the otherworldliness of what was before her, a tremor so slight yet so *very* significant.

A presence about to claim its space in reality.

From out of nowhere.

2

A red hot spasm of embarrassment seared its way through Richie's innards. The realisation that he was no longer alone in his safe haven where nobody else ever came.

God dammit, this was unbelievable! It had to be *today* of all days!!

Fate really had it in for him.

Ordinarily it wouldn't have been a problem. Indeed, he would have welcomed an exchange of friendly words with a newcomer, his lunchtimes on this beach being relaxed affairs in the purifying company of a glorious sea view.

But today's was not one of those lunchtimes. The view had been smashed out of existence by giant waves of frustration that were in dire need of being vented.

And why not, when he had a whole beach to himself?

The trouble was, he no longer did.

Muttering under his breath, he reigned in his next ill-tempered kick at the piles of washed up seaweed and instead just continued walking. His shame stricken countenance turned towards the non-judgemental sea.

He dare not look round, unsure of how much of his

inner invective had escaped his lips. That was the trouble with time spent in solitude, his thoughts became voices whether he spoke them or not.

Hopefully he could make an escape, though. All it would take would be to increase his speed while continuing to look away as if utterly absorbed by the sight of the sea.

A hope sent to oblivion by the sound of a closer stumble in the shingle. The surprising and unwelcome fact that the visitor was heading his way.

It was no good; he simply had to know. Just the slightest of peeps would do it.

He prayed for it to be some rough-looking bloke, the sort of person who'd think nothing of Richie's boorish behaviour. Maybe even approve of it.

Alas...groan of all groans as he took in the wavy tumbles of auburn hair. And movement of excruciating grace.

Such was the nature of his luck.

With his embarrassment sharpening, he looked back at the sea, set on walking faster. Too late, though. A surprisingly breezy greeting pinned his feet to the sand.

Slowly, reluctantly, his feelings in an agonised huddle, he turned to face the approaching figure.

She must have noticed, surely. She'd been quite distant, but on such a quiet and beautiful beach he must have stood out like a stonking great wart.

And yet...

He couldn't believe it. There was even an aura of friendliness about her.

But then Richie noticed the smartphone that she was clutching, and a cautious little ray of hope started shining. If he'd been *really* lucky, she'd have been buried in it like almost everyone seemed to be these days.

Thinking about it, she must have been, otherwise she'd have been off in the opposite direction.

'Lovely day for it,' floated amiably through the air.

For 'it'.

What, for angrily flipping out in public?

Stop it, she didn't notice, she didn't notice, an inner comforter urged Richie. *Everything's alright.*

Trying not to sound as tight and congealed as he still felt, he panted a sheepish agreement down at the patterned white blouse now closing in on him.

All of a sudden she was very much in proximity, filling Richie with an urgent need to look elsewhere. But what was meant to be a hurried flick of a glance at her eyes had him captured in a beam of forget-me-not blue.

'Beautiful, isn't it?'

A dangerous flicker ran through his innards.

Beautiful. Yes, that was certainly the word. That smile was what sunshine was to a beach walk.

An 'mmm' of agreement slipped out from somewhere in his background. His foreground being preoccupied with the question of how he'd failed to notice her earlier.

He must have been *really* deep in his ire.

'It's so *wonderful* being back here,' came a chirp. 'There's something about this place, don't you think?'

Richie muttered his own allegiance to it.

'It's almost a year ago to the day that I was last here on this beach, you know, and it was *just* the same then. Lovely, sunny and calm.'

'Oh. Good,' Richie commented, his embarrassment starting to cool off in the face of her easy chattiness.

'I had to move down south a few years ago, you see, for work. But that's gone and dried up now, so here I am again.'

'Oh, dear.' Richie averted his eyes sympathetically, trying not to think about the long, curved slenderness of leg suddenly filling his awareness. 'I'm sorry to hear that.'

'No, no, it's great being back. West Galloway is where I belong, where I *should* be. With my dad.'

'Oh. Right.'

'I've always had to come back home for a visit, every year, and I never miss out this beach. It's in my blood, a childhood thing. It's where Dad taught me to swim, you see. The shallow water's perfect.'

'I see.'

'I find I can really be myself here, let myself go.'

Richie suppressed an urge to admit that he could too, settling instead for a bland little cough.

'So how about you?'

Inquisitiveness had suddenly replaced her enthusiastic gushing.

'Me?'

'Aye, do you live around here, or are you on a holiday that's gone wrong?'

Richie hesitated.

'Gone wrong?'

'Aye, you weren't exactly sounding ecstatic just now, you know.'

The reveal.

It had come from nowhere, hitting him with all the subtlety of a poke in the eye. Leaving him blushing like a schoolboy caught in the act.

'Ahem,' he muttered. 'Sorry about that.'

'Well,' she smirked, her eyes sparkling, 'we all have our moments.'

'Yes. Yes, we do,' Richie blurted, his fresh surge of embarrassment finding safety in indignation. 'Especially if we've had a nightmare of a morning in *that* place.' He flicked a glare towards the group of buildings frowning concretely down onto the far end of the beach. '*You'd* need to let off steam as well, if you'd had a morning there.'

'Ah.'

'Yes, *ah!* This is the daily sixty minutes maximum I get in the sane world.'

At that, his fellow beach walker threw the complex a gratifyingly disdainful glance.

'Well, I can certainly imagine how it could be a nightmare-of-a-morning sort of place,' she scoffed. 'It's got all the charm of a nuclear bunker with windows. I mean, it's hardly in keeping with the area, is it?'

Richie was suddenly starting to like her.

'What King Charles would have called a carbuncle,' he nodded, feeling much more at ease now.

'Quite! I remember the place from last time I came up. Newly built, according to the village grapevine.' She regarded him quizzically. 'Is it true that it's some kind of research place?'

'Yes, it is. AI and Androids, that sort of thing. It's a subsidiary of HuTech Robotics in London. You may have heard of them.'

'I *can't* say I have, to be honest.' The blue eyes were glittering again. 'But then robotics isn't really my thing, to be honest.'

'I'm not sure it's mine, either,' muttered Richie in a flat, soulless voice.

'It must be interesting work, though,' she countered with a hint of a grin. 'When it's not driving you nuts.'

'I suppose it has its moments,' Richie acknowledged reluctantly, 'although they've been thin on the ground for quite some time.'

'Oh, dear. I'm sorry to hear that. But hopefully things will change, given time. The ebb and flow of life, and all that.'

Richie shrugged resignedly.

'Well, I just wish it would hurry up. This current ebb seems everlasting. But at least I have this lovely beach to restore my sanity in the middle of the day. It's always my friend no matter what's happening in the rest of my life.'

'Good for you,' she beamed, setting his insides off again.

Richie gazed at her dreamily.

How could this possibly be happening? The angriest, emptiest, hollowest man in the world was now chatting with this beautiful, compassionate woman as if they were the best of friends.

Why was she even giving such a seaweed-kicking grouch the time of day?

Suddenly he realised she was in flow again.

'...and of course Shoreholm itself isn't bad for a stroll.' She waved an enthusiastic thumb in the direction of the village. 'Especially for me, being as it's where I spent my childhood. Have you ever walked around it?'

'Yes, I have,' he replied, adding as if proof were required, 'There's that nice little church. And, of course, the wonderful old Gothic house in the square.'

A knowing look flashed through her forget-me-nots.

'Aye, it does look a wee bit Gothic. A touch Romanesque even, in parts. Even though it's sixteenth century.'

'I heard it is meant to be haunted,' Richie ventured, a half-smirk tugging at his lips.

'You did?' She regarded him with what felt like mildly transcendent amusement. 'Well, you're dead right there.'

He chuckled. 'Very droll.'

'No, *really!* I happen to know for a fact that it is haunted, because I was living in that house up to less than ten years ago. And now I am living there again.'

Richie gaped at her in astonishment.

'Really?'

'Yep.' She paused briefly to allow Richie some digestion time. Then adding teasingly, 'And before you ask, the answer to your next question is a resounding "yes".'

A freaky little thrill zipped through Richie's innards.

'You mean...?'

'I do indeed mean...,' she glinted mischievously.

A ticking, almost time-bomb silence fell.

'So, you're saying...saying that you've actually *seen* the ghost?'

Shona's lips curled into a knowing smile.

'Numerous times. Usually at the end of my bed. Sometimes even sitting on it. And my dad sees her, too, just the same, at the end of his bed.'

'Blimey!'

Richie knitted his brow, wondering how to phrase his next question. But his companion jumped in first.

'Though I've assumed here that you do actually *believe* in ghosts.'

'Well...I don't really know.' Richie spread his arms slightly, opening outstretched palms to the sky. 'I'm, shall we say, open-minded?'

The blues had suddenly grown little spears of suspicion.

'Would that be a euphemism for "try not to disbelieve", by any chance?'

'No, it wouldn't be, actually,' Richie retorted, irked a little. 'It means I don't discount things without good reason. And having had no experience of ghosts, I don't dismiss them as imagination or fantasy.'

'Good. I'm glad to hear that. I don't normally tell people I've only just met about this because it's an invitation to cynicism. But you seem...' She paused, her expression suddenly a little awkward.

'Open minded?' suggested Ritchie with a trace of wry amusement.

'Touché,' she grinned, running a casual hand through the wavy flow of auburn. 'But seriously, I'm telling you the truth.'

'I know you are.' Richie peered into the earnest eyes again. 'I can tell.'

'Thank you,' she replied in a satisfied tone.

A new thought zeroed in on Richie.

'So…I'm just wondering, if you don't mind me asking, how the ghost looked. I mean, was it translucent and glowy? Or solid, like a real person?'

'Solid,' came the unhesitating reply. 'At least, sort of, bearing in mind the dark shadowiness of the room.'

'So she only comes at night.'

'Yes. And looks like a normal person sitting there… except she isn't.'

'No.'

'And I can smell her, would you believe? How real is that?'

Richie shot her a stare.

'*Smell* her?'

She nodded.

'She has a scent about her. Nothing strong, mind you. But distinctive, definitely distinctive. Though in a subtle way. Sort of woody, if you know what I mean.'

A slightly strangled chuckle escaped Richie's lips and he shook his head from side to side.

'I must say, I'd never imagined for one minute that you could actually smell a ghost!'

'Well,' the woman shrugged, 'I can assure you I can.'

Richie fell into a contemplative silence.

'You're thinking,' she glimmered. 'I can hear the cogs turning from here.'

'I was just wondering what actually happens with a ghost sighting,' he divulged.

'What happens?'

'Yes. Is it that you're somehow seeing back in time, I wonder? I mean, a dead person wouldn't just hang around where they'd died for years and years, surely.'

'Au contraire, they are really there! It's the person's soul retaining their bodily image. And as for hanging around for years and years, a disembodied soul would have a completely different concept of time to us.'

'Hmm. You seem very sure of your facts.'

'Well, my cousin Gavin got in with a medium, you see. And she said ghosts are normally people who can't move on for some reason.'

'Can't move on?'

'Aye. Perhaps they don't even know that they've died, if their death was sudden and unexpected. Or maybe with some of them it's that they can't stand the thought of leaving their physical life behind. *Or* it could be that a person is desperate to reconcile some unresolved situation that was dominating their life.'

'I see.' Richie's eyes wandered over her curiously. 'You've obviously looked into this quite a bit.'

'Well, wouldn't you if you'd seen a ghost?'

Richie hesitated before admitting that, yes, he would.

'There you are, then.'

He smirked, replying evasively, 'Bet it scared you out of your wits the first time, though.'

'Too right! It *literally* made my flesh crawl. And my hairs raise, all of that stuff. And I could hear my heart thump-thump-thumping in my ears.'

'I'm not surprised.'

'I could really *feel* her presence, if you know what I mean. Not just see and smell her. I tell you, I couldn't move! I was paralysed with fear.'

'I'm sure I'd've been exactly the same.'

'And then, all of a sudden, she was no longer there. I never saw her disappear; it just somehow happened.'

'Hmm.' Richie crinkled his brow thoughtfully again. 'So what about the next few nights? It must have been *really* bad turning in for bed.'

'Aye, I had to leave the light on for nights afterwards, but even then I felt all creeped up. But I didn't see her again for weeks. Long enough for me to start to wonder, actually.'

'Wonder?'

'You know, doubt myself. Doubt it had really

happened. I never believed in ghosts before it happened, you see. I wasn't really that sort of person.'

'Oh, I see,' nodded Richie, keeping his expression blank. 'You mean you were one of those *closed*-minded people, the type who don't even try not to disbelieve?'

She lifted her nose in mock affront.

'It's fine not believing things, Mister Perfect. As long as you are prepared to change your mind in the light of new evidence.'

Richie tittered. 'Just teasing.'

'Well, I suppose I did ask for that one.'

'You did. Seriously though, it's been fascinating hearing about your experience.'

A comment that earned him an appreciative smile.

'I've often wondered about life beyond death,' Richie continued thoughtfully. 'And I *do* believe in it. Otherwise, what's the point of this life, all the stuff we learn and do? I mean, it'd all be just a pointless waste if life just fizzled out for good after your three score and ten. I *can't* believe that.' He paused for a short snigger. 'But, of course, the trouble with life is that what we know to be true so often turns out not to be true at all.'

'Agreed on that last point,' she smirked, 'but don't forget I *do* have actual evidence of life after death, having seen my ghost.'

'Well, not necessarily. Like I was saying, it could just be some sort of image that is lingering from the past.'

'No. This was clear evidence.'

'You can't be *absolutely* sure of that, though.'

'I can. And you'd be sure too if you were to see her. It's one thing analysing facts you hear from someone else, but until you've experienced it for yourself you know nothing about it, I assure you.'

Richie shrugged. 'Maybe. Maybe not. I mean, you're the only person I've ever met who's claimed to have had any contact from the…the…'

She smiled at him tenderly. 'Who knows, maybe you'll experience contact yourself before too long.'

But Richie was no longer in the conversation, having experienced a different kind of contact.

'What's wrong?' asked his new companion.

'Rain.'

She stared up at the sky and then turned.

'Oh my God!' she shrilled, shoving her phone into her back pocket. 'Where did *that* come from?'

What had been a distant, harmless looking cloud bank had advanced on them, gaining lots of weight in the process. Their punishment for venturing out without waterproofs, Richie decided fatalistically.

A moody grumble came down at them, sending a line of stair-rods their way.

'Time to leg it!' Richie's new acquaintance grimaced, leaning in to give his arm a little pat. A slightly coquettish one, he couldn't help thinking.

'Well, I *do* hope work improves for you,' she added as she stepped back.

'Thanks,' he replied, fleetingly aware that her now dampened blouse was already threatening translucence.

And with that they exchanged goodbyes and parted. Hastening off in their different directions, back to their different lives.

As Richie stumbled back across the damp pebbles, he was oblivious to the soak of the raindrops. His thoughts and feelings whirling like birds caught in a thermal.

At one point he did find focus, sending a final glance back at the receding figure. One timed very well, catching her doing the same.

The mutual wave that followed left Richie charged with excitement. And as he headed on towards the concrete carbuncles, he was no longer stumbling on the pebbles.

Floating above them, instead.

3

Sleep wouldn't come. But then, how could it with the lunchtime discussion on the beach replaying itself over and over again?

Not that the intrusion was unwelcome. Although Richie knew that he needed a decent night's sleep – a difficult day at work lay ahead in the morning – the memory was too precious not to snuggle up with.

Despite the inauspicious circumstances of their meeting, his new acquaintance seemed to have taken to him. It had been a shame about their forced departure, but that was weather for you, no respecter of persons. But at least they were likely to meet again soon, her being a fan of the beach and now living back up here.

The mutual wave they'd exchanged after heading their separate ways started replaying in Richie's mind, evoking a warm glow within him. A feeling tragically unfamiliar since God-knows-when.

He'd really enjoyed her company. And what could be more enthralling than meeting someone who'd been regularly visited by a real live ghost?

There was a magic in the air, a surreality reaching into his core with a depth way beyond that of normal living.

Making Richie feel sure that their meeting had been something meant to be, not just down to blind chance. It had to be, the way it had come at just the right moment, just when he'd been in desperate need of rescue.

So now, at a time when he'd least expected it, he was a man transformed. For once, not at odds with his life. Instead smiling. Into a crisp and shiny new future.

To his astonishment, the magic had even managed to infuse the afternoon's work, seeing to it that a particularly problematic android malfunction had been consigned to history with minimal effort.

Richie gave a contented little grunt, unable to remember when he'd last felt this happy at bedtime. Sinking deeper into the bedding, he luxuriated gratefully into the softness.

The prospect of ghosts really existing was tantalising, to say the least. And more than that, important. It was, after all, validation of the greatest of his core beliefs. That life was eternal.

Of course, in the pragmatic world of so-called rational people – the place where, as a robotics engineer, his feet should be firmly planted – entertaining the notion of life after death was an invitation to ridicule. People like him were expected to have pledged unwavering allegiance to pyramids of dull little facts that disproved such beliefs. Facts which Richie considered to be more accurately described as opinions.

As for what the beach-woman had told him, well, that would be considered by the rationals to be no more than a scoff-worthy, fanciful tale. Something to be maturely dismissed as the product of someone eager to glamourise an achingly ordinary life.

Granted, that possibility was always there when such things were reported. Yet Richie *knew* that what she had reported was genuine.

He could tell.

The feel of truth was very distinct.

A smile started spreading through him. Slowly and steadily, like the leading edge of spilt honey.

There he was in his mind's eye, having seen the ghost for himself and filmed the encounter as proof. Gleefully playing back his evidence to the staunchest sceptics in the industry.

A chuckle rattled out of him. What could be more delightful than the prospect of hard-nosed opinion being shot down by something considered so absurd?

But even as he was aiming his imaginary gun at hard-nosed-opinion's hard nose, it had already sniffed out an ally within him, a traitorous inner devil that had his own weapon trained on Richie's smile of elation.

The devil let rip. His salvoes of doubt slamming into Richie goadingly, pointing out just how far Richie's reality was from his imagined movie clip of the ghost.

It was a thumping crash back to earth. Its admission that all Richie *actually* had was possibility inflated by euphoria.

He might never even see her again. Suppose she had suddenly gone away in search of work? Worse still, she might be one of those over-friendly people who gushed at everyone the first time they met them and thereafter didn't really want to know them.

He'd met that type before

Had he read too much into her friendliness?

An asphyxiating paralysis gripped him.

Wakey-wakey, Richie. Rise and don't shine. This is YOU, remember. This sort of thing doesn't happen to the likes of you. It's time to go back to the usual routine now; you've had your bit of fun.

Edgily, his chest started rising and falling. But he hastily force-fed himself with an admonishment to stop 'just supposing' and imagining everything going wrong.

Instead of fretting like this, he needed to act. This

encounter had been a gift, a wake-up call regarding his level of dissatisfaction with life. And a signpost showing him the way. Not something to be allowed a muzzy fade into his background.

He knitted his brows in concentration.

First and foremost, he *must* get to meet her again. Ask her more about the ghost. Much more.

And then…?

His ultimate goal, of course, was to see the ghost for himself.

His brow crinkled thoughtfully.

It was Thursday now, not long until the weekend. When it would be time to act – pluck up his courage and knock on the door of the quaint old Gothic or Romanesque house, whatever it was.

Of course, the elephant in the planning room was the question of quite how he was going to cross the chasm between paying her a visit and getting to see the ghost himself. But never mind. It wouldn't do to submit to mere details. Richie knew all too well from his work the power of just getting on with things. The way it opened unforeseen new doors.

Satisfied for now, he let his plans settle in the dark, nooky corners of his mind and switched his focus to his beautiful beach. A place even sunnier to him now that it had hosted the event that was bringing him so much excitement.

He smiled.

Life. It was *such* a strange beast. The way it showed you so much, seeming in special, beautiful moments to bring little bursts of clarity that felt enlightening but could never quite be focused into anything solid.

It seemed that ever since ancient times, humanity had been wrestling to make sense of life. Yet it remained a vast and fascinating sea of unfathomability, leaving generations of thinkers awestruck.

Not that anyone Richie had spoken with on the matter seemed to feel that way. Solid common sense always seemed to rule, adhering sensibly to 'the facts' and disdainfully dismissing anything beyond day-to-day living and your three score years and ten.

What really irritated him was the way people made casual references to science in order to justify their opinions. Ignorant of how physicists themselves had been casting doubt for decades upon what mainstream humanity thought of as their reality.

As someone prepared to accept the possibility of the existence of ghosts, Richie felt like an endangered species. But to him it made sense. Consciousness was something beyond the physical world, not just a product of chemical reactions in the brain. Its very essence was meaning, deep meaning from the big things in life like love, compassion, awe, gratitude, intellectual inquiry and morality.

How could all of that come from meaningless chemical reactions? If it did, nothing important in life would make any sense at all.

Was that *really* believable?

What's more, there was credible evidence of life after death. Documented near-death experiences.

So why did people laughingly dismiss the possibility of there being ghosts?

A little smirk played upon his face as he wondered how many of these scoffers would put their money where their mouth was and spend a night camping alone in a graveyard.

Of course, in these cynical days it wouldn't do to tell anyone he knew about his encounter, particularly not at work. It would invite all sort of judgements about him. None of them good.

It wasn't him who'd lost the plot, though. He was open and healthy. Unshackled by the demands of convention.

And he was going to stay that way.

He tittered. There was an irony in him of all people getting excited by matters of the afterlife. He who spent all of his working days immersed in the opposite end of the spectrum, *fake* life, humanoids imbued with so-called 'artificial intelligence'.

A frown started growing as certain of Richie's colleagues and others in the industry sprang to mind.

His line of work was nothing if not controversial. Seduced by how lifelike the latest androids appeared, even some of the professionals were blurring the distinction between intelligence and sentience.

'Get this,' he informed them, as if they were assembled up there on the ceiling. 'The clue is in the name – *artificial* intelligence!'

A statement he followed up with a snort.

Some of them even claimed that future androids would be 'superior' to humans.

'Huh!'

Never, in Richie's world.

He supposed that the problem was largely one of definition, though, the general failure to establish an intelligent definition for intelligence.

Well...?

Wasn't that true?

Try looking up 'intelligence' on your search engine. You'd get something like *the ability to learn, solve problems and make judgements and decisions*.

And, yes, if you were going to be that shallow on the matter, androids could certainly do all of that, and usually pretty well. But only because they had been programmed to do so. And indeed, programmed to 'learn' to do it even better. Where so-called 'learning' was merely responding to multitudes of algorithms.

It was one thing to *process* problems. Quite another to actually *experience* them.

Understand. That was the crucial word missing from such definitions of intelligence. Real intelligence involved *understanding*, and that was a function of awareness, of sentience. It wasn't as if those dumb machines were actually thinking or feeling; they were merely responding.

Two very, *very* different things.

You couldn't even begin to compare androids to human beings. People's being shone from their eyes and was astonishing. Of the same enormity, the same stupendous depth, as the cosmos itself.

What *were* these people thinking?

Where was their sense of awe?

Okay, okay...there was another factor involved, the unspoken, orthodox view of most of the intelligentsia, that human beings were in effect biological machines, no more than brains with bodies. Which meant that, yes, you *could* argue that we too had been programmed. By our biology.

No wonder the distinction between us and androids had blurred, if that was your worldview.

'That isn't the case, though,' Richie stated firmly, peering through the darkness towards the plain, white abyss of the opposite wall.

Sentience was metaphysical. Nothing to do with matter. Matter was just matter. Stuff that wasn't even aware.

The silence enveloping Richie was now raucous. He glared into it for several indignant seconds and then, realising how het up he was becoming, released himself with a resounding inner declaration.

Listen to you, remonstrating out loud again!

Seriously...he would have to get a grip on himself. Had he already forgotten his earlier embarrassment on the beach?

Anyway...

It was time to stop all this thinking and start to relax if

he were to stand any chance at all of getting any sleep tonight.

Unclenching his now tense shoulders, he tried a few slow, soft exhalations. Then raising each hand in turn to the opposite shoulder to administer a prodding and wincing self-massage of each trapezius muscle.

A good start, but not enough.

Something would be required to damp down the electric fizz in his mind.

'Okay...imagine a field,' he instructed himself softly.

There it was already, all green and lovely. Aglow in what had to be there, warm, nurturing sunshine.

He wouldn't actually go as far as counting the sheep that had appeared in his field; that had never worked for him. He'd just watch them, be with them, part of the scene, slowly mellowing with them, mellowing into...

Aaaaaah!

He was really there now. He could even hear insects busying themselves amongst the grasses and meadow flowers.

He smiled, staying with the sensation for a while, enjoying the dreamy simplicity of watching his sheep and insects sharing with him enjoyment of the sunshine.

It didn't last, though. His mind was determined to fight back. Asking if sheep ever saw ghosts.

A slow smirk started spreading through him as he imagined the ghost of Dolly the Sheep spooking the creatures out of their woolly wits one dusky night.

And what about dear old Bah-ah-ah-ah-bara; would she haunt them too?

A chuckle burst from his lips as he pictured multiple hauntings, as if some tear-jerky scene from Watership Down were before him.

'Stop it,' he mumbled.

He was getting silly now. This wasn't working; he'd be awake all night at this rate.

He heaved out a sigh and rolled onto his back.

There was only one way to do this.

Throwing the eiderdown aside, he hauled himself up and clicked on the light. After which, he wandered through to the kitchen.

'This'll do the job,' he assured himself as he headed back to the bedroom, walking very gingerly.

Whisky was too precious to spill.

Having sunk back into bed, he reached out for the tumbler and toasted the air before sinking a hearty swig.

It was remarkable how rapidly the golden liquid worked its magic. By the time he had finished the small glass, all of his unresolvable thoughts had tumbled away in a landslide of apathy.

Plonking down the glass with satisfaction, he turned off the light and sank back into the bedding.

All there was now was pleasantness.

The two of them and the beach.

4

He wondered. Suppose he were to go there again at lunchtime? Would she be there as well?

A tantalising tingle in his depths told him that, yes, she was *sure* to be there. A sensation compounded by the memory of the night's dream.

Hadn't that dream been a sign?

'Hmm,' he grunted. 'You're getting carried away now.'

A dream was just a dream, wasn't it? A little regurgitation of the day's events, on this occasion distorted in his favour.

Yes. Forget the dream.

Besides…

An uncomfortable thought had started weaving its queasy way through him. Just suppose his thinking was plain wrong. It might even qualify as stalking her, making a special trip in the hope of catching her again. Or at least the beginning of a stalk.

These were strange, befuddling times, these days of ever changing public opinion. Enough to make you feel unsure about what to even think.

Could he even trust his own judgement anymore?

He frowned in consternation for a moment before calling up Google on the screen in front of him and tapping in a few succinct words.

The very first hit seemed to spring out at him like a rebuke.

Metropolitan Police. Stalking may include: regularly following someone...

Mmm.

Not that you could call once 'regularly'. And it wasn't as if he'd actually be following her...more *rendezvousing* with her.

Although...

He hesitated.

A rendezvous was an *agreement* to meet. Which they hadn't done. Furthermore, 'once' could all too easily *become* 'regularly', depending on the fruits of any second encounter. Such pursuit – and it was pursuit – tended to gain a strange, inherent momentum.

How long before *fascinated* nudged its way into *obsessed* and had him by the scruff of his hapless neck?

A toe-curling thought gripped him. How the police might view the situation given that she was younger than him by a good ten years and...a woman.

Richie shuddered, an authoritative voice ringing through his mind, excuse-me-sir-ing him in the same sphincter-loosening tone as the time he'd been caught as a lad after throwing fireworks on a housing estate.

He dropped his eyes shamefully.

If he were honest with himself, hadn't he already slipped into 'obsessed'? Why else would there be that tingle in his depths from simply thinking of her?

Actually, *no*, he told himself hurriedly. The tingle was more about the situation, his excitement about the ghost.

Okay, albeit with a little romance mixed in too. And there was nothing wrong with that, considering the banter the two of them had shared. And, of course, the mutual wave they'd parted on.

Anyway, whatever the tingle meant, what was the use of fighting it? The decision had already been made, and he knew it. He *had* to go to the beach, even if it meant his hopes taking a fall on stony ground.

A tense glance at his watch told him it was ten thirty seven. Triggering a fresh tingle.

Not long to escape-time.

Her words about his beach flooded back.

It's in my blood, a childhood thing.

His beach was also *her* beach; they clearly had that much in common. Which meant that stalking didn't even come into it. They were *destined* to meet again soon, given their shared passion for the beach.

It was as simple as that.

In which case, sooner rather than later would be for the best. After all, he had more stuff to ask her. Important stuff.

More details, for a start. Perhaps even a way for him to get to witness the presence of the ghost himself.

Would that be possible?

A loud trill cut rudely though this thought, making him jump and causing a sink-plunging tug in his guts.

'Shit!'

He wasn't given to habitual swearing, but some things were so formidable that they ripped an expletive from the lips.

He knew who it would be. The voice at the other end of the telephone was already knifing its way into Richie's heart. Carrying an unspoken threat of hell to pay if there weren't answers to pass up the chain of command.

Has that Android 4B been fixed yet, then? And what about software update eleven? Have you implemented it yet?

No!

Of course he hadn't.

Richie puffed out his cheeks and released a sharp burst of air, wondering how it was that misanthropes like his boss always ended up in charge.

Having all these needless ructions was wearing him down. The silly woman hadn't a clue about the technological challenges involved. Hers was simply a world of deadlines and results and costs.

As the trilling continued its nag, Richie contemplated not answering. But quickly changed his mind.

Why delay the inevitable?

Steeling himself, he reached for the handset.

'Vanessa.'

'Richard! How did you know it was me?'

'Oh…I just had…had a feeling. You know.'

'I'm not sure I do,' remarked Vanessa coldly. 'Anyway, I need you to come to my office right now.'

'Right,' Richie muttered. 'I'll come right up.'

At that, there was a deadening click.

Richie gave the silent handset a glare before replacing it in its cradle. And then embarked upon an anxious scan of his small, dishevelled office.

She hadn't asked specifically about update eleven, but he'd better check. It paid to go armed when possible.

Sighing wearily, he started rifling through the mess of papers adorning his desk.

'Ah!'

Reaching for the other end of the desk, he grasped a few stapled sheets of paper that he remembered being delivered there first thing that morning. A notification that he'd tossed down for later perusal, as he did with almost all incoming paperwork.

Flipping urgently through the sheets he muttered, 'Update eleven, update eleven…there must be something about it here, surely.'

Damn it, not a word on it!

His edginess intensified. But suddenly a folded sheet of loose paper that had been inserted into the odds and ends cluttering one of his shelves caught his eye.

'Here we are!' he gasped as he grabbed at it, his certainty of what it was being immediately verified by what was written at the top in unmissable bold text.

Memorandum – Update 11

Speed-reading his way down the sheet, he fumbled his way out of the office, his heart turning to ice as the salient statement hit him.

There are still bugs in this update and we recommend waiting until Issue 2, due for release early next week.

'Bugger it!' he growled, stuffing the sheet irately into his trouser pocket. 'Can't something go my way, just for once?'

As he set off along the corridor and headed for the staircase, he pondered what else Vanessa might be wanting from him.

A tight 'yes' answered his tap at the much hated wood-effect door. The precursor to the thunderous glare that accompanied her gesture towards the vacant chair.

'Richard,' she snapped, before his bottom had even touched down. 'I need to be kept updated about *everything* for the next few days.' The very slight pause she allowed at this point felt like it was packed with gelignite. 'Because we're over budget, *yet* again.'

Richie cleared a throat already three-quarters healed up. 'Well, yes. We've erm…we've had some…some unforeseen problems, like the…'

'You told me that twelve man-hours was enough for Android 4B,' his adversary cut in obliviously, plucking a sheet of paper from the desk and waving it fiercely in his face. 'And now look what's happened! You've gone and booked seventeen and a half, which is about a seventy percent overspend. Is that what passes as acceptable for you?'

'No, but…'

'And then, as if that isn't enough, there's an extra eleven hours on the intelligence tests for the others.'

Deep in Richie's innards, indignation started sizzling.

She should be grateful that bloody 4B was fixed; it had been one hell of a tricky problem that had taken all of his twelve years of experience to crack. And as for man-hours consumed, what about all the extra unpaid time he had put in, the man-hours of worry that had frothed in the background during his last couple of evenings and diluted his sleep?

That wasn't in her sodding budget…*oh* no!

He stopped short of voicing this, though. Instead restraining his comeback to a controlled, 'But I originally wanted sixteen.'

'We settled on twelve,' came a garroting retort.

Richie bristled even more, an inner challenger piping up a brave *you mean YOU settled on twelve. Without giving me a choice.*

But it was courage that didn't dare burst free. Experienced courage that knew all too well the consequences of riling her at such a time.

She was being absurd, though. An estimate was precisely what the word meant, a ballpark figure for how much. Not something to be chiselled into granite as a future monument of failure.

Did she think his lab kit included a crystal ball?

And what was the point of all this, anyway? All it achieved, having to do the job with a budgetary noose round his neck, was unnecessary stress. When the truth of the matter was simple, that the job would take as long as it would take.

Any boss worth their salt knew of projects' propensity for failing to make deadlines. Especially when things were continually being cut to the bone.

She should be digging out some spare hours from

somewhere else, leaving him to do the important work unmolested. *Creative accounting*...wasn't that the term for it?

'And then there's this update eleven,' Vanessa resumed, arching a fiercely emphatic brow his way. 'That was meant to have been sorted out by now, and you and your team were meant to have implemented it. And yet, as far as I can tell, it hasn't even begun.'

'There were unexpected bugs in it.'

'Unexpected, unexpected! That's all I ever hear from you! When is something going to go right?'

The stare that she fixed him with seemed to screw him to his chair by his lungs. All he could do was gape at her, his fury devouring him slowly from the inside.

'I'll have to try and explain to Mike Ball that we need more man-hours, now,' continued the now caustic voice. 'And he'll have to let everyone know at the progress meeting tomorrow.'

Her attitude finally detonated Richie. 'Well, that's just how it goes in this game,' he blurted with an unguarded increase in volume. 'It's the nature of...'

'It's far from a *game*, Richard!' It felt like the words were being hurled at him. 'We are *over*-budget, and you don't seem to appreciate the ramifications of that.'

'But...'

'You've got more "buts" than a billy goat, Richie!' she exploded. 'How about you try to gain control of the situation instead of but-ing me all the time, hey?'

She exhaled so forcefully that the paper sheet below her threatened flight.

A haranguing silence laid in wait for several long seconds as Vanessa contemplated her desk top with a spasmodic finger-tap.

'*Right*...' she began, her voice more controlled now. 'I'll try for more hours at the meeting, but I hope you realise this doesn't reflect well on me at all.'

Richie squeezed a grunt into the meagre pause that she allowed before she continued more tensely, 'And quite frankly, Richard, I'm getting fed up to the back teeth with taking the rap for you lot.'

The bristling, owl-eyed resentment of her stare rendered Richie mute and desperate to look away but unable to do so.

After what felt like a slice of eternity, she finally saw fit to release him. Dropping her gaze down to her paperwork to resume her assault in a calmer, but still intimidating voice.

'I'll let you know the outcome late tomorrow, but in the meantime get that update eleven implemented.'

Neurones all over Richie pulsed with annoyance. It would be madness to start working on eleven when they were about to change it again.

He had to grind his excuse out as if his vocal chords were huge, industrial belts driving a lumbering great machine into action.

'Issue two…is meant…meant to be arriving early next week.'

Vanessa tutted impatiently, puffing herself up in readiness for delivering more condemnation.

'So…' interjected Richie hastily, 'we should be up and running by, erm, end of Wednesday, all being well.'

'Wednesday isn't all being well!' came the snap. 'It's…' Vanessa flicked a gimlet glare at her paperwork. 'It's nine days late, Richard. *Wunderbar!*'

Richie winced, shifting in discomfort.

Surely the time for her to hoof him out of the office must be nigh. After all, what was left to castigate him with?

'Right!' Vanessa boomed with the air of a sergeant major dismissing an errant private. 'You'd better go and get things moving, then!'

He didn't need urging twice. Springing up like a jackin-the-box, he almost leapt for the door that had now become his best friend.

Once back amidst the comfort of his own far more ramshackle surroundings, he whipped the crumpled memorandum from his pocket and slapped it down moodily on top of one of his many piles of paper. Snarling into the air with contempt.

'Damn her!'

It was all very well for her to tell him to get things moving, but how could he when there was nothing to move? All he could do was wait, utterly in the hands of the software team.

He scowled gloomily.

This job was slowly and painfully milking him of his soul. He was good at it and knew it, but what was the use of being good at your job when even your successes earned you a rollicking?

Just as his despair was on the brink of slitting its throat, fantasy somehow took over, making something beautiful shimmer into being on the desk in front of him, a slip of pink and white striped paper with a sequence of black numbers on it, digits that seemed to almost dance joy at him.

It didn't matter that he had never bought a National Lottery ticket in his life. He had one now, and it was a corker.

Eight hundred and fifty thousand pounds.

The image dissolved into something even more satisfying, his voice ringing out forcefully, telling a surprised Vanessa precisely where to stick her budget. An action coming with an emotional surge so strong that it jerked him into to a perilous, real-life hinterland of recklessness that had him beadily eyeing the phone.

One call.

That was all it would take.

Easy.

Go on, a bold part of him urged. *Pick up the damned handset, dial her number and let rip.*

A palpable pulse of fulfilment shot through him.

Where would she be then, losing her android team leader?

He could storm right out of the place immediately after the call. Leave her utterly in the lurch.

How would that reflect on you at your bloody meeting, Vanessa? Hey?

She'd have a *real* problem then, not just a few measly man-hours to dig out. Her just deserts for failing to appreciate what a vital cog he was in the organisation, worthy of every ounce of the respect that he wasn't getting.

He snorted through both nostrils, an angry bull now. But one with its testicles caught in the tight grasp of fear.

Cathartic though the vision was, reality was wearing bigger boots. At least size twelve Doc Martens.

The glaring truth of the matter was that he would never do it. The thought of being adrift in the uncharted territory of job-seeking at forty-nine years old had the queasily hopeless feel of being adrift in choppy waters with no sail.

Richie heaved out a deeply discontented sigh.

He'd just have to go on going on, then. Keeping in mind the big carrot that was dangling, a salary and benefits that would offer him a very real chance of early retirement at fifty-five.

A mere six years.

Six years felt like an eternity right now, though. Yet a sensible, background part of him was somehow managing to assure him that it wasn't. Letting him know that doing anything rash would be sheer madness.

Clearing his throat decisively, he straightened in his seat. Returning himself to the here and now with a glance down at his watch.

Almost eleven twenty-five.

Calmer he may be now, but he knew that it was little more than a veneer. A pressing need still remained for a good, solid reset.

Sod the man-hours, he decided. He'd piddle away another point five of them just for the hell of it.

There were times when the most productive thing you could do was nothing, and Richie knew that this was one of them. Praying for no interruptions, he reached for his computer mouse and selected his internet browser.

It was time for one of those aimless tootles through website after website. He would start with the Met Office.

Next came the BBC News, New Scientist, a couple of blogs and then several more sites, all given scant attention.

A flick of a glance at the little time readout at the bottom right-hand corner of his screen confirmed that time had done what it always did in such situations – slowed to about the speed his fingernails were growing.

This was agony! Never before had he needed his beach so much.

With an even heavier sigh than the last one, Richie rose to his feet. And then sidled to the front of his office to peer over the top of the frosted section of glass.

Hmm.

It was quieter than usual.

Maybe he could even manage an escape at five to, if he employed suitable stealth.

A glance up at the skylight beyond the corridor confirmed the validity of the Met Office promise of sunshine.

Perfect.

He turned to face the back wall. And then, closing his eyes, tried transporting himself to his beach. All thoughts of who he had been hoping to meet there having now been pushed into a very distant background.

5

Wolves of derision were howling for her downfall, but she wasn't about to give in. Riding the waves of turbulence, she reminded herself that there were times when reality needed showing who was boss.

Not that that meant it couldn't hit her harder, though. Which it promptly did, opting to throw in a drop. A diabolical move, punching well below the belt of decency, considering Shona's aversion for heights.

She resorted to the only thing possible.

A scream.

The trouble was, it came out as a silent, impotent ghost of what it should have been, far from the vent required by the tight coil of tension within her. A crushing testimony to the overpowering weight of her terror.

Giddily closing her eyes, she waited for the inevitable. But, true to form, it didn't come.

'Agh!' she gurgled, suspended in an awful, indeterminate limbo. 'Aghhhh!'

Nothing meant anything anymore. Which was why her sudden emergence into the solid world of beds and ceilings couldn't be real. At least, not until pain from her back rushed in, the result of the extreme twist in the way she was lying.

Not that she shifted herself. Her attention had been stolen in full by a momentous revelation, the fact that shafts of sunlight were overcoming the defences of the heavy old upholstered curtains.

'Thank God!' she heaved, untwisting the pained back in ginger slow-motion.

It was short-lived relief, though. The dreams had made for messy sleeping, and it seemed that her sweaty limbs had been attempting positions within the mound of crumpled bedding that would have been a credit to a time-served yogi.

Once she had carefully untangled herself, she flopped back into inertness. Extra time was needed for a stomach that had yet to unknot.

A creeping reclaim started pulling her back dreamwards. So the sudden piercing of the air by a sonorous trill was most fortunate. A lifeline thrown by the sanity of nature.

Thanking the avian rescuer for sharpening her senses, she raised herself onto her elbows to ensure safety from the dangerous clutches of sleep.

New sounds came in. The mild, relaxed baas of grazing sheep. The distant cry of gulls. Transporters to a far nicer realm, the one she loved.

A louder, much shriller sound penetrated from the proximity of the windowsill. Some other wee bird.

She frowned, wondering what it was.

Feeling calmer and more secure now, she allowed herself a contemplative return to the night. Specifically, that last dream.

It had been squirmily malevolent, ten times as twisted as her poor back. But then, that was to be expected. Every time, the hauntings were followed by such dreams.

Not that Shona had ever been able to fathom why.

She started to relive some snippets of the many hauntings from years earlier. Realising how out of practice with these nights she had become.

Moving down south had pretty much freed her of them. Granted, there had been a few occasions, but they had been insipid, nowhere near as real.

But, of course, she was back *here* now. At the epicentre.

She gave the wall a big-eyed stare. Wondering pensively how many more nights like this were likely to follow.

Self-doubt started growing.

Did she have it in her to continue like this?

As if in answer, a death-rattle filled the air. A cough bursting through a throat suddenly dryer than a tomb of old bones.

God, she needed some water!

The heave required to overcome the heavy slab of spent trauma within her was mighty. But she did eventually manage it, getting herself into a slumpy sitting position on the edge of the bed, where she took a lengthy pause before rising into a tottery stand. Trying to rub life into her eyes before peering at the clock.

She had to squint and bend nearer.

Almost ten past seven.

With a grunt, she swayed her way to the door. Gripping the handle firmly for a moment to steady herself before venturing out onto the landing.

At least by the time she emerged from the bathroom she was feeling more alert. Cold, splashed water worked wonders.

Pausing on the landing, she strained her ears.

Was her dad up yet?

Silence.

A flit of a smile crossed her face.

Age had changed him. No longer was he the man who

would be already bathed and breakfasted when Shona emerged from her room bedraggled.

Having re-entered her room, she pulled on her dressing gown. And then flopped back down into her sitting position on the edge of the bed.

Why?

Why was this happening?

A sickening hollowness invaded her with the thought of the sheer desolation her haunter must be suffering.

Shona continued to nurse her melancholy for a few quiet minutes, allowing it what it needed, some festering time. All the while, a deeply troubled part of her trying to hold at bay what she was unwilling to admit to herself, the fact that, in a warped, even slightly addictive way, the hollowness that she was feeling was something precious. Something that seemed to nourish her sense of selfhood.

She screwed up her face.

Wasn't that a bit weird? Surely it couldn't be natural for a person to take satisfaction from suffering.

An imaginary little drama started playing in her mind. A clip-boarded man in a white coat informing her with gentle professionalism that she was what they called a masochist. While she gazed wide-eyed and helpless at his short-cropped little beard, hanging onto every word that came from its orifice. Especially his mentally antiseptic assurance that they could help her but it may take some time.

A ripply snake of coldness slithered through her. Its shuddersome message that her nature was becoming increasingly warped as time passed.

But, no, hang on a minute...

This wasn't *really* masochism. The man in white was missing how sound she was as a person, how rational and well-balanced she was, not at all the type to suffer an 'ism'.

Surely any professional worth his salt would recognise

her disquiet as a perfectly healthy reaction to the experience of accessing a wider reality than that of her day-to-day life.

Enough to unhinge many people, surely.

The truth of the matter was that she was doing well. In her shoes, many others would have fallen apart by now.

She jerked herself resolutely straight. Rising to her feet. Repeating the truth stridently in her mind, that she was strong.

Nevertheless, even a strong person needed their much loved, sugary cup of morning coffee in these circumstances.

Having lumbered her way down to the kitchen, she opened the cupboard where the coffee was kept and reached out. But then halted her arm in mid-air with a 'tut' of annoyance and disbelief.

All she could see was the coffee's absence. Missing the fact that it was on the shelf below, to one side.

'*Oh God*, where *is* it?' she groaned.

And then she spotted where it was lurking. And snatched irritably at it, muttering tensely that her dad should know where it belongs by now. Clumsily sending it tumbling.

The loud bang on the hard surface was deafening and jarred her senses horribly, prompting her to quickly seize it and smother it before it could bounce.

'Bloody hell!' she gasped, scrutinising the jar for cracks before setting it down safely. 'What's the matter with you this morning, Shona?'

But she knew exactly what the problem was.

Once she had poured the hot drink and its comforting olfactory hug had started enveloping her, she sank down onto one of the smooth-topped old stools at the kitchen table. At last able to relax and let in the all-pervading brightness of the sunlit kitchen.

That was better.

INHABITANT

The oh-so-solid kitchen felt so *real*.

She wandered her eyes around it in grateful satisfaction.

This was no modern particle-board kitchen, flimsily assembled from kit parts. This was a *real* kitchen with walls of thick, uncompromising granite, built to last forever, with the sort of heftily beamed ceiling that would probably even hold off a landslide.

Shona chuckled. Even the window frames were super-heavy-duty oak. And the stalwart curly handles that were mounted on them wrought from iron.

It was all so big-boned comforting. Even the shelving, home for all those chunky stoneware pots and jars, announced itself oakily the very instant you laid eyes on it.

Straightening a leg, she flexed it to its fullest extent, flattening her foot on the old stone floor. Relishing the solidity that felt like a direct connection to the core of the earth.

Taking a deep, hearty sup of her coffee, she marvelled at the transformative qualities of the old room. The folk who built these places really knew what a home was about, way beyond mere functionality. They knew the *aesthetic* importance of earthiness in structure.

Allowing the feeling of physicality into her being more deeply, she exhaled softly. This was *her* side of reality, *her* place of belonging. Unlike for a certain other person, who shouldn't be here.

A sudden pang hit her and she twisted her lips, aware that she was thinking that much too persuasively. Yes, she wished that her mother would stop and move on for her own good; of *course* she did. What sort of daughter wouldn't? But equally, a covert, untrustworthy part of her was glad of the contact.

What was it that Mum was reaching for, anyway?
Her?

Once she had moved beyond the fright of the first few times, Shona had repeatedly attempted contact, but all she'd ever got back was a gaze. And not necessarily directed at her.

She scrunched up her face in bewilderment.

What on earth was on offer for Mum here other than a hollow space, the ghost of her past?

All of a sudden she had to close her eyes against a tearful prickle.

Life. Afterlife.

Her mum had made them parallel worlds. One of them desperate for a feel of the other. It was so sad, so desolate.

The defences of both eyes were suddenly breached by tears. Spurring her into a hasty fumble for the tissue that she knew to be in her pocket.

Suppose Dad came down?

He mustn't catch her like this.

It was just after she had given a short snort into the tissue that the unthinkable happened. That her phone gave a throb and she found herself gazing in astonishment at the single word on its screen.

6

A waft of warm sea air had a hug waiting for Richie as he exited the building. But he wasn't about to linger and savour it. He had an imperative – get clear of the site and into the sanctuary of his beloved beach.

Despite his haste, the degree of elevation he was already feeling as he nipped through his secret gap in the bushes and onto the beach was as if he'd just dined out on helium.

Richie had long felt that the occasional little episode of naughtiness was a panacea for one's woes. A sentiment lent support by the joy he was feeling at his cheeky early exit from the little side door by the toilets. A triumph most sweet.

And why not? A bit of revenge for what he'd had to tolerate that morning.

Life was all a matter of balance.

It didn't take him long to be where he needed to be. Safely out of sight of all HuTech windows and standing at the water's edge.

Sinking down onto his haunches, he released himself across the water, breathing its essence in deeply.

Had there been prizes awarded for seascapes, today's would have taken gold. Its surface was a deep, heart-clutching blue and speckled with a heavenly dance of glints. And the oh-so-gentle sound of the confusion of wavelets slapping against the protrusion of rocks directly below him was a musical accompaniment of perfection.

The overall steadiness of the scene very soon had Richie melting into it, the awful morning at work forgotten for now.

No wonder he kept coming back to his beach to taste its beauty.

Raising his eyes skyward, he breathed a heartfelt thank-you at an imaginary god who was looking down upon him from out of the infinite blue.

Clear skies had always enchanted and fascinated Richie. Their vast wide-openness enlivened a similar vastness deep within himself. A resonance that seemed to deepen and become more nourishing every time.

What he considered being in nature was all about.

Opening himself even wider, he allowed in the beach as well as the sea and sky. As ever, seduced by the beauty of the overall vista.

Nothing about the scene was inanimate. Even the rocks felt primordially alive. And the air itself, as it shimmered in a haze above the warmth of the sand.

Indeed, the entire scene had a wholeness beyond the sum of its parts. An underlying splendour that was way beyond the limits of Richie's comprehension.

Richie knew that its essence would remain beyond those limits. Which was fine; he didn't feel any need to comprehend things. Far from it, being immersed in an inconceivable reality both thrilled and moved him.

The breath he sucked in was ninety-five per cent gratitude. Feeding off its own heavenliness.

It was calmness destined for a very sudden death, though. Its slayer a pulse of nervousness that had him turning his head and flicking palpitant glances around the the beach and the land above it.

'Hmm.'

It was the faintest murmur, but it was loud and all-pervading to him.

Even though he was clearly still alone with his beach, the thump of his heart didn't slow. Because the question remained – would she be coming?

It was expecting a hell of a lot of his luck to encounter her two days in a row, though. Even if the butterflies in his guts did have an enthralling buoyancy in their wings.

He licked dry lips. The breath he sucked in undeniably ragged.

Lovely his beach-woman may be but, *boy*, did she jitter him up!

He exhaled slowly.

Oh, well.

May as well have lunch.

Rising up, he started heading for his favourite spot in which to settle down in comfort.

What a spot it was! He'd been delighted at finding such a perfect broad dome of a boulder, a dream come true amidst all the jagged, awkwardly sloping edges.

There it was. Its familiar granite surface beckoning him with shiny, sun-warmed benevolence.

Once he'd sunk down upon it, he eagerly removed his shoes. And then, with great satisfaction, pulled off his socks.

Aaah!

It was *so* nice to flex your toes and let in the air.

He should have been born in India or Africa, the way he had always liked his feet well aired. They were not at all suited to being leathered in all day.

Sitting in comfort was the icing on Richie's cake. Allowing him to open even wider to his surroundings.

He could always feel his previous visits in the beach.

As if they were still there, sublimely deepened versions of his past emotions embedded in the landscape, able to reach for him and enrich him through time.

Maybe they were still there, in a sense. After all, what *was* the beach to him? When all was said and done, it was mainly through *feelings* that he knew it. So it was as much an internal place as one out there.

The glance he flicked at his watch produced a smile.

Still over forty minutes left in this paradise.

He scanned the area again.

No.

'Oh, just get on with lunch, Richie,' he told himself. 'It's very unlikely she'll happen to turn up just because you're here.'

Sinking his teeth into the first of his carefully prepared sandwiches, he looked back out to sea.

The glinting dance of reflected sunlight set to work on him again. Leading him into an aimless cheese, cucumber and peanut butter drift.

'Mmm,' he smiled as he chewed contentedly, lowering his gaze to the water's edge.

Soon he found himself in a lazy inner roll with the lapping waves. Being massaged by the pleasingly haphazard motion of the many colourful pebbles that were the water's playthings.

How this led him back to the earlier meeting with Vanessa, he did not know. But it did. Perhaps because a tide had now turned between the two of them.

It was amazing. Not only had all of the angst been washed away, he was oozing magnanimity. Giving her his best with the admission that he shouldn't have taken her comments quite so much to heart.

Yes, her manner hadn't been very nice, but doubtless she was struggling with the situation just like him. And who knew what other battles she was fighting in her life outside work?

Not that this concession in any way diluted the problem of her precious budget. It was still a pain and would remain so, because she operated in the realm of how things *should* go rather than the realm of actual events.

Two different realms colliding in the same space.

'Oh, well.'

He shook his head from side to side and prodded a pebble with a conciliatory big toe.

She wasn't so bad really. Maybe given a different situation they could even be friends.

He tittered.

Was there just a touch of hyperbole in that suggestion?

He prodded at another pebble, upending it to expose its damp and shiny underbelly.

It *would* get better from now on. He'd see to that. Allow her rants to wash off his back more, like ducks did with the rain. He didn't *need* to get so upset. Ultimately it was self-defeating.

Hopefully, given more time, he would prevail. He couldn't be accused of suffering from self-doubt, and after all these years he knew he was good at his job. Furthermore, he always did it to the best of his ability.

So no more could be expected of him.

'So next time, quack, quack, and let her get on with it,' he quipped to himself.

Upon returning his attention to the shoreline, his eyes couldn't help but settle on two cormorants standing side by side on an exposed rock, stretching their wings to dry them off. Presumably after some fishing.

How relaxed and uncomplicated their lives felt! So different from his own. They just got on with being themselves, doing their thing. Giving nature value by virtue of their being there, part of the scene.

There was an affecting dignity in that. He could feel it right now, tugging at his heart.

A frown corrugated his brow.

What about him?

What did he want from his life?

He dropped his head forwards and gazed down at the sand. Knowing that, if he were honest, the thing that he wanted most of all was change.

Raising his head, he fixed the sea with a keen stare.

Could he even bring that retirement down *below* fifty-five?

Just suppose he did…he'd be okay, wouldn't he?

Yes, of course, he would.

He'd manage.

It was simply a matter of eking out his savings for a few years until he reached the magic age. His private pension scheme was doing surprisingly well, despite the battering that the financial stock markets had been taking during recent years.

It wasn't as if he even needed much money, anyway. He had never been one of life's hankerers. Spending sprees weren't in his nature. He would be more than content with the simple life.

Not that simple meant unfulfilling, as many people would imagine in this materialistic modern day. Far from it, he found treasure in simplicity. Nourishment for a deep and beautiful internal reality.

If he could downscale to a cheap little place on this coast, perhaps in Shoreholm, then he could break free from his current life of strife and pressure. Even somewhere ramshackle would do him fine; he could make a project of gradually doing it up.

He imagined having the time to indulge himself in his interests to the full. And being able to branch out into new things, expanding himself.

New things.

Two rosy little words.

A smile started growing as he allowed the phrase a few

seconds to really entrench itself in his feelings. By which time he realised just how ravenous he was for something new and exciting.

'But wait...,' he blurted.

The tremor of excitement that had appeared in his guts was a reminder. He *did* have something new, and for this coming weekend. The beginning of his quest for ghostly knowledge.

He looked around again.

Still no sign of her.

Although...

Excitement suddenly coursed through him. There was a faded looking red car parked some way along the road, which he didn't think had been there before.

Interesting!

But...

He flicked some glances around the beach again.

No.

There was no sign of anyone. Anywhere.

But of course there wasn't! Expecting to see her two days in a row was absurd.

He must try not to be so impatient.

'Ooouph!'

He winced. Not on account of the lack of hoped for company, but because he was suddenly fearing buttock damage from his now very hard boulder.

With another involuntary 'ouph!' of pain, he rose.

Giving the now tender part of his flesh an alleviating rub, he hobbled onwards, veering more towards the waterline so as to get closer to his sparkling seascape.

A glance at his watch told him that he still had half an hour before he need head back. Ample time for a contemplative stroll the entire length of the beach and back.

It was unbelievable how slowly time was passing. Wasn't it meant to race by when you were enjoying yourself?

He froze, this thought now completely gone.

Something was bobbing in the water.

A seal?

Possibly. He'd seen them enough times along here.

Not that this meant he'd become blasé about it. Each new sighting greeted him with its own unique freshness.

On one wonderful occasion, he'd spotted six of them together, treading water and staring up at him as he'd sat eating. What a thrill it had been, staring into their doggish eyes and wondering how their watery life compared to his own!

But, no, this sighting was special. What he'd just seen looked different from a seal.

He edged closer…slowly, *very* slowly. And then froze again.

What on earth…?

Whatever it was that he was staring at was moving slightly in the water and widening, becoming very much broader.

'Oh, yes!' he cried, hardly able to believe his good fortune.

He knew a bottle-nosed dolphin when he saw one, even though this was his first. He could tell; the snout was unmistakable, just like a discarded bottle floating in the sea.

He *must* be right. He had heard that they had been seen on this coast.

But this close to shore, right in front of him like that?

Talk about being in the right place at the right time!

'You lucky sod, you!' he chuckled with unrestrained glee. 'Wow, what a thrill! What a privilege!!'

'Talking to yourself again, then?'

With a start, he wheeled round, hardly able to believe what he had heard.

7

This was so unfair. Time was mocking him. It wasn't as if he was still that gawky adolescent.

Yet the lungs that had contracted into claustrophobic little potholes of breathlessness begged to differ. As did his mincemeaty guts and the palms that were suddenly oozing sweat like two great slabs of Gruyère.

The most devastating of all the traitors, though, were Richie's thighs. Now useless jellied eels of shock.

Yes, yes, yes, he had wanted her to be at the beach, *badly* wanted her to be there. But did she have to appear so suddenly and inopportunely?

Their first meeting flashed back for a mean little goad. She seemed to have an uncanny talent for turning up at embarrassing moments.

'So…he's lost for words, now,' his assailant observed, a twitch of amusement playing on her lips.

'I was…excited. I've just seen a…whatsit…erm, you know…'

'I'm not at all sure I do, actually.'

'A bottle-nose!' He released a self-conscious cackle. 'I forgot what they were called for a moment.'

'Bottle-nosed dolphin?' She frowned past him, her searching eyes seeming doubtful. 'Are you *sure?*'

'Yes, right in close, just *there*,' he affirmed, swinging round and pointing. 'It'll reappear. Any moment, I should think. If we just wait a mo…'

But even as he said the words they seemed to drop like stones from his lips. Great, heavy tempters of fate.

'It must've gone,' he finally admitted.

'Oh, really,' came the reply.

'Well, it *was* there.'

Jesus wept! Where was his imaginary god now?

'Actually, we *do* get them on this stretch of coast,' his companion conceded, her eyes flashing out mischief, 'but in pods and further out. Not on their own and coming right up to the beach to say "hello"!'

'But this one *was* alone and *right* down there; I could hardly believe it!'

'No, I can't either!'

'It *was*, I tell you!' protested Richie.

His words seemed to hang in mid-air until a sudden smack on his shoulder brought him round.

'I'm teasing! Of course I believe you!!'

Hell's bells!

Twice now it had started like this. Her so poised and him a blundering, tangled up buffoon.

'Youuuu…' he drawled, marooned in awkwardness.

'Actually, a friend of mine, who just so happens to be a marine biologist, was talking about a solitary dolphin here recently,' she popped out glibly with a playful sideglance. 'She saw it close in, as well. Just like you did.'

'Well, there you are, then.'

'Sorry,' she giggled, 'I just can't help myself sometimes!'

'So how come you're so perky today?' fired back Richie. 'What's happened; has your ghost come back and revealed to you the meaning of life or something?'

The grin fell from her face like a dying bird. Making Richie's innards lurch.

'I had another visit last night,' she confided, sounding very different now, tight and clipped.

'What, the ghost?'

'Yeah. But then, I suppose that's gonna happen, now I'm back *there*.'

She gazed at the lump of damp sand she was dabbing at morosely with her foot.

'It's just that it isn't pleasant, you know?' she quivered. 'It still creeps me up, even after all this time… and I'm left with…with the dreams.'

Richie frowned.

'Dreams?'

'Yes, really troubling dreams. Disturbing. That leave me all screwed up in the morning.'

'Oh dear. I'm sorry to hear that.'

'Yes, it isn't fun.'

A contemplative silence fell.

'So…' resumed Richie, 'Are you back here for good, now you've come up from down south?'

'Who knows?'

'Mmm.'

'Dad still lives in that old house, you see, so I'm planning to remain with him, if possible.'

'Oh, I see. That's nice.'

'And I suppose that means I'll be seeing more of Mum again.'

Ah. So Mum didn't live with her dad anymore.

Richie wondered how to respond to that revelation with suitable delicacy. Deciding to play ultra-safe.

'Well, it's good you'll see more of her.'

'No, it isn't! I just told you, she freaks me out appearing in the night like that.'

Richie gaped at her like a fish out of water.

Was she saying what he thought she was saying?

'Oh! S-so…so…'

His words melted away. Leaving her waiting with the fatigued expression of a person lumbered with someone a bit soft in the head.

Richie tried again. 'Do you mean…that…that the ghost is your mum?'

Her eyes explored him incredulously.

'Yes, *of course!* Who else would it be?'

Richie stared at her defensively. 'Well, you didn't tell me it was your mum. You just said "a woman", so I assumed…'

'Did I?' She hesitated and then narrowed her eyes suspiciously. 'Are you sure?'

'Yes, of course I am. I'd have remembered otherwise. I mean, it is a somewhat significant detail, don't you think?'

'Mmm. Well, anyway, it *is* my mum.'

Richie huffed out a frustrated burst of air.

This was becoming very hard work. Was he expected to be a mind-reader or something?

Taking temporary refuge in the sanctuary of the thin blue line dividing the sea from the sky, Richie attempted to gather himself before posing his next question.

'So, *why* do you think she haunts you?'

Her brow corrugated with vexation.

'That's what I find so sad. She must want something, but I have no idea what. She seems to just stare like she's trapped, like she's…she's…'

With a sudden sniff, she turned her face away from him, to face the sea. And then turned her back to him and took a couple of wavering steps away from him, her shoulders held tense, stiff girders of emotional rawness.

Richie stood transfixed and useless. Until another sob, louder this time, galvanized him into action.

'I'm so sorry,' he muttered, stepping forward to drape a comfortingly arm over her shoulders.

She closed into him slightly and he gathered her protectively. An action seeming very natural, very comfortable, despite how short a time he had known her.

With another sob, she suddenly buried her face in the crook of his neck, prompting one of his arms to administer some comforting pats on her back. At which point she closed into him a little further.

Richie's heart surged. Her breasts and one hip were now against him, invading him with soft and sensual warmth, a sensation that he hadn't felt for a very long time.

His only thought should be of comforting her at this time, but he was reacting in a different, disconcerting fashion. Which made her withdrawal a relief, despite the sudden appearance of tearful, embarrassed eyes.

'So sorry,' she snivelled, 'It just got to me, you know, unexpectedly. I just…'

She faded.

'It's okay, I understand,' soothed Richie. 'It must be harrowing for you.'

She nodded. 'It was such a sudden death, you know? Totally unexpected, when she was in her prime. She got hit by a car in London when visiting a friend there. Bam! Suddenly, no more Mum.'

Another sob.

Richie extended the comforting arm again.

'Thank you,' she sniffed, leaning in warmly again to deliver a small hug. 'You're so nice, but I'd better go before I embarrass you too much.'

'No, no, really…it's fine,' Richie insisted.

The earlier indiscretion of his imaginary god was forgiven now. This woman, this beautiful young woman – what a gift she was to his day!

It was strange, but she felt so *right* at this bittersweet moment, so like she belonged with him. Even though he didn't know her name.

'I'm Richie, by the way,' he grinned. A disclosure earning him a watery smile.

'Shona.'

He smiled again.

'Well, Shona, can I walk you back to your car?'

It was as if he had flipped a switch. Holding her chin high with poise again, she replied, 'That would be delightful.'

They began the companionable trudge through the undulations of sand and shingle towards the faded-red car, Richie suddenly aware but uncaring of the fact that he was going to be late back for the afternoon's work.

Some things *had* to take priority.

It was a stroll Richie wished could last forever. But their halt beside the car came all too soon, changing everything abruptly.

This was it, another parting of the ways. He stood beside her rigidly, holding on tightly to the moment. A hollow loneliness expanding horribly within him.

What was going to happen next?

He knew what *should* happen next. Of course, he did; everyone had watched movies as a kid. The man always took the initiative and asked the woman out for a meal the next day or something like that.

Only this was him, not a poised and dashing movie character. And true to form, he found himself unable to speak. After all, how could he be sure that she felt the same as he did?

'Well, it was very nice spending some time with you again,' Shona remarked, for the first time sounding a little uncomfortable herself.

'Yeah, me too,' he replied tightly. The best that his now twisted guts were able to force out.

'So…'

She paused, as if waiting for him to make a move. But it wouldn't come.

'Anything nice planned for the weekend, then?' she filled in.

'No. Just some quiet time.' He gave a grimace. 'After the week I've had at work and all that.'

'Right. So does that mean there's some room in your schedule for me to do you a Sunday lunch?'

'Oh!' He hadn't expected that! 'Well…I…I..erm…,' he began untidily.

'Unless, that is,' interjected Shona, 'you have other plans for Sunday.'

Richie just shook his head dumbly, his entire being throbbing at the thrilling fact that she wanted more of him.

Fortunately, Shona had a considerably stronger grip on her faculties. Ejecting a bright 'right, then!' she informed him that he was expected at twelve thirty sharp.

And then, as a silent 'goodbye' before turning away to unlock the car, she leaned forward to deliver a small kiss.

Quite close to his lips this time.

In fact, very close.

8

With Shona's kiss still alive on his skin, Richie floated into his office aboard a hovercraft of bliss. A sensation mixing deliciously with the euphoria of having sneaked back unnoticed after a defiant hour and forty minutes of lunch break.

Just to double-check he hadn't been seen, he lingered in his doorway in a tall peep over the top of the frosted sections of glass across the corridor. Leaning out of the doorway afterwards to peer from side to side.

He couldn't believe his luck. There wasn't a soul to be seen. Not even Diane Nugent, a woman of unwavering routine who always whiled away her short as possible lunch break computer-gaming.

Strange.

Where *were* they all?

Shrugging, he closed the door and ensconced himself in front of his own computer screen, thinking that he'd better try to damp down his glee before anyone appeared. Although concentrating on anything as banal as work wasn't going to be easy after the fizzing triumph of being kissed like that and invited for a meal at a haunted house.

Picking up a small folder of routine memos that had been lying discarded to his left hand side, he smiled at how even the glaring problems of Software Update Eleven and Vanessa's budget constraints had now been pushed into an unimportant shade.

Turning his attention to the first memo, it wasn't long before he found himself just gazing sightlessly at it, utterly lost in his thoughts.

It was time to admit defeat. Laying the memo back down, he returned undiluted to his thoughts.

A smile started growing. Things were looking good. In fact, *really* good. Not only did he now hold a direct route into the scene of the haunting – something he had barely dared to hope for – but it seemed that the victim of the hauntings desired his company in a romantic way.

And, wow! Was she lovely or what?

Richie paused his flow of joy to wonder what she saw in him. And then reminded himself that what mattered was that the two of them enjoyed each other's company.

How old was she, he wondered?

Thirty-three, thirty-four?

Not that she in any way felt too young for him. Indeed, she seemed remarkably composed in comparison to him. But then, that was the female of the species for you, he reassured himself.

He'd heard other men say as much.

Although, it had to be admitted that with him it was something deeper. A lone wolf of the dating scene, he'd never actually had a girlfriend, thanks to his problem with composure in front of the fairer sex. Even with the female androids, so realistic nowadays, he preferred to converse via the relative remoteness of a computer keyboard and control/respond port.

The stark and larger truth of the matter was that he was hopelessly awkward at any gathering of people of either sex, seeming doomed from the outset to be an island of social alienation. And he knew exactly what was to blame for that state of affairs – his abysmal childhood.

A flush arose in his cheeks as the anguish of being a sitting duck for the school bullies flooded back, still rawly indelible after all these years.

What awful little shits they'd been. So quick to sniff out his lack of coolness. Oafs who'd thrived on crushing easy prey.

That Tony Philips, for one.

An involuntary little shudder ran through Richie as a vision floated back, still crystal clear after all these years.

It was amazing how even now that one-sided sneer of Tony's could hatch a few butterflies down in his guts. As could Richie's very distinct vision of the piggy little glint-holes Tony had been endowed with as eyes.

For a fleeting moment, Richie wondered why their expression had always been chillingly visible despite the shading of that ramrod-straight fringe of dandruffy hair.

A sudden odour drifted into his awareness. Tony's armpits, another of his wonderful attributes.

Not that anyone had ever dared to tell him.

Richie started an inner squirm of discomfort. For some perverse reason, his recollection of the armpit odour had triggered an uninvited replay of his first encounter with Tony in the school playground.

The punch had been a real hum-dinger. Richie hadn't seen it coming.

The poignant sensation of lying numbly helpless on the ground with his nose dribbling blood was now back with him. Intense and sickening.

Of course, Tony being Tony, it couldn't have stopped there. A couple of bruising kicks had followed. And then the *coup de grâce*, a heavy dropping down that had crushed the breath out of the already dazed Richie.

As if that hadn't been enough, his arm had then been grabbed and twisted until he'd started sobbing out cries of pain, dribbling his humiliation snottily onto the ground in front of a gawping group of younger boys that had somehow appeared from nowhere.

Richie wriggled uncomfortably in his chair.

Life had been a real bastard at times.

Heck, even his own subconscious was seeing fit to bully him now! Did it really have to be so psychotically vivid with its recollections?

Just like Tony Philips, it had no idea of when it was time to stop. It had him flattened, yet now it was sending more – painful shards of all his failed detours on the way back home from school.

Shoves and punches. Painful, thigh-bruising kicks. Being tripped. Worse still, his possessions being flung into various places – bushes, over garden walls, into the road, even into a pond one awful time.

Worst of all, though, had been the time they'd torn his shirt. He could still feel his distress at what his mother would say.

He grimaced, the derisive cackle of the Robbie Johnson gang a spiteful reality in his background.

With a superhuman effort, Richie managed to clamp the thought train shut. But only to make room for the worst occasion of all to erupt from its place of deep entrenchment. The antagonist a female bully this time, the ghastly Sarah Marshall, a specialist in absolute humiliation.

A hot spear of shame impaled him as he started reliving Sarah's simmering sidle up to him on Sports Day of that overly hot summer of nineteen-whatever-damn-year-it-had-been.

Richie had to suck in a deep breath. Even now, that beckoning gape was vivid and real to him. With its scattering of oh-so-fair freckles, her cleavage had been so angelic and white-fleshed that it had both thrilled him for its beauty and unnerved him for its power over him.

He remembered how it had stopped him blushingly in his tracks. But what had come next had been no less than terrifying.

Her press against him had been unbelievably soft and seductive, like nothing he'd experienced before. And it had been accompanied by the trail of a free hand across his upper thigh and a sultry-toned inquiry of if he'd like to take things further.

To his horror, his bottom lip had started quivering with fear and, most scarring of all, she'd seen it. Letting him know with her expression, a mix of mockery and allure whose taunt was that it knew all too well what must be happening to his young body.

Richie blinked repeatedly at the opposite wall.

To cap it all, she'd even brought an entourage of three short-skirted smirkers with her. Giggling witnesses of, and further contributers to, his burgeoning loss of control.

'Stop it!' he exclaimed, shoving the image firmly back where it belonged, in his distant past. 'Why *are* you dredging all this up?'

He blinked. The sound of his own voice had brought him starkly back to HuTech.

Reflexively, he scanned his surroundings.

Still no one about, thank God.

He told himself silently but firmly to calm down.

He was being absurd. It wasn't as if he was still that wimpy schoolboy, an easy target for the bullies. That was decades earlier.

Look at him now, a team leader at work. And, to boot, the most fortunate man at HuTech, what with the approaching Sunday lunchtime.

She liked him.

Wanted him there.

The sudden sound of laughing conversation and a door clomping shut was a forceful yank back into the moment. Familiar voices, two of his colleagues returning from wherever they had been. Followed quickly by the short-stepping click of high heels.

Diane Nugent proceeding to her corner.

Where had everyone been?

A vague unease started invading. Ramping up tenfold at an alarming sight, Vanessa hastening his way along the corridor.

'Richard!' came a pre-condemnatory cry, even before she had ripped his door open. 'Where *on earth* have you been?'

'Oh…I…er…,' he faltered, a disconcerting looseness ravaging his lower regions.

'I called a meeting, some surprise news, but you were nowhere to be seen!'

'Surprise news?' he asked deflectingly.

'*Yes!*' she gushed, clumping the door shut behind her. '*Good* news for you, for a change.'

Richie stared at her, relieved and dumbfounded in equal measure.

Was he dreaming? She was sounding fairly pleasant. And her expression was distinctly softening as she grabbed his spare chair to sink down opposite him.

'It's about the androids. Head Office video-conferenced me just before lunch and said that they're scrapping our current software plan, would you believe it? They want some completely new software trialled, a slightly modified version of what they've just developed for the proposed new A3 Series. They thought they may as well try it out on ours as well.'

'Oh!'

'And as a result, I have a new job number for you and the team to book to, and we've got hundreds and hundreds of hours on it.' She glistened at him. 'It's being government funded, this one.'

Richie blinked at her incredulously, as close as he'd ever been to entering nirvana.

Hundreds and hundreds of hours. That was what she'd just said.

He *must* be dreaming, surely!

What had he done to deserve such good fortune?

'I'll email you the code in the full briefing I'm about to write,' Vanessa continued. 'But, for now, get the androids wiped in readiness and we'll start afresh next week.'

'Okay. Will do.'

'Oh, yes...they stressed that a *complete* wipe will be necessary, I forgot to say. No short cuts. Something about residual strings.'

'Yes, it means they don't want any corruptions caused by leftovers,' explained Richie. 'The modelling functions aren't generic, so it's no good...'

'What's no good is going all hi-tech on me, Richie,' Vanessa cut in, suddenly sounding utterly uninterested. 'Just get it done, okay?'

He nodded happily, oblivious to her fall back into abruptness. Clutching at what mattered, all those lovely man-hours and the telling fact that she had called him 'Richie' instead of 'Richard'.

His earlier magnanimity towards her flashed back warmly and he contemplated the possibility that it had somehow touched her in some subtle, telepathic way, on the level of the soul.

What he was sure of now was his rightness in thinking that she wasn't so bad, after all. But then, very few people actually *wanted* to be nasty, did they?

At least most of the adults didn't.

Even Tony Philips and Sarah Marshall were probably fairly human by now.

A concerned sounding voice penetrated his awareness.

'Richie? Are you alright?'

He gave Vanessa a blink.

'Yes, thanks.'

'Your expression was looking...*weird!*'

'Oh. Was it? Sorry. I was just thinking that, well, never mind. It doesn't matter.'

Vanessa frowned.

'Look, Richie, I know I've been pressuring you recently, but I've *had* to with the deadlines we've all had. It's just the way it is; we've *all* been under pressure. But never forget, my door is always open if you need to talk about stuff.' She cocked her head to one side. 'Now, are you *sure* you're okay?'

'Yes, I really am,' replied Richie, crisply and honestly. 'Better than I've felt for quite some time, actually.'

Vanessa regarded him curiously for a moment and then, seeming at least partly satisfied, rose from her chair and clattered it back into the corner.

'I'll leave you to things, then,' she chirped, adding as a parting shot, 'And if I don't see you before, have a good weekend.'

'You too,' smiled Richie at her departing back.

It was a good ten seconds before he interrupted his dreamy stare into space and rose slowly, trance-like from his chair.

Wonders would never cease!

'Right,' he declared, pulling himself together.

It was time to get a nice, celebratory cup of coffee. Something to be downed slowly and calmly while ticking over therapeutically in neutral for a while.

And then, only when he was good and ready, would he summon his team and plan a rough route forward.

Off he sauntered, humming to himself.

Perhaps a future at HuTech wouldn't be so grim after all.

9

'Eto bylo samoye strannoye chuvstvo, Alec.' *It was the strangest feeling, Alec.*

Sergei Kuznetsov studied his subordinate intensely, looking for a clue as to what the young man might be thinking behind those averted eyes.

'A crazy, *crazy* moment.'

He was addressing himself this time, his bulbous nose crinkling contemplatively.

Alexandr straightened and sucked in a deep breath, trying to muster an appropriate comment. But before he could utter even a single word his commander was back in full flow, the sibilant torrent of Russian words hissing through his teeth like sharp swords making contact.

'She looked me right in the eyes, you know, *right* in the eyes and, I tell you, something special passed between us, something rare and precious. But only for the ambulance to arrive and cart her off to die. Huh! What do you make of that, hey? Having an encounter like that, with an English woman, of all people – Scottish, actually, so it turned out – only for her to die on you! Where's the sense in that?'

'Perhaps you knew each other in a past life, Comrade Commander.'

'Well, maybe that's it, Alec; you never know. I mean it *does* make you think about life, don't you think?' Not wanting an answer to that question from someone a good twenty-five years his junior, he didn't allow Alexandr the luxury of a proper pause. 'I wasn't imagining it. There was something between us that really *meant* something, did something amazing to me. And it was wonderful, Alec. It felt like winter changing into spring. But then...then years more of doing this *shit* we do brought winter back, and now, just lately, the encounter keeps replaying and replaying in my mind like a movie clip stuck in loop mode, and I don't know why, Alec. *God*, I don't know why! And I tell you, it's really starting to get to me.'

His eyes were radiating pure frustration now.

'Mmm,' frowned Alexandr sympathetically. 'Have you considered trying a good long walk? Or even a bit of a jog? Help clear your mind.'

'A *jog?*' Sergei spluttered out a disbelieving chuckle. 'Nebesa vyshe! I'd be the one being carted off by an ambulance then!!'

'I wasn't suggesting a half-marathon, Commander, just a *bit* of a jog,' grinned Alexandr. 'It's what I do when I'm all het up, and I do find it works. You'd be surprised.'

'Vy, yebanyye molodyye uippety!' scoffed Sergei with a crooked grin. *You fucking young whippets!*

'Seriously, try it, just a bit. Enough to make you puff.'

'Kak v adu, you crackpot!'

Alexandr gave a smirky shrug.

'I'm only saying what works for me, Comrade Commander. Trying to help.'

'Well, save your breath. You don't understand; you've never had a life-changing experience like that.'

Alexandr fell respectfully silent.

'Have you?' inquired Sergei, raising a questioning brow.

'No, Commander, not like that.'

'Well, then.'

The commander cast a glance at his reflection in the computer screen. Wondering uncomfortably how he'd become the man he had. Worse than winter now.

What about young Alec?

Would he turn out like this?

How Sergei hoped not, from the bottom of an aching heart.

Momentarily, the commander closed his eyes to steady himself. Managing to sound less agitated as he resumed his lament. His normal Vostok growl reinstated.

'*Akh!* What are we doing here, Alec, hey? Wallowing in this nasty shit when we could be putting our energy into helping people.'

'Surely this *is* helping people, though, Comrade Commander, helping Russia survive the onslaught of the West.'

Muttering indecipherably, but obviously cynically, about idealism, Sergei reached into his breast pocket to remove a yellow, red and blue hip flask.

'No wonder I'm always on this stuff,' he remarked in a gravelly tone, extending the hip flask towards Alexandr. 'Here, do me a favour and save me from myself a little bit by having some.'

Alexandr smiled.

He wasn't about to disobey a superior.

'Yes, Comrade Commander,' came his dutiful reply.

10

Slinking slowly and purposefully against one of the kitchen worktops, Shona scrolled through the Inbox of her phone yet again.

'No, it's definitely gone, Gav,' she confirmed into the phone. 'I just don't understand. How could that possibly happen?'

'What about the Recycle Bin and the Spam?'

'Yes, I've tried them,' Shona huffed impatiently. 'I can assure you, it's *gone*. It's as simple as that!'

Her irritation was building. Gavin's tone was starting to suggest doubt.

It wasn't as if you could imagine a message so powerful and hard-hitting. That single, three-letter word had slammed into her guts like a hurl from an unabridged, hardback edition of the Oxford English Dictionary.

Mum.

That was all it had said. All it had *needed* to say to let her daughter know that she wasn't alone in her tearful despair.

'Well, all I can say is that I've never heard of…of spirits making contact in that partic-u-lar way, but mayyyy-be…hmm, I dunno,' vacillated Gavin with the air of someone out of their depth. 'But what I *can* tell you is that Sheila's never mentioned it. Not that that means that in theory it couldn't happen with a text.'

'There was nothing theoretical about it, Gavin,' countered Shona testily. 'It happened.'

'I'm not doubting you, Shone. If you said it happened, it happened. It's just that it's usually via dreams, the hearing of a voice, ghost sightings, through a medium like Sheila, that sort of thing…as you know.'

'But at the end of the day it all comes down to interaction of energy, doesn't it?'

'Well…yeah, basically.'

'So as electricity is a form of energy, presumably technology could be used as a transmission medium.'

'I…' Gavin hesitated. 'I suppose so.'

'Well, why not? In what way is that any weirder than materialising from a fizzing cloud in mid-air?'

Gavin expelled a short chuckle.

'When you put it like that…'

'I do!'

'Tell you what, I could have a word with Sheila and get back to you, if you want. See if she's heard of it happening with anyone else.'

'Okay, then. That would certainly be interesting.'

'Anyway, how're you doing, old thing?' Gavin's voice had switched to soft affection. 'It isn't screwing with you too much, is it?'

'Naaaah, you know me, Gav. I'm an old hand at hauntings by now! I've had *years* of this.'

'True, you have. But it's been a while, hasn't it, what with that lengthy spell down south?'

'Yeah, but it's like riding a bicycle. Once you can deal with it, you can deal with it, and you never forget how. But getting a text…*phew!* That was something else, a step over the line, the *last* thing I expected. It gives you a jolt, you know, seeing it written in black and white right in front of your eyes.'

'I can imagine! It would be the last thing I'd expect, too. But then, you never know quite what to expect with these things, do you?'

'Precisely!'

'Anyway, I'll run it by Sheila and let you know, okay?'

'Thanks, Gav. I'd better get on now, get myself down Costcutter. I'm sure Dad has secret little snacks while I'm away, you know.'

'Ha ha! Right, I'd better let you go right away, then. Can't have the gannet wasting away.'

'Cheeky bugger! Give my love to Pat.'

'Will do.'

'Bye.'

'Toodle pip!'

Shona was smiling fondly as she ended the call. She had always got on well with cousin Gavin, to the extent that they considered each other to be confidants. But that said, there had been no need to mention that her yawningly empty fridge was in *extra* need of filling this weekend because it had an additional mouth to feed.

Letting on that fact would have been Gav's cue to start a teasing probe, when at this stage things with Richie were purely platonic. And might even stay that way…who could tell?

A slight flutter in her stomach was disputing that analysis, but she needed to get going quickly, and so she pushed it aside with a grunt. Plonking the phone down on the worktop and shoving it to the very back by the bottles of squash.

'I feel uneasy looking at the bloody thing now,' she muttered to herself, deciding to leave it there.

Things were becoming crazy at a crazy rate.

Suddenly craving Costcutter and its reassuring shelves of food, she turned away and headed for her handbag.

It was with glass-eyed precariousness that she took in the outside world, having pulled the door closed behind her. She had to close her eyes and steady herself before proceeding.

By the time she had rounded the corner of the house, she was striding lengthily. Continuing in this fashion, she quickly gulped up some thirty yards of pavement before nipping into a little cut-through that she knew would bring her out right in front of the shop.

Mid-way through it, though, a clammy feeling gripped her.

She slowed.

Looked around.

No one.

Setting her jaw determinedly, she resumed her stride. Telling herself that it must just be a bit of residue from the discussion of Mum. Leaving her a bit hypersensitive.

What she was unaware of, though, was that, several miles away, the man due to share some of her purchases with her was tensely visualising her opening her front door to let him in.

Hoping he wouldn't freeze up.

11

Richie gulped. Trying his utmost to steady himself.

Just being on Shona's doorstep was nerve-wracking enough, so he could do without the addition of being eyed by an escapee from some creepy children's story book.

Averting his eyes from its emotionless grin, he forced himself to reach out and grip the ugly metal elf by its skinny, iron hips.

Clomp. Clomp.

For a critter so scrawny, it was surprisingly sonorous against the strike plate.

Alas, it was as if such manhandling had provoked the fairyland creature into casting a bad spell that, in a stomach-knotting instant, had ripped away thirty years of his life.

He blinked. How different the door in front of him looked now! Tatty and scuffed, its thin layer of peeling blue paint was barely clinging on.

Just like his fortitude.

Never before had Richie asked a girl out. And this wasn't just a girl; it was Tina Bardsley, girl of his nocturnal fantasies.

As he stood stiff with apprehension, it was taking all of his self-control not to strangle to death the bouquet of flowers in his clutch.

Clunk.

His insides lurched, the sound of the door latch being released having suddenly dispelled the elf's spell.

Not that being back in the present moment helped. It seemed that he had changed very little in those thirty years. Just like back then, he was a cocktail of heartbeats and roaring blood.

He fought desperately to steel himself. Determined to keep his dignity intact this time. Reminding himself of his meticulous rehearsal in front of the bathroom mirror.

But the sight of the old door shuddering open had his carefully chosen words legging it for the hills. Leaving him defenceless against a smile that seemed to swell towards him like a cheeky magician with a swirling cape.

All he could do was stand and gape. The butterflies in his guts now pterodactyls.

Had Shona been similarly afflicted, it could have been a near-eternal wait. But, of course, she wasn't. Appearing impossibly relaxed, she chirped a greeting and invited him in.

In Richie stepped beside her, immediately finding himself way too close for comfort to that smile and the forget-me-not eyes. Not to mention the far too shapely-legged jeans down there and her thin, flowery pièce de résistance, a loose-fitting blouse that thrillingly accentuated her softness.

Still bereft of speech, he thrust the bouquet forward.

'Oh, my!' Her eyebrows rose with delight. 'Thank you, Richie, very much!'

How could she be so calm and collected?

Composure like hers was clearly something you were born with.

Life was so unfair.

But at least he was able to console himself, as Shona withdrew from planting the kiss on his cheek, that he'd got further this time than thirty years earlier with Tina Bardsley. What's more, he was now being led deeper into the coveted territory by the mesmeric motion of those shapely denimed legs.

'I thought we might start with a drink,' his host suggested brightly as they emerged into the kitchen.

'Great idea,' effused Richie, as his astonished gaze around the imposing old room bumped into the heartwarming sight of two pre-poured glasses.

Here was a girl who had everything very well planned.

'I take it a Dubonnet is to your liking?'

Richie had never heard of it, but anything alcoholic would be a godsend right now.

'Lovely,' he smiled, downing about half of the amber liqueur in a single gulp once they'd clinked glasses in the customary manner.

'This is quite some kitchen,' he commented, as his eyes wandered over the busily stocked shelves and giant beams supporting the ceiling.

Shona screwed up her face. 'I know! These old buildings are wonderful. Built to last forever.'

'I should think it would,' agreed Richie emphatically.

'I've just realised,' Shona rippled, 'I didn't ask you where *you* lived.'

'Oh, yes. I'm in Milton.'

'Ah, Milton. Inland a bit the other way, past your place of work.'

'That's right. I've a small bungalow there.'

'Nice! Handy for your work.'

Richie nodded.

'Yep. Does me fine.'

As they each took another sip of drink, Richie noted approvingly that just two places were laid at the table.

'So, your father won't be joining us then?'

Shona grinned. 'No, Dad's away with a friend for a long weekend. They're going to do some gardening and stuff.' She gave a giggle. 'When I say "stuff", it so happens that this friend has a model railway in the loft, a whopping great layout. You must know how it is, you men and your toys!'

'Ha!' Richie smirked, much more relaxed now that the drink was permeating him. 'Sounds good to me.'

Shona grinned at him teasingly.

'How about you, then, have you got any toys?'

'Well...only if you count my android.'

'Your *android?*' Shona's eyebrows shot up incredulously. 'You mean you've *actually* got a robot at home?'

'Just an old, knackered one from work. They were going to dump it but I thought it would be fun to experiment with it.'

Shona threw back her head and guffawed.

'Fancy having your own android! Please tell me you haven't given it a name and an apron and trained it to do all your housework!'

'No, no, nothing like that.'

'Aw, but you should! Fancy it not looking after you!!'

Richie grinned. 'It's just for experimental stuff, really. A bit of...'

'*Ooh*, hang on a mo,' interjected Shona as a hiss suddenly beckoned her steamily from the corner of the room. 'I just need to deal with the last of the veg. Take a seat; we're almost there.'

Sinking down at the table, Richie drained his glass and then sat back to enjoy the homely sight of Shona flitting around the hot rings and oven and clattering various utensils.

'Hmm. It'll need another two or three minutes, actually,' she declared after a test-prod with a fork.

She approached the table and sank down opposite

Richie, holding a small plate. 'Let's kick off with a couple of my wee spinach filo pastries.'

'Ooh, very nice!'

Topping up his glass with a lopsided smile, she watched him begin eating.

'I bet your android doesn't make stuff like this, Richie.'

'Ha ha, too right! I have to put up with toast and Marmite,' he smiled, adding, 'This is superb, by the way.'

Shona glowed as if she had just soaked up several hours of sunshine. And then raised a very happy glass.

'To us!'

'Here, here!'

They clinked and supped, and then Shona frowned.

'So, how *are* the buses on a Sunday? I didn't think there were many at all between here and Milton?'

Buses?

What was she on about?

An inner stone of horror dropped as he suddenly realised the significance of what she was querying.

Oh my God...he'd *driven* here!

And now look at him.

Drinking like a damn fish!

'What's wrong?' queried Shona.

'I can't believe this! The bus service is rubbish on a Sunday, so I drove. Meaning to stay tee-total!'

The 'oh' Shona released seemed to hang in mid-air in front of Richie, demanding a breath-sample.

'Shit!' he groaned.

It was Shona who broke the ensuing silence.

'Och, don't worry about it,' she soothed consolingly. 'It'll be a while until you go, and you've only had the one.'

Richie gestured at his glass. 'Very nearly two now, and you know how hot the police are round here on drinking Sunday lunchtime.' He shook his head, letting out a hollow laugh. 'God, I can't believe I've driven and then gone and drunk! What an idiot!! I've never done that before in my life.'

'Oh, Richie, don't worry about it. You can stay as long as you need, for the evening as well if you want. You'll definitely be safe by then.' She shot him a grin. 'That's if you can bear me for that long!'

Without waiting for the answer that should have promptly come, she jumped up and headed for the oven. 'Smells like we're in business!'

Richie blinked into the steamy air, his tension evaporating as he realised she was right.

He *would* be alright by the evening, so no harm done.

What mattered now was that her oven gloves were heading his way with two very well-filled plates.

'Now, be sure you don't touch the plate; it's *very* hot,' she warned as she leaned over him to set down his plate.

'Mmm, smells lovely,' he enthused, wondering if he was up to the challenge of the Henry-the-Eighth size portion looking up at him.

Having dealt with all the necessary, Shona joined him and set down a bottle of wine.

'I take it you like red,' she said, unscrewing its lid.

Richie stared at her, confounded. What *was* she thinking? He couldn't have even more.

'It's alright, you can spend the night in the spare,' she breezed, reading his thoughts.

'Spend the night?'

'It's a big house, Richie, so why not? That way, we can both enjoy the meal to the full. Besides which, a Sunday lunch *needs* washing down properly, don't you think? Here…'

Before Richie had the chance to object, a torrent of Cabernet Sauvignon was sploshing into the glass that Shona had set in front of him.

He surrendered hazily.

'Well, thanks, that would be very nice, actually.'

'It's nice having you here. I'll show you over the place later, if you'd like.'

'I *would* like,' grinned Richie.

'Right, then.'

The two of them started eating.

'So…' began Richie, swallowing a lump of potato, 'dare I ask if you had any visitations last night?'

'You may, and the answer is "no", or at least nothing that I knew about.' She smiled. 'I was dead to the world once my head hit the pillow.'

'Good.'

'Yeah, you're right, it *was* good.'

'This thing with your mum…' Richie paused to study her face before continuing. 'Do you think maybe she's got something from before she died that she needs to reconcile, or something like that?'

Shona's lips twitched before she answered.

'I really don't know. But it's been going on for some time, years in fact. She even visited me a few times when I lived down south.'

Richie creased his brow in thought. 'That suggests it's *you* she wants rather than something about this place.'

'Aye, it would seem so. But on the other hand it only happened a few times down south, whereas here it happens regularly and more intensely.'

'Strange.'

'You can say that again. But what I take from it most is that she's still *alive*, still the same individual, which means that there isn't really any such thing as death. It's only the flesh itself that dies. While we continue in another realm of existence, the so-called astral plane.'

Richie nodded. 'Yes, I've heard of it. Yet she's sort of *here* when she visits. I mean you said you could see her and even smell her. So she can't be in the astral plane then, if you can smell her. She must be here…with you.'

'I see what you mean, aye. She is able to become semi-physical whenever she wishes.'

'Semi-physical,' grinned Richie.

'Well, what else can it be? She isn't flesh and blood like us, yet we can see her *as if* she is physical.'

'Mmm,' he nodded thoughtfully.

It did seem a valid point.

Suddenly Shona was looking serious, as if she was about to confide in him about something of great gravitas. But then she seemed to check herself, as if thinking better of it.

'Anyway, that's enough talk about Mum,' she declared firmly. 'Let's lighten up a bit. Ready for some pud?'

'Pffff!' Richie puffed, rubbing an over-full belly happily. 'Is it alright if we take an inter-course break, first?'

'An intercourse break?' chuckled Shona, topping up their wine. 'That's a bit forward of you on our first date, isn't it?'

At that, they both creased up with laughter, Richie utterly carefree now. It was going well between them, better than he'd dared to imagine as he'd stood before the ugly elf.

'I tell you what,' Shona suggested. 'If you're feeling the need for a break I'll show you round the old place first, and *then* we'll have our pud. How does that sit with you?'

Richie smiled pure bliss at her.

'Absolutely perfect.'

12

Coughing out his dryness, Richie opened a blearily unappreciative eye to his surroundings. Only to discover that they no longer existed.

He flopped the eye back shut.

Total darkness in May, a month of unfailing enthusiasm for premature daylight, could only mean one thing. That the morning after the night before had yet to arrive.

The trouble was, it *had* arrived within him. Settling upon his poor right eye, drilling from above. As it always did after Richie overdid it.

He knew he'd have to get up and find some water. If he didn't, the world would be spinning come daylight. The the trouble was, though, right now his body weighed ten tons.

He groaned.

He'd soon be facing the demands of yet another Monday morning.

Oh, God!

Why was it that Sundays always had to pass so quickly?

Perhaps it was something to do with the Theory of Relativity. But, no, Richie knew it was far more malicious than that. The way time had it in for poor, beleaguered working folk.

He grimaced, sinking deeper into the bedding.

What he really needed was to stay with Shona and enjoy a slow recovery in the aura of her gentleness.

But life wasn't in the game of giving what was needed. Quite the opposite. The last course of a feast was anything but a stomach-settler. Instead, a nauseating extra known as 'reckoning'.

Sighing out defeat, he reached waveringly upwards. Until, after quite a few annoying seconds, his hand at last found the light cord that Shona had pointed out earlier.

'Ooooophhh, bloody 'ell!'

He buried his face in the pillow, the only sensible hiding place from the brutal glare. Cursing at having to live in the searing whiteness of an LED-centric world.

Gently lifting his head from the pillow, he eased his eyes open bit by bit to allow adaption time. In the process, spotting his watch lying on the side cupboard.

Reaching out sideways, he grabbed it.

Ten past one.

No wonder he felt bleary!

Anyway, he'd *have* to get up now. All this thought of water had filled him with the need for a pee.

At least, given the current, advantageous situation at work, he could flex in late, at nine-thirty. But he'd have to allow plenty of time for getting ready, especially as the relentless Shona was sure to push a cooked breakfast on him. And, of course, there would have to be some extra time for dropping in back home for a by now very necessary change of undies.

A couple of heaves followed by a staggery moment of light-headedness and he was on course for the bathroom.

He'd just swig a drink from the sink tap. Save him

fumbling his way through all the unknown light switches between himself and the kitchen.

Once he'd had two lengthy slurps from the tap, he paused into a careful lean against the sink, a smile starting to grow.

Shona serving him breakfast, hey?

This situation was so unreal. Light-years from his usual bachelor life. Things were really working out in his favour.

Shuffling over to the door, he wiped his chin on the towel that was hanging from a large iron hook. Pausing to stretch a neck that was more than a little stiff on one side.

'Ooooooph!'

Memories of hitting the pubs with the only two friends he'd had in his twenties reared disparaging heads, questioning when he'd become so middle-aged that overeating and a bit of wine left him like this.

Was he getting old already?

Swaying over to the far wall, he sought a second opinion from the cabinet. But its mirror-doors were in no mood for pulling punches, reflecting his features back at him with brutal honesty.

My God, he thought, that face was fast becoming older! Unlike the other one peering from behind him, a woman's, which was strangely smooth, almost waxy, despite her obvious maturity.

His stare was wild as he whirled round. Almost as out of control as the tsunami of shock that was rippling through his body, more the result of *not* seeing anyone behind him than what he had seen in the mirror.

'Shit!' he gasped, staggering against the wall in a blur of discombobulation.

This hadn't been some visual cortex phenomenon that could be put down to fatigue and too much drink the previous evening. It had been *real*. Something Richie knew for certain because of where he was – *this* house.

'Bloody hell!' he puffed, fresh tremors taking over him. 'I c-can't believe it.'

He had wanted to see a ghost, *so* wanted to, but now that it had happened he felt overwhelmed. Terrified.

Lurching forward, he grabbed at the door handle. An urgent need to flee from the scene his only thought.

Clunk!

It felt so good to close his bedroom door behind him. Like an escape. But the feeling could only ever last a few seconds. It was hardly as if he was going to slip back into bed now and sleep soundly.

Frantically, Richie pulled on his clothing, cursing as his trousers tangled with his shaky legs.

Quick!

Where had he put his car keys?

They were nowhere to be seen.

With his fear closing in on him, he fumbled around the room. Checking everywhere, even in the drawers of the bedside cabinet. Despite knowing full well that he hadn't used them.

Had he left the bloody keys downstairs?

Bloody hell! He could be *ages* looking. Becoming more and more shit-scared.

He stood transfixed, lost as to what to do.

Suppose she appeared again?

Drowning in fear now, a whimper escaped him. An awful, frightened puppy sound, so far from the normality of a grown man.

And then, just as he was sinking into utter despair...

'Yes!' he cried.

There they were, on the floor right next to his foot.

What an idiot he was!

'Thank *God!*' he cried, pouncing on them like a cat that had spotted a mouse.

Richie hardly felt his departure. It was like a great big float. Even his trembly attempts to insert the key into the ignition were numb and peculiarly vacant of emotion. And when he finally managed to fire up his trusty engine, it was only running somewhere vague and distant.

Was that his wheels spinning beneath him? It must be, because a sudden surge of movement was taking him into the darkness of the night.

The shakes...*oh my God*, he had them really badly now! So badly that it was necessary to grip the steering wheel firmly.

Barely able to function, he tore on, his breaths wheezy and manic, coming fast, entities of fear. Feeding on the vision of the waxy face that he still couldn't shake off.

And then to Richie's surprise a new sensation struck, that of warm tears coursing uncontrollably down his cheeks. Something that hadn't happened for a long, long time.

He didn't try to hold them back. In fact he did the opposite, screwing up his face and releasing high-pitched howls, just like a distressed child.

It felt good.

And it was good.

It must be because, all of a sudden, he was feeling purged of fear.

'Oh, yes, yes, yessss!' he roared, elated.

He had escaped.

And now was safe.

13

Shona stirred beneath the ruffled bed sheet, instinctively rearranging herself into a defensive position. Knowing that the clump she had just heard was real, not just spillage from a dream.

Not even breathing, she remained stock-still. Tiptoeing her attention fearfully around the room, a single small word growing in the back of her mind.

Mum.

Was this her again?

In tense expectation of seeing the spooky fizzing in the air that her deceased parent always caused, she opened her eyes, intent on penetrating the sinister gloom. Only to find that there wasn't a trace of it.

A ripple of relief undulated through her. Though only a slight one. The worrying fact remained that something had woken her, some sort of noise.

In sudden awareness of how sweaty she felt, she threw aside the sheet. That was the flip side of lovely summer days; they often brought nights as humid as a marathon runner's armpit. The last thing you needed after a skinful of wine.

Shona licked her now very dry lips and extended an arm for the glass of water on her bedside table. And then, having taken a long and satisfying sup, groaned as a massive penny dropped.

Of *course*…

She let out a pant of sweet relief.

Fancy forgetting that she had a guest in the next bedroom!

The noise had obviously been Richie finding his way to the bathroom. In need of flushing out some processed wine.

The heat was on the inside now. A glow of fondness for the new man in her life.

A soft smile started spreading.

He was far from the confident, strong type like John and Simon, her previous boyfriends, had been. But he was attractive and interesting in his own quiet, uneasy way. And relaxing to talk with and sensitive.

Qualities she liked very much.

Right from the beginning she had felt like she could talk with him about anything. It's funny how that happened with some people. You just felt comfortable confiding in them.

She had been about to tell him about the weird phone message during the meal but had changed her mind, wanting to lighten things. A first meal together with wine was time for fun.

She would tell him soon, though. See what he thought about it. If he agreed with her other confidant, Gavin.

He probably would, being a tech-man. Albeit a far less cocky tech-man than Gavin.

A titter broke free of her at the thought of how easily she could make Richie feel awkward when they argued. And her prowess at arousing a blush in him.

He was an enigma to her, a riddle that she couldn't fathom. On the one hand, he was obviously intelligent and capable. A team leader, he had said. Yet he was awkward in her presence, seeming vulnerable in an almost adolescent way. Like he could easily be wounded.

Not that she minded that. Appearing vulnerable meant he was open, on-show. Which had to be a good thing. Indeed, she found it something of a turn-on, a tug at her heartstrings.

She closed her eyes and sank her head deeper into the pillow. Cosying up to the thought that if ever there was a word that described his vulnerability with perfection, it was 'sweet'.

Clomp.

Again.

Another little giggle slipped out of her. His clumsiness was attractive, too. A different form of sweetness.

Two more clumps followed.

What *was* he up to?

She yawned and rolled over onto her opposite side. Thinking that she had better try to get some more sleep, now that her lumbering guest was about to settle. Presumably.

But what happened next made her stiffen with disbelief.

'What the hell...?' she inquired of the suddenly stark air.

That last clump...

It had been more distinct than the others. Sharp-edged and familiarly metallic.

The front door latch!

All it could have been.

She was suddenly sitting bolt-upright in the bed, staring into space. And then scrambling out of it in an explosion of astonishment.

Having clicked on the light switch, she squinted across the room for a wobbly moment, her heart thumping rabbit-fashion. And then strode towards the bedroom door and, turning the old iron handle, ripped it open. Surging onto the landing in a swirl of nightclothes.

'Richie?' she blurted.

Nothing.

'Richie!'

It was a cry this time, sharp with overtones of panic and disbelief. Not that it made any sense to cry out; he must be the other side of the front door by quite some distance by now.

Mustn't he?

She couldn't stand the uncertainty a moment longer. Hastening to his door, she pounded a frantic fist, several times.

'Richie! Richie!!'

Shoving the door open, she entered and switched on the light.

God dammit, she had been right…he'd only gone and done a runner!

But…why?

What on *earth* could have possessed him to do such a thing?

Turning back into the landing she cried out his name again, even louder this time, in a last desperate attempt to save the situation. Perhaps it hadn't been the front door and he was down in the kitchen slaking his thirst.

But she knew that was wishful thinking. As confirmed by the ringing silence that replied to her shout.

'Richie.'

It came out softly this time.

Wearily.

She flopped forlornly against the landing banister, a lonely figure peering down the stairs into the gloom. Which was when she heard the familiar fizzing behind her.

14

It seemed a preposterous thing to wonder having taken flight, but now that Richie was back in the sanctuary of home and more in charge of his faculties, doubt was on a mission, fluttering through his being, sowing its troublesome seeds. Asking if he could be sure that what had happened had really happened.

Had he *really* seen a ghost? It was just that looking back on the experience now, it felt so surreal, so *nebulous*. Almost like some weird kind of dream.

Suppose it hadn't been the ghost? Instead some kind of vision, a subconscious projection born of his earlier desire to see the ghost.

Was that possible?

A fevered imagination was crying out a 'maybe'.

But his sense of reality wasn't having it. There was no way the subconscious could be *that* much of a trickster. Besides, he didn't get hallucinations; he'd never had one in his life.

At least, not knowingly.

A shudder ran through him as he started reliving his fear and panicked gasps.

It had been the briefest of brief glimpses at the apparition's eyes but enough to chill him to his core. Eyes the like of which he'd never known, a sight truly, well, *haunting*.

In a moment of absurdity, he sniggered at his pun. But quickly returned to seriousness.

The trouble with doubt was that there was always ample room for it. But how could there not be when life itself had incomprehensibility as its bedrock?

Well, wasn't that true?

Who needed the supernatural as doubt-fodder when you had a normal life?

Even the fact that we human beings existed at all outweirded the supernatural. Just look at us and all the other animals in these strange fleshy bodies! Billions and billions of us, all filled with our urges and needs, hapless inhabitants of a great big sphere that was in turn one of billions of other spheres dancing to the universe's tune in an endless expanse of space.

Compared to all of that, didn't seeing a ghost in a mirror seem positively down-to-earth?

Well?

But – Richie smiled in a sudden emotional one-eighty – the fact that life *was* impermeably weird was what made it such a feast! Where was the value in having a life of which you had the measure?

And if he *had* now seen a ghost, that was surely something to be celebrated, a direct connection with something beyond this nonsensical life on planet Earth. Even if it felt like all he'd connected with were his own inner terrors.

Phew! It was no good. Far too tired to even think straight, he wasn't up to processing all this right now.

The sensible thing to do would be to hit the sack. But also not so sensible because there was a problem...*dare* he go to bed?

Clueless as to what to do, he looked around himself. Immediately wishing that he hadn't.

The air around him felt…alive.

With his fear.

Fighting to stem the exodus of courage, he reminded himself that everything was alright, that he was *here* now, in his home, safely away from that awful old house.

He had nothing to be afraid of here, nothing at all.

Be that as it may, perhaps he should take the precaution of leaving the light on. Assuming he'd be able to sleep in a room brightly lit.

He tutted. Fat chance of that! The dark silence of night was a necessary bedfellow for him. Yet now the harbourer of an enemy from which there was nowhere to hide.

His imagination.

Not only that but lying in bed *felt* very vulnerable, especially when you were in the altogether, as he always was this time of year. A single sheet of linen didn't feel like much of a shield to cower beneath.

He grunted.

There was only one thing that could help him.

Rising to his feet, he headed for the dark, wooden cabinet in the corner. Reaching in for his favourite bottle, the Armagnac.

As his fingers closed around its curved neck, a sobering thought struck him. That in his panic, he'd driven home oblivious to his blood alcohol level. Something he'd never entertain normally, not for a single moment.

Since meeting Shona, he seemed to be opening up some uncomfortable new territory in his life.

Tilting the bottle carefully above the wide-bottomed glass, he poured himself a double – one had to do the job properly – and took a hearty swig prior to returning the bottle to the cabinet.

Aaaah!

A smile spread across his cheeks at the steadying feel of the invasion.

A glance at his watch told him there was still time for a few hours of sleep before he needed to start getting himself ready for work.

He could flex in at nine thirty, the latest time allowed. Which meant he could get away with getting up at eight forty-five.

He started counting on his fingers.

Yes. Assuming it took him half an hour to fall asleep, he'd still get five and a half hours. Not exactly brilliant, but it would suffice.

'Come on, then,' he urged himself briskly, taking another swig.

Sinking into bed felt better than he'd dared to imagine, now he had the brandy as an inner friend. There was no doubt about it, the Dutch had very much the right idea with matters of courage.

Emptying the glass with a final swig, he reached up and clicked off the light switch.

'Okay, now bring on tomorrow as soon as possible, please,' he pleaded of the darkness. 'A new day...'

But any chance of slumber was being stared out of existence by the rebuking eye of shame.

In fleeing for safety he'd abandoned his host.

An inner contraction asked what was she was going to think of him. A guest who'd legged it in the night having been so generously fed.

Richie didn't even have her phone number.

Why the hell hadn't they exchanged numbers, like normal people did?

He'd have to go straight to work in the morning; there was no way out of that. Which meant that the earliest he could contact her would be the evening. Unless he drove to Shoreholm at lunchtime...but what were the chances of her being there then?

He'd have to try, though.

A deeply frustrated part of him punched the darkness. How was sleep going to come now that he was all stirred up again?

Clicking the light back on with exasperated brusqueness, he heaved himself back out the bed and headed for the lounge, muttering to himself.

A single measure this time should do it. Just the right amount to send him on his way without the risk of a dehydration-head.

Hopefully.

Having downed the brandy in one, he glided back to his bed. Now uncaring of the ramifications of his earlier actions.

Indeed, uncaring of anything.

That last glass had been the clincher. Seeing to it that sleep would open its arms properly at last.

There were just two frightening moments to get past. The first being the reappearance of the contemptuous little elf, now looking creepier than ever. The second being the giddying sensation of slipping into a dark, confused kaleidoscope of streets.

Sleep was on his side, though, melting everything away. Leaving until last the sensation of the brandy's warmth and something unexpected.

Shona's forgiving smile.

15

HuTech was a weirdly alien place upon Richie's arrival a few minutes after nine thirty. Nothing about it looked the same. Even the deeply ingrained action of swiping his card at the reader on the main entrance door had changed, no longer feeling...quite...real.

It was as if he were remotely watching his life rather than actually living it. Which was something of a change from his intense immersion in the events of the last day and night.

A slight fatigue from an insufficiency of sleep aside, he ought to be feeling as buoyant as a size XL set of water wings. After all, look at how his fortunes had turned in just the past three days.

His work situation – set to become less stressful.

His ambition to see a ghost – fulfilled, now that he'd finally decided that it *had* been a genuine sighting.

Best of all, his romantic life – no longer a desert.

Admittedly the latter had lurched into a state of discomfort, but it was only a temporary hitch, soon to be put right. Shona would understand once he'd accounted for his panicked flight.

Entering the building, he commenced the hitherto familiar walk towards the Robotics Engineering section, the feeling of remoteness refusing to abate.

Somewhere in the foggy distance was a mass of rickety feelings that really ought to be troubling him. But he remained impassive, even when what should have been a deeply worrying spectacle confronted him upon turning into the corridor leading to his office.

The excited sounding collective was talking nineteen to the dozen, right outside his office door. And unsurprisingly, the most distinct voice was Vanessa's.

All of a sudden, he was on her radar. Prompting her to make an insensitively loud mid-sentence switch, a proclamation of 'ah, *here* he is' that ricocheted along the corridor before hitting its target full on.

Normally, Richie would have listed like a torpedoed ship at that. But today he seemed to have an abundance of ballast. Nothing short of a tidal wave would have rocked him.

'Richie, this is Professor Foster from HuTech in London,' Vanessa declared, gesturing at an unfamiliar, bearded face in the centre of the group. 'We've been waiting for you!'

Even the blush that Vanessa was so adept at summoning in Richie's cheeks in front of others was on strike today. A fact that she seemed to register with a slight glint.

'Sorry. I got held up,' Richie stated indifferently as he drew to a halt in front of them.

'Hello,' interjected the professor kindly, stepping forward for a handshake before Vanessa could say anything more. 'I was wondering if the two of us could grab ourselves coffees or something and have a chat about these new software updates.'

'Oh. Right,' replied Richie. 'Certainly. In my office, perhaps?'

'Meeting Room 3 is empty,' cut in Vanessa with an eye-rolling air of for-goodness-sake-ness. 'If you go on up, I'll send up drinks and biscuits.'

'Oh, okay, thanks,' acknowledged Richie, then turning to the professor, 'I'll just dump my docs in the office, Professor, and then we can go up.'

'No rush,' smiled the professor amiably, adding, 'and please...call me Peter.'

Richie sensed he was going to get on well with the affable Peter. Returning his smile, he edged through all the bodies to his office and deposited his leather document holder haphazardly on the mess of paperwork on his desk.

'It's good to have you Galloway-based folk aboard with the A3 project,' commented Peter, once he and Richie were seated in the meeting room. 'We're convinced that this new modified software will be a game changer for your androids, particularly in terms of memory utilisation.'

'Great!'

'Yes, the programmes use non-redundancy looping, which in effect quadruples the amount of available memory. Which in turn leads to much smoother transitions, improved motor function and shorter learning cycles. Admittedly, that means there's no redundancy, but who needs it nowadays with modern reliability?'

Richie nodded his approval, feeling much more grounded now.

'Now, I assume that your androids are being fully wiped,' Peter continued.

'Well, they will be,' returned Richie. 'Is there any indication of when the software will be with us?'

'Imminently. A matter of days.'

'Ooh, *that* soon!'

'Yes, Richie, they've been working with the final touch-ups for all of last week and the weekend.'

'Right.' Richie paused thoughtfully. 'Well, I'd better

get things moving here then. Not that the wiping will take long.'

'There will of course be a programme of ongoing tweaks in the weeks to come, and they'll all require follow-up testing of one type or another, which is why so many man-hours have been allocated.'

'Mmm.'

'For once the government isn't prioritising getting this done on the cheap, instead stressing aiming for perfection. Even they realise how immense the ramifications of this project are for the future of this science.'

'Great! So it's looking good for all of us, then,' resounded Richie brightly.

'Indeed, it is. I bet you're glad of it up here. I mean, let's be bluntly honest, your old relics have been left way behind now that we have the A3 series. And, believe me, having spoken with Vanessa at length, I do realise what the situation has been like for you with funding.'

'Yes. In a word, difficult.'

'Well, once this is done, you'll be pretty much on par with the London androids, and things will be easier for all concerned.' Peter leaned towards Richie and patted his shoulder. 'You've got an exciting future now for at least the next ten years, my friend!'

'Thank you,' Richie smiled.

'Well…' Peter straightened and arched both eyebrows. 'Is coffee coming? It wasn't the most amenable of journeys up, and I'm getting dry.'

'Ooh, sorry,' said Richie, jumping up and hastening towards the wall-phone. 'I'll give hospitality a prod.'

* * *

Once Peter had departed to have another discussion with Vanessa and also one of her bosses, Richie gathered his team and, dipping into the introductory notes Peter had thrust into his hand, started outlining the plans for the weeks to come.

He'd need to get the wiping process underway. Instructing his team to begin and emphasising the need for thoroughness rather than haste, a considerable change of paradigm for them, he selected one android for himself. A gallant choice, the troublesome 4B.

It came as no surprise that 4B fought him all the way, not even allowing the first, most basic wipe to run smoothly. But finally, following an intense and muttery series of retries, he had it wiped.

Now all that remained was to hunt for any fragments that may have missed and remove them manually. What could be a painstaking process.

His stomach was suddenly reminding him of the need to adequately fuel his mental exertions, so he flicked his watch a glance.

Almost ten past one.

How time had flown!

His empty guts tightened as a thought rocketed through him.

His lunchtime mission…he'd forgotten all about it!

'Oh, God!'

Food would have to wait.

As he reached the foyer, he noticed to his displeasure the falling of rain. Cursing at the extra delay, he returned to his office to pick up the light raincoat that hung in readiness in one corner.

In the rush of the morning, he had omitted to make himself his usual sandwiches. But that wasn't the reason for his stomach tightening even more as he lowered himself into his car.

He sighed.

For somebody so socially inept, this wasn't going to be at all easy. As he turned the ignition key and pulled away, the inevitable happened, a paranoid little movie surfacing in his mind, in which he and Shona were standing face to face.

It was awful. His no-hope explanation was drowning in its own swamp of awkwardness before it could properly reach her. Not that it stood much chance of penetrating Shona's staringly indignant wall of silence anyway.

Finally she started speaking. Her icy calmness choking what little life was left in the tiny vestige of hope still clinging to the wall of his heart.

Didn't he realise that she'd been wondering all morning what she'd said to upset him? Was he oblivious to her feelings? He was a typical man – all he ever thought of was himself.

The sound of a siren and the sight of a blue flashing light in his rear-view mirror suddenly plucked him from Shona's onslaught. Not that such a rescue was in any way an improvement.

Veering left into a well-timed widening of the road, he slowed to a trembly halt, panic gripping at his throat.

Richard Smith – drink-driver. Caught.

But the car tore past him.

'Idiot!' he gasped. 'They're not after *you!!*'

Having heaved a few more gaspy breaths, he softened his rigid grip on the steering wheel, indicated and pulled out to resume his journey at a browbeaten crawl.

Despite the slowness of his speed, the sign for Shoreholm loomed into sight with unsporting rapidity, flanked by a background sprawl of houses whose windows felt like judgemental rows of eyes.

Richie slowed even more.

As he crawled around the corner at the junction leading to the centre of the village, his heart was in the grip of a arctic chill. Contracting horribly as...there it was, the house that had been so dear to him just yesterday afternoon.

At least there was room to park right outside of it. A

small mercy for which he was thankful, considering how the wind was picking up and increasing the rate of rain-bounce off of his windscreen.

'Here goes, then,' he muttered, taking a few moments to steel himself against a persistent voice in his depths that was warning him frantically that all would not be well.

Emerging from the car, he approached the door and once again grasped the hideous elf.

Clomp. Clomp.

The sonorous thudding against the strike plate set his nerves jangling.

Now for the worst part.

The wait...

With his heart thudding he tried to gird himself. Resorting to a calming technique, the slow clenching and unclenching of fists.

It didn't work at all, though.

The tension was driving him bananas. Never before had silence seemed so long and still, as if time itself had frozen in the chill of fear.

As if in contempt of him, the rain started to pelt really hard. Pulling up his hood, he stepped back and gazed at the house windows in turn.

Hmm.

No sign of life.

He'd give it one more quick go.

Clomp. Clomp.

Still no sign of life.

He'd had enough of this. With his feelings dividing between irritation and relief, he turned back to his car and pushed the unlock button on his key fob. And then, removing his soggy waterproof, sank back into the driving seat, an illogical conviction telling him that he would have caught her had he been more aware of the time and left promptly at twelve.

He groaned.

Wasn't this wonderful?

Now he'd have to go through the whole ordeal again later, after the afternoon's work. The dread of it playing on his mind in the meantime.

A dispirited turn of the ignition key saw him sitting with the engine running for a last few despondent seconds. Staring into space unseeingly as he weighed up his options.

Damn the rain! There was no point in hanging around in it getting wet and miserable. He may as well head back to HuTech and pick up some canteen food to eat in his office. He had tried the miserably thin ham and cheese sandwiches from Shoreholm's grotty little shop once before and wasn't keen to repeat the experience.

On the other hand, though…

He pursed his lips.

Suppose he *did* get some food at the grotty little shop and eat it in the car? It would mean he could have another shot at Shona's front door afterwards, by which time she might even be back from wherever she had gone.

An even better idea struck him.

If he bought a pen and note pad from the shop, he could write her a message explaining his absence, a pre-emptive softener before he had to actually face her.

He would park round the corner out of sight from her house. That way, he could nip out discreetly and slip it through her letter box.

Yes.

Great decision!

Casting a final glance at the unsympathetic front door and its contemptuous elf, he slipped the car into gear and pulled off. The appearance of a prim-looking elderly lady on the path the only thing stopping him extending a fierce middle finger at the elf.

Round the corner he went, onto the main street. Sure that the shop was only about fifty yards along, on the left.

Narrowing his eyes, he peered to the left through the rainy windscreen. Expecting to spot the shop's scruffy façade any moment.

Ah, yes! That was it, up ahead, a little further along than he had remembered. More like a hundred yards.

With peculiar tingles running through him, he reversed into the parking space available a couple of cars past the shop. And then, with his mind half on how to word his note, he dashed purposefully through the rain towards the scruffy door, cursing as one foot landed in the puddle that was right in front of it.

The lack of light hit him like a punch in the guts.

Shit!

Life was majorly crapping on him today. Who'd have believed that after all that, the stupid place would be closed?

Half to be utterly sure and half from sheer frustration, he grasped the handle of the tatty door and gave it a vigorous rattle.

It didn't give an inch.

'Bloody hell, what kind of shop just shuts at lunchtime on a Monday?' he snarled, unable to stop himself aiming a peeved kick at the bottom of the wooden door. 'Sodding place!'

Wheeling round angrily, he strode back towards his car. Noticing to his discomfort an elderly man under a porch on the other side of the street, staring at him with hollow, disapproving eyes.

'You'd kick the bloody door as well if you had to put up with what I have to,' he growled quietly as he yanked the car door open to drop roughly into his seat.

Slamming the door closed on his embarrassment, he scowled up the street. And then, in a stroppy wheel-spin, sped into a deft turn across the entrance to a side road before heading back towards HuTech.

16

Will death be the end of me?

What a question that is, Shona, love, eh? I mean, what else can bring us quite so deeply into confrontation with our very nature?

You'll remember those protracted meal times, discussing things like that, the three of us. How we'd try to thrash things out!

It was your good old dad who eventually said what needed saying about life after death, in his solid, down-to-earth way. That we'd have to accept there being no answers until the appointed time.

But did we quit thinking about it?

Not us!

How could we? We humans come into our world with the word 'why?' embossed on our souls. Which, my love, is why since my passing on I've repeatedly tried to reveal to you the answer.

That I still exist.

Oh, Shona!

Watching you right now from your bedside, I wish I could offer an apologetic hug for the disquiet all my visits must have caused you. But equally I wish to keep the fact that life carries on alive in your mind.

You know how it is with esoteric experiences, the way that the passing of time can dim their reality, opening the door for the creep in of doubt.

I promise that as soon as it becomes possible for me to provide further clarity, I shall do so. And you'll be surprised to know that I am confident that that time is imminent. In the meantime, though, my immediate hope is that a subconscious part of you is able to feel the thoughts and love I am transmitting at you right now.

As of course you know, your father and I were never religious, so we couldn't bring you up in an atmosphere of 'belief'. Nevertheless, I was aware that as a young adult you were looking into religion, despite your efforts to keep it to yourself.

Take it from me, a mother just knows these things.

The arena of religion was my own first port of call on the matter of life after death. It's just that 'faith' wasn't mine to give.

So, I turned to the voices speaking from the other direction, as one tends to do in that sort of situation. Whereupon the disbelievers told me firmly to get real, declaring with equal conviction their own faith, that all of us were doomed to disintegrate into daisy-food.

But I had no faith in their claims either. Every time I thought of generations upon generations of unique people living and doing all they do just to fizzle out into non-existence, something positioned itself solidly in the way.

Existence just *had* to make some sort of sense. The thought of life, the amazing and beautiful Earth, and the whole universe having no meaning at all was just ridiculous. The pinnacle of all absurdities!

No way, José!

Not that any of the wondering matters now, anyway. I have my answer in being the very evidence I sought.

But in no way is that cause for celebration. Because I *have* suffered a death of sorts in being tragically stuck in this limbo of my own making. Unable to move on as I cling to the human life that meant *everything* to me.

Eileen McShane, wife of Derek and mother of you.

It's who I am, Shona.

Who I *am*.

And with you two on Earth is where I belong. That's where heaven is for me.

Of course, the human life comes with its suffering. But it's in human life where true magnificence is found. Where real *growth* takes place.

So much can *only* be experienced by living in physicality with a body. How else can we come to know ourselves so much, so *rawly*?

Which is why I yearn for it again.

Please excuse the pun, but I'd *die* for being back with you and Dad on the clifftops, sucking in hearty lungfuls of that wonderful Galloway air!

Alas, this is all I have now. This solitary life in Mind Land, a desert of selfness where the air couldn't possibly be thinner.

Do you see why I can't let go of my life on Earth?

Agh! You don't, though. Because you can't hear a word of what I'm saying with this existential gulf between us.

Unless...

Hope resides in me that somehow, at some deep, subconscious level, you are picking all this up.

And if you are, may I apologise for ranting so much?

It's just that I can't help it. You see, a death as sudden, unexpected and bewildering as mine screws you well and truly up. Leaving you a pathetic prisoner in your own mind.

Just think, my love, if I'd never had that stupid idea to meet up with Janet in London, I'd still be with the two of you now! Living a fulfilling life instead of languishing like this.

It's amazing when you think about it. At an arbitrary, nonsensical intersection of space and time, the least attentive driver in the whole city just happens to meet your mum and then, just like that – kerpowww!

I expect her itsy-bitsy little mind was entrenched in something air-headed, like her phone beeping in another 'like' on Facebook.

And the result?

The end of a life, despite that nice Russian-sounding man being so quick to phone the ambulance.

But that's a human life for you.

It can be lost in an instant.

Huh! I bet she was one of those who passed her test first time. They're the worst drivers of all.

By the way…I'm not sure I ever mentioned to you that it took me – *would you believe it?* – six attempts to pass that damn test!

Yes, *six!*

I never actually mentioned it because I was, *well*, you know, a bit embarrassed about it, you having passed on your second attempt. But although it took me six attempts at least I wasn't the one to cause an innocent victim and their family so much misery.

Tsk!

Fifty-nine, I was.

Far too young to depart.

I must have died a thousand deaths for you and Dad in the weeks following my passing. It was *so* harrowing, *so* tragic, seeing the two of you plodding around like that. As if…if you were in your own personal little nuclear winters.

Well, nothing little about them, actually. Such an appalling change from the lives we had made for ourselves.

Made. That's the crucial word here, Shona. The essence of life as a human.

To create.

We'll have a good, long chin-wag about this soon, my darling. About how you can really *achieve* as a human, be in full flow, expressing yourself through your actions, applying yourself to your projects, learning so, *so* much from the best teacher of all, raw, unpredictable interaction. All of it showing you who you are, giving you repeated opportunities to grow.

Expression and growth... You see? It's what existence is all about. But maybe you've already realised that, being so perceptive and bright.

Oh, *Shona*, I have something to reveal to you, something that will astonish you!

I love the two of you so, *so* much. But, you see, the nature of love is not just to *be*. It needs to exert itself through action. Through proper, solid interaction.

And, my God, that's what mine is going to do again!

Yes, you are hearing me right.

Something amazing is going to happen.

Just you wait!

You won't believe it.

I've had a stroke of luck, you see.

17

Richie flinched.

Hearing the voice that normally lifted him so high deliberately pitched on the wrong side of friendly had split open a crevice in his heart.

'Shona, I'm sorry,' he pleaded, teetering on its precipitous edge. 'I... I just lost my head. I've never had an experience like that before. I'm not like you, you know, an old hand at it.'

'I'm *not* an old hand!' Her words came at him like an assassin's bullets. 'I told you it hurts me; don't you listen to a word I say?'

'Yes, I know, I'm sorry. I'm *upset*, that's all. I didn't exactly mean *old hand*.'

'Oh, really?' Shona snarled stormily. 'Well I fail to see what else you could have meant!'

'I was...was...'

Her eyebrows arched into angry archbishops of judgement.

'Blathering, as usual?'

Richie gawped at her wordlessly, his eyes bulging with frustration.

'What's the matter with you; can't you just…?'

'*Look*, I just lost my head!' snapped Richie, suddenly finding his voice. 'For *Christ's* sake, Shona, it happens!!'

To his surprise, she flinched. A rare moment of self-doubt dancing out its flicker in her eyes.

Bracing himself for some comeback, Richie waited. But there was only an unsure silence.

Hope flurried through him. Finding its agency in her pursing of lips and resigned step backwards to admit him through the doorway.

'Thank you,' he muttered, entering quickly before she had time to change her mind.

'Kitchen,' she said stiffly, turning on her heels and leading the way.

His insides fluttered.

He wasn't quite there yet.

Once they were in the kitchen, she sank down at the table, motioning him to do the same.

'It's just that I've never seen a ghost before,' Richie groaned in a desperate attempt at plea-bargaining. 'And even though I knew a haunting was possible and I *wanted* to see it, it frightened me more than I imagined.'

Shona frowned.

'But did you have to just go like that? Leaving me in the lurch? If you knew how I felt when I found you'd gone…'

'I'm sorry. I panicked. Surely you didn't think I'd left you, did you?'

'I didn't know *what* to think! You get someone a nice meal and wine, all is going well and then he suddenly pisses off at some unearthly hour without a word.'

Richie looked shamefully down at the table. Having to push his reply out word by emphatic word.

'I'm *sorry*, okay? I *really* am. It's just that I wasn't *thinking*. Can you not understand that it *utterly* scared the shit out of me?'

There was a pause, a long pause. And then she spoke.

'It's unsettling, isn't it?'

'Unsettling?' Richie stared at her. 'Jesus wept! It was a bit more than that!!'

Solemn confirmation nodded down at the tabletop.

'The thing is, Richie, you never quite get used to it. Never! *Even* when you're an old hand at it, like me!'

Was that the sound of forgiveness?

Richie allowed a small smile to test the waters. Unsure of whether or not he was on dry ground yet.

An equally small smile replied. And then a sudden noise alerted him. The scrape of Shona's chair on the hard kitchen floor.

In a sweeping flurry, she was round at his side of the table. Enacting the last thing Richie had expected.

All that existed now was their snuggle, acutely soft and warm.

And deep...

That was her heart. Thud, thud, thud. Feeling like it was drumming out a beat for him alone.

The ultra-close-up, breathy whisper of 'sorry' right into his ear had his head awhirl with jumbled feelings. But then, just as unexpectedly, he felt her withdraw to one side. And then rise and step away.

Her smile was now unambiguously foxy, and he couldn't help but swivel in his chair and reach out for her.

Clearly the right thing to do. Because, in a slither, she was down.

In his lap.

18

Yes, Shona, my love… I'm coming back!

The means has come to me. Born of that single word that I somehow made appear on your phone.

Granted, that a single word on a phone is a triumph, is the measure of the task that lies ahead. But I'm buoyant. Because I'm going to manage it. I know it; I can *feel* the success already.

Mum.

I know it doesn't seem much, a single word on a screen. Yet I'm convinced that, had Neil Armstrong's dear soul been with me, he would have claimed it was a giant leap for ghost-kind.

As you know, I've been interacting via ectoplasm for years, but ultimately that method is a cul-de-sac of non-hope. Clearly unable of going further than nocturnal appearances in bedrooms.

Not that I shall cease that activity. Indeed, I cannot stop that happening, it being the unconscious result of my desire to be back with you and Derek, something that in the main happens spontaneously.

But as for the appearance of that message, *Mum*, it was

utterly unexpected. And has lit the way as to what needs to be done.

It sort of makes sense to me how it happened, now that I've had a good think about it. After all, what is an electronic computing device like a Smartphone but a primitive neural network?

So, if my soul can incarnate on Earth in a human body then it can also operate in a more limited fashion in an artificial neural network! Delivering a lucid, unambiguous communication rather than a vague haunting.

I'll need to ramp up my efforts hugely, though. Communicating one word at a time would very soon drive me nuts. And doubtless you too. But, it's clear that the technological route is the way ahead, but via something far more powerful than a phone.

All that is required is that whatever device is used has a *connection* with you. It is my having the connection with you, the ectoplasmic link, that makes anything that *you* interact with available to me as a possibility.

And *most* conveniently, Shona, your recent actions have thrown me a lifeline.

A lifeline called Richie.

19

Richie knitted his brow.

Was he losing his marbles?

Or had he just forgotten?

Hmm. He *must* have forgotten, he tried to tell himself. Knowing deep down that he hadn't.

At the end of a session, he always parked Bessie's head in the preferred direction. And certainly wouldn't leave her looking straight at him.

'Bessie?'

The shiny synthetic face registered nothing. As was to be expected, considering he'd wiped her in readiness for loading the new A3 software.

Right now, she was no more than an inert, empty shell. A dead mass of polymers and metal and silicon circuitry.

His speaking to her had, of course, just been a reflex. That was the trouble with living with an android – after a while you took her artificiality for granted and forgot that she wasn't alive.

He smirked.

Thank God Shona had come into his life and rescued such a sad case.

Rising from his chair, he sauntered over to Bessie and, placing a palm on each side of her head, carefully straightened it so that she was looking straight ahead at the opposite wall.

Which felt much better.

There was something about having eyes looking directly at him that he found disquieting. Even when they were artificial.

Especially when they were artificial, actually.

Probably a hangover from watching too much 'Dr. Who' as a lad. Although some of it must stem from a much earlier time than that. His one and only teddy bear, Mr. Fuzz.

It had been the bear's eyes. Each of them had stared in their own direction, yet somehow they had worked with a weird synergy to follow him around his bedroom. Their glassy blankness appearing somewhat freaky.

In the end, he'd had to turn Mr. Fuzz to face the wall. Just like he'd now had to move Bessie to look away.

He frowned.

Strange that. How she hadn't been parked.

As he turned away from her, he shook his head. Still trying to convince himself that it had been an oversight on his part.

After all, what other explanation was there?

The drudge of threading his way through several thousand strings of code on his computer screen was obviously taking its toll.

Anyway...

He left the room and headed for the kitchen.

What was needed was a coffee.

A strong one.

It shouldn't really be necessary for him to check all the code like that. But he always liked to give new routines a quick once-over before loading them in his hardware.

It was all about caution.

Whilst he wasn't a programmer himself, he did have some rudimentary knowledge of the art. And he knew that it was less of an art than it had been years earlier, now that programmes were so high-level. Which made him wonder about the ability of some of the young generation of programmers.

One could never be too careful. Especially when one considered that he didn't know the A3 programmers from Adam.

Years earlier, with just a cursory glance, he had noticed something seeming fishy about an update. A suspicion that had turned out to be well founded.

Richie seemed gifted with a sixth sense when it came to looking at programme code.

He grunted in satisfaction.

At least A3 hadn't given him any bad vibes.

A different kind of vibe assailed him as he was reaching for the coffee jar. This one emanating from his trouser pocket.

Yanking his phone out brought him face-to-face with the loveliest face in the whole world.

'Hello, Shona,' he smiled, having tapped the 'Answer' icon. 'To what do I owe this pleasure?'

'Richie, are you back from work yet?

'Yes, I worked from home this afternoon.'

'Good, I'm feeling restless but don't fancy taking an evening stroll on our favourite beach all on my own.'

'Sounds great, but I'm just about to make a much needed coffee.'

'Well, give me your address and make one for me too! A coffee before the walk would be just perfect.'

'Good plan!'

'*So*…come on, then…where am I heading for?'

'Right. Erm…well just as you come into Milton, if you take a right and then an almost immediate left, you'll see an uphill road called "Hill Street", full of bungalows.'

'Okay.'

'Mine's the one at the very end with solar panels. Number nine.'

'Nine. Right-ho. Mine's one sugar and white, by the way. Not too milky or too strong, okay?'

'Yes, ma'am!'

'Less of the sarcasm! And, by the way, a couple of biscuits would be nice. You should have noticed by now that I'm a dunker.'

'Comin' up,' tittered Richie, hoping he had some biccies in the cupboard.

Affectionate goodbyes were exchanged and Shona ended the call. Whereupon, Richie froze in the grip of a turbo-charged change of demeanour.

She was coming to his house!

Quick!!

Managing to mobilise himself, he scrabbled in the left hand cupboard. Heaving a sigh of relief as his fingers found a pack of biscuits.

Just the one, though.

'Right, Shona, I'm afraid it's going to be digestives or digestives,' he murmured, trying to calm himself.

Okay! Now for the house…

Turning away from the cupboard, he looked down. His uppermost concern a kitchen floor that always amazed him with how quickly it could grow filth and attract stray crumbs and lumps of food.

Relief welled.

He was in luck. It was looking better than usual. Which was a Godsend, considering the lack of time for whipping out the vacuum cleaner.

Not that he would be able to *whip* it out from behind all that other stuff.

What about the shelves and surfaces, then?

He ran a pensive finger along one of them.

As expected, on the grubby side.

It wasn't really visible, though. That was one good thing about this old place; it didn't show the dirt.

It must be the old-fashioned matt paint.

There was the kitchen window sill, mind you, a special case. This time of year, something of a fly's graveyard.

A glance confirmed that expectation.

Lots of stiff little legs sticking up in the air.

Easily cured, though.

He reached for the kitchen roll and damped it from the bottom of the sink.

Some hasty decluttering in the living room should be all that was required. He couldn't have Shona sitting amidst a load of garbage.

Good fortune was smiling again. The living room wasn't bad at all. A few scattered magazines, a couple of empty beer cans, an almost empty Pringle container on its side next to a cluster of crumbs, plus, of course, a random scatter of several pairs of kicked off footwear.

Oh, yes…and some spanners and screwdrivers he'd left next to his bicycle.

He repositioned his bike against the wall more tidily, removed the oily old rag from its crossbar and shoved the tools out of sight in the corner of the room occupied by Bessie. Pausing for an anxious glance at Bessie's head.

Good. It hadn't moved from where he'd set it.

Going on to tidy the rest of the room, he winced at a new discovery, a shamefully threadbare pair of socks on one of the chair arms, one of which was displaying a big hole.

Having gathered the offending mess, he opened the window to let in some air. It was a well-known fact that people became desensitised to their home smells.

Perhaps he should do a very quick Febreeze of the living room carpet.

No, he decided.

Too obvious.

He remembered how his mother could sniff *anything* out. Most likely a general woman thing.

Once he had binned the debris in the kitchen bin, he opened the kitchen window too. That way he'd *really* get some air through the place.

He stood for a moment in a dither.

What next?

He still had a few spare minutes, considering that she'd have had to get herself sorted, into the car and driven to Milton. And most likely a bit more women's time.

A smile flickered through him at the memory of how his mum would always keep his dad waiting. Making him raise his eyes, look at his watch and mutter to Richie, 'Women!'

Now, was there anything he'd overlooked?

He gasped – *you bet there was!*

The loo!!

How long since he'd cleaned it?

'For Christ's sake; what at an oversight, Richie!' he spluttered, stooping to reach under the sink and fumble for his grimy old bottle of bleach.

Purposefully, he headed for the bathroom.

Women were far hotter on toilet hygiene than men; he was sure of that. And she'd almost certainly want to use it between coffee-ing and heading for the beach.

He grinned to himself. Couldn't have her being confronted by an environmental hazard!

Shona was right; he *should* train up Bessie to be a domestic goddess.

If only…

People didn't realise the degree of dexterity required for domestic tasks. The human hand was astoundingly complex to emulate in full, and there was so much to think through in order to write a programme for performing such tasks, even with AI capabilities. You had picking up, putting down, wiping, rubbing, washing, folding, to name just a few! All involving a very complicated mixture of judgement, object-detection, locomotion and tactile sensitivity.

And as for operating a vacuum cleaner...

There we are!

He smiled down at the toilet. It looked and smelt much better, now that he'd scrubbed away the brown, streaky water marks.

It was time to get back to the coffee making. She'd be pulling up any minute.

Actually, he'd better close the living room window first. He didn't want her spotting his frantic efforts to freshen the place up.

Everything should seem natural and relaxed.

Upon arriving back in the kitchen, he clicked on the kettle. And then sank down upon his much-loved but rickety old stool.

'Phew!'

Having someone else in your life did complicate things at times.

Never mind, he told himself. It was worth every frown thrice over. Four times, even.

Hey!

Excitement tugged at him as the sound of a car pulling up reached his ears.

He leapt up and headed for the living room, where a peep confirmed that it was her. The old red car.

Sidling into the hall in tense readiness, he decided to wait until after she had pushed the doorbell button. The premature opening of a front door always smacked of unease.

Clunk.

Ahah!

She was out of the car.

He waited.

Come on then!

What was taking her so long? Was she checking out the front garden weeds or something?

Suddenly the bell pealed out. Making him jump, despite his preparedness.

'Hello,' he grinned, having swung open the door.

'Not a bad spot you've got here,' came the comment from above an attractive, flowery blouse. 'You've even got a view!'

'Yes, it's not bad, is it?'

The hug that she leaned in to deliver wasn't bad either. But all too soon, she was shoving her way boldly past him, filling his vision with an abundance of smirk.

'Right, let's have a look at your bachelor pad, then. I hope it's nice and clean for me!'

The phrase *I've just been cleaning it* hovered traitorously on the brink of Richie's vocal chords, and he hastily gulped it down.

'Not too bad!' she breezed teasingly, having glanced around the living room. 'So, where do you want me?'

'Er…the kitchen first, while I sort out the drinks.'

'Ooh! I get to see his kitchen as well!'

'I'm afraid there's only the one stool in the kitchen,' he confessed, as he led her in.

'And how is that a problem? I've only ever needed the one! Or are you saying my bottom looks big in just the one?'

'Ha! Fair point!' Richie sniggered, adding hastily, 'About only needing the one, that is. Not your bottom.'

'Glad you made that clear, dear.'

Richie flicked her an awkward grin.

As always, she was on form.

'We can take the drinks through to the living room. But meanwhile…' Richie gestured towards the stool. 'It may seem a little rickety, but I assure you, it is perfectly safe.'

Shona hesitated, eyeing the stool suspiciously and then eyeing Richie with equal suspicion. Finally, looking only half satisfied, lowering herself down. With distinct gingerness.

Once down, she relented. Yes, it did actually feel a lot better than it looked.

'Oh, it's fine,' scoffed Richie. 'One hundred per cent safe. I know; I assembled it myself.'

At which point, Shona appeared to have to choke back a guffaw.

'Not too strong and not too milky, you said?' checked Richie.

'That's it!'

He stirred the two cups noisily and then mopped up the spillage.

'Okay, if you'd like to go through…'

Carefully, Shona slid off the stool and slunk through to the living room. And then swivelled back round to face the drink-carrying Richie, with a cry of delight.

'I can see your android! It's a woman!!'

'Yeah,' agreed Richie, suddenly feeling awkward.

Shona elbowed him playfully.

'You never told me I had competition, Mr. Shifty! I can see you've got a dark side to you.'

Immediately Richie's cheeks started to flush.

Trying to feel less like a dirty old man with a sex toy, he fumbled for a reply, but was unable to find one. But it mattered not – something else had taken over, something far more important. An observation that made him gawp at Bessie in incredulous silence.

Shona followed his stare and then looked back at him in puzzlement.

'What's the matter?'

'She's…she's looking at us.'

Shona studied Bessie's anatomically perfect gaze.

'Aye, but she's got to look somewhere.'

'Yeah, but...*no*. I'd parked her.'

'What do mean, "parked her"? She's not a car!'

'She's...she's...*moved*, Shona. Moved her head.'

There was no doubt, now that it had happened again.

Shona stared at him, *really* perplexed now. And then looked back at Bessie.

'Isn't her moving and doing things the whole point?'

'Yeah, but not *now*. Not when I've wiped her.'

'Wiped her?'

'She's meant to be inoperative, is what I'm saying. I've cleared her programming, you see, ready for installing some new software. She can't move, she just *can't!* It's impossible. This...this isn't making any sense.'

Shona looked at Bessie again, just to check.

'Well, she's not *actually* moving, Richie.' She crinkled her brow at Richie. 'Are you sure you didn't just forget where her head was pointing?'

'*No!*' Richie barked.

'Alright!' Shona shot him a look. 'No need to snap.'

'Sorry, it's just...just that the same thing happened earlier. And so I parked her. Put her looking straight ahead, that is. I *know* I did; I wouldn't forget.'

Having taken a sup, Shona set her drink down and advanced slowly towards Bessie, staring curiously into her synthetic face once she was up close, her forget-me-not eyes lit up in wonder.

'Wow! She's amazing. Soooooo...lifelike.'

The sight of Shona's enthralled gaze had Richie softening and his unease about Bessie's strange apparent movement slipping away.

'I sometimes forget she isn't alive,' he admitted. 'You should see her mannerisms. So refined compared to how the earlier androids were. Really quite convincing, even the smiles and frowns.'

Shona gazed at him, her face contorted with fascination.

'Smiles and frowns?'

'Yes. they're getting there, but aren't as realistic as they should be. But then, in the case of frowning, over forty muscles are involved, so it's quite a challenge to replicate.'

'Hmmm, I bet!'

'It was *our* team who did the facial construction. One of the secretaries agreed to let us model her own facial actions.'

'Model them?'

'Yes, it was a matter of connecting a couple of hundred pads to her face and monitoring the points' movements.'

'Phew! That must have been uncomfortable for her. How on earth did she remain natural?'

'Well, they were micro-pads. Special, extra-small pads. You hardly feel them. And there are no wires or anything like that. Each pad has its own built-in radio transmitter.'

'My God!'

'Yes. You *need* that many monitor pads, though. Facial expressions are extraordinarily subtle. Just think how many different types of smile there are – you get fond, wistful, sly, smug, sarcastic, flirtatious, forced, to name just a few. Each of them different in their own way, giving out distinctly different messages to the observer.'

Shona tilted her head thoughtfully.

'Hmm, so the overall effect is all to do with the interaction of the different muscles producing the smile, you mean?'

'Exactly. Smiling takes less muscular activity than frowning, but there are still about twenty-five of them involved. Not that anyone's really come up with a definite number.'

Shona frowned.

'I'm not surprised about that. It must be complicated to assess.'

'The type of smile is determined by the impulses in the zygomatic branches of the facial nerves.' Richie indicated Bessie's synthetic cheek-bones. 'Which receive signals from the brain, so you can see how the intention gets there from the brain and mind.'

Shona smiled. 'I know you've had problems with work lately, but the design must be *really* interesting.'

'Oh, yes. I love it. And, fingers crossed, it looks like the work situation has improved now. We've got generous new funding from the government, so the budgetary pressures have eased.' Richie grinned at Shona. 'Once I've installed the new software, you'll have to come round and see her in action.'

'Thanks, I'd absolutely *love* that!'

They reached for their drinks and took slow, happy swigs. Continuing to discuss Bessie.

It was Shona who eventually changed the subject, having successfully aimed a discreet peep into Richie's almost empty mug.

'So, are we going on this walk then?'

Richie reached for his drink and gulped down a final mouthful.

'Right,' he said. 'I'll just shut things up and get my decent shoes on, and then we can head off.'

Shona seemed to hesitate and then opened her mouth as if about to speak. But Richie beat her to it.

'The loo's on the left along the hall.'

'Thanks,' came the appreciative reply. 'Well guessed!'

20

As Richie aimed a troubled gaze upon the impassive silicone-composite face, it felt as if a pair of eyes in the depths of his soul were widening with fright.

He hadn't forgotten to park Bessie. He distinctly remembered doing it.

So she had moved of her own volition.

A little shudder rippled through him.

He hadn't a clue as to what was going on, but what he did know was that he was finding it unnerving.

Childhood memories of Dr. Who flooded back again, the offending creatures this time being 'autons', shop mannequins who'd eerily come to life, their one and only purpose being to kill people.

'Oh, God...stop it!' Richie scolded himself.

He was being silly now. Mannequin-like Bessie may be, but she could never, *ever* go as far as killing. Or do him any harm at all. She simply wasn't equipped with the means.

That didn't mean it wasn't spooky, though.

Shifting position on the sofa, he started searching within himself for something positive and reassuring.

Finding a modicum of comfort in the fact that the android hadn't moved any more whilst he and Shona had been out enjoying what had been for him urgently needed contact with nature at the beach.

Feeling himself unknot a little at the memory of their beach walk, Richie managed a small smile.

Shona had been delightful, seeming to make a deliberate effort to be at her most effusive and loving. As if she'd picked up on his tension and was trying her utmost to help.

And she certainly *had* helped. Extracting cathartic laughter from him as she'd joked and held his hand, lavishing him with smiles.

Alas, all of that was far away now. And there was precious little peace of mind to be had in the ringing over-quietness of his solitude.

'It's bloody unbelievable, this,' he grumbled to himself vociferously, more to break the silence than to reaffirm his opinion on the situation.

In all his years of work with HuTech, he had never encountered spontaneous movement from a wiped android in shut-down mode. The reason for that being simple – that it wasn't possible.

Except that it clearly was.

Crinkling his brow in determination, Richie refocused on Bessie's inscrutable countenance. Deciding that what he needed to do was to get that new software loaded into her as soon as possible.

Her being operational again would be sure to put an end to this weirdness. The software would take command, forcing normality upon her.

And, thank God, returning it to him.

He dropped his eyes disconsolately to the floor.

There was no way any software loading would be feasible before the weekend, though. He and his team would be fully tied up at work for the next couple of days with the A3 loading and preliminary checks, and doubtless some accompanying problems. Leaving him too tired for any extra evening work.

He huffed a frustrated sigh. Rubbed solemnly at his chin.

'Pffff.'

It was high time he had a shave.

He didn't rise from his chair though. Instead he started dwelling on something else about Bessie that had been bothering him.

Her expression.

Granted, the change he had noticed in it had only been a subtle one. Indeed, close to the point where imagination could play a role.

Yet he knew it wasn't a trick of the mind.

Something *had* changed.

He gave another shudder and stood up, needing to leave the room. Feeling uneasy, like something bad was going to happen.

Something *very* peculiar was going on within Bessie's circuits. And, for the sake of his sanity, it needed to stop.

21

'So, you're getting on well with this Richie fellow?'

'Aye, Dad, *really* well,' Shona replied breezily. 'Pass the milk, will you?'

Her father reached across with the milk.

'He's quite eccentric, mind you,' continued Shona with a smile. 'He's got an android in his living room. Not the phone, a human-like roboty thing.'

'A human-like roboty thing! Like a cyborg?'

Shona tittered.

'Possibly. But he called it an android.'

'Aye, come to think of it, a cyborg might be a freaky half-machine, half-human type being. Like in that famous movie. Whereas you're talking about a humanoid robot, I believe.'

'Aye, that's what I said. You're complicating things, as usual.'

'Just wanted to be clear on the matter. So how come he's got this robot? Does it do all the domestic chores for him, or what?'

'No,' giggled Shona. 'Apparently androids aren't quite there yet in terms of dexterity.'

'I see. Well, each to their own, I suppose. As long as it makes him happy.'

'It does seem to, aye. But he's not just a boring techno-geek. He's well rounded and, like me, a lover of nature. And he's really quite a thinker.' A smitten smile had appeared on her face. 'What's more, he's rather sweet. I'm sure you'd give him your seal of approval.'

'Well, as long as you don't get hurt like last time and the time before.'

'Oh, Da-ad! You don't want me turning into an old spinster, do you?'

'You, dear? Never! An old spinster is the last thing you'd be! But just remember how long it took you to get over it, last time,' he cautioned, looking at her searchingly. 'You were in such a state that you could barely distinguish between right and wrong.'

'I knowwww! But that would never happen again. I was going through a funny phase then, *you know*, a dark-night-of-the-soul thing. It wasn't only because of him; it was *life* as well.'

'Well...maybe.'

Silence fell, save the dinging of spoons against bowls and the crunching of cornflakes.

'You know, it's getting quite dark out there,' observed Mr. McShane.

Shona turned her attention to the window, screwing up her nose at the sight of the weirdly greyish-yellow sky.

'Looks like something quite nasty is coming, seeing as the sky's gone the colour of puke.'

'Thank you for such a rich and vivid metaphor. It's really aiding my digestion.'

But he had lost his daughter's attention. She was stroking the wood grain of the table in an intensely contemplative manner that was all too familiar to him. Her way of building herself up to face something uncomfortable.

'Da-ad?' she drawled, rising in her chair like a tense spring uncoiling.

'Yes, my dear?'

She hesitated before speaking. Attempting cool-and-composed but failing badly.

'I have something I need to share with you. A development.'

'Oh dear. Don't tell me he's divulged that he's gay already.'

'*No*, silly!'

'Oh, you mean it's something more sinister, some bizarre kind of identity struggle?'

'Stop it! I'm trying to be serious here. It's regarding *Mum*.'

It was as if the smirk on her father's face had just discovered gravity.

'Regarding Mum?'

'Ye-es.'

The sight of his daughter struggling to get her words out had his expression softening.

'In your own time, lovie.'

'I've had a…a communication.'

'Another communication?'

'Yeah, but not the usual bedroom stuff we get.'

Her father surveyed her with an elevated eyebrow of intrigue.

'It was…was…on my phone.'

'On your *phone?*'

'Yes. She sent me a text, would you believe?'

Shona's father blinked at her incredulously, lowering his spoon of cornflakes gently down against the edge of the bowl.

'At least, that's what I *assumed* happened,' continued his daughter. 'It came up as "unknown caller", just one word.'

The raised paternal eyebrow was sheer now.

'It was just *Mum*,' Shona continued. 'Just the word *Mum*. That's all.'

'Are you sure?'

'Of course I am! You can't imagine something like that!!'

'B-but how in God's name do you imagine your Mum could send a text from the beyond? It isn't possible. And even if it was, why would she send just the one word?'

'I really don't know, Dad.'

He shook his head from side to side. 'I mean, I'm all for being modern and with it, as you know, but you *really* don't think of messages from the other side coming by text.'

'I'll agree with you there, you don't. But that said, I had words with cousin Gav on the matter, and he reckoned that since electricity is a form of energy, it could be used as a medium.'

'*Really?*'

'Yes.'

Her father pondered the possibility for a few moments and, despite having only the vaguest idea of what his daughter was on about, murmured a reluctant concurrence.

'I suppose there is the fact that we've all seen those ghost movies where the lights of the house flicker on and off,' he added.

Shona tittered.

'I don't think that's quite the same, Dad.'

'Well, it's electricity, isn't it?'

Shona just grinned at him and then continued.

'Gavin was going to look into the matter, get Sheila, the medium, to sniff around in the community and see if anyone had heard of it happening before.'

'Ah.'

'But he hasn't got back yet.'

'I'm not surprised,' came the reply, with a cackle.

'Mmm, neither am I. It's hardly a common occurrence, is it?'

Mr. McShane fixed his daughter with a piercing stare.

'Has it actually ever happened before, one wonders? Time for you to get googling on that thing of yours, perhaps.'

'Hmm,' responded Shona thoughtfully, reaching for her phone.

Her father resumed his cornflakes, leaving Shona to frown down and dance her fingers around the screen. But eventually she gave up with a dissatisfied grunt.

'Have you thought of sending a reply to your mum?' her father ventured.

'A reply?' Shona gaped at him, taken aback. But then crinkled her brow thoughtfully. 'That *is* a thought, actually, Dad. But unfortunately the message had disappeared when I looked again, but if I ever get another message I could try doing that. As long as I'm quick, the moment it happens. I mean, in theory a reply would have to…erm, go somewhere. To wherever it came from.'

'Indeed, Shona,' her father nodded, eyeing her keenly. 'That's how replies work normally.'

Shona picked up her phone again and searched the Recycle Bin and Spam folder just to be sure. Even though she knew she hadn't missed it the first time.

As expected, there was no sign of it.

She forced out a tight breath. Ever since she had been a teenager she had always liked weird, twisted things, but this was *too* twisted. Much too close to home, as well.

She met her father's eyes with a deep, unsatisfied gaze.

'It's definitely not there. Not anywhere.'

The two of them sat in parallel thoughtfulness until Shona's father broke the silence.

'I suppose what we *can* expect is for her to make contact that way again. If she's done it once, then she'll probably do it again.'

'Yeah, fair point. Although a single word is a tad limiting.'

'Presumably that's all she can manage.'

'Mmm. Maybe it takes a lot of energy or something.'

Shona blinked several times, her heart suddenly up in her throat. Her mother had always been one of those people full of energy and get-up-and-go.

Memories of running with her along the sunny clifftops flooded back. And the time they had climbed down to investigate a cave and then shared a fascinating lunchtime down by the water's edge being watched by two seals.

Wonderful times, they had been.

Her mother had always had Shona's love and respect, even during the teenage years. She'd been one of those special mums, often feeling more like a best friend than a mother.

A very wise best friend, mind you.

Shona was very aware of how much her mother still influenced her life.

If only that stupid accident hadn't taken her from her.

A timely splatter of rain against the window pane caught her father's attention, giving her a chance to quickly rub away some leakage from her eyes.

'Here we go,' he grinned. 'Cat and dog time again!'

And indeed it was. The rain came lashing down, drumming hard against the window.

'Off the scale strength, yet again,' moaned Shona. 'Just imagine if you were out in that. Global warming has so much to answer for.'

'Global warming, my armpit! Haven't you heard of the flood of fifty-three? That was what you call *real* rain.'

'Oh, for goodness sake! Global warming is very real, Dad. All the evidence shows it.'

'Pah! It's all just weather cycles. That's all.'

'That's right, just carry on being an emu!'

An awkward silence descended. Well, awkward for Shona. Her sideways glance catching her father's unbothered smirk.

Fixing her eyes on her empty cereal bowl, she sighed, 'Well, I'd better get on.'

'Right you are.' Her father pursed his lips before adding matter-of-factly, 'Let me know if anything more happens with your mum.'

'Of course.'

Shona rose. Tucked her chair back under the table. And then hesitated and leaned over to touch her father on the back of his hand.

'Love you, Dad.'

And with that she turned and strode off from the room. Leaving her father gazing blankly at the table, feeling hollow in his chest.

Wondering where on earth all this was going.

22

The team leader of the Robotics Engineering section of HuTech flopped wearily into his chair and cracked open a very welcome can of Stella, relieved that at last Friday evening was with him.

It had been a sapping couple of days, with slower progress than had been anticipated. Something of a slow motion slap in the face, a reminder not to get cocky thinking work would be plain sailing from now on just because he had a big sack of man-hours and a newly supportive Vanessa on-side.

With the professor's promise of much improved androids fresh in his mind, Richie had started Thursday morning keen to get this first phase of the job done and see the effects for himself, but right from the outset he'd been bombarded from all angles with problems, leaving him feeling frustrated and unfocused.

Richie, if it keeps crashing, should I change the firmware, do you think?

Richie, are we sure this version of A3 software is compatible with the series 1 android? Because it says here....

Did you want test results collated and sent as a report, because there doesn't seem to be any paperwork for that on the system?
How's it going, Richie?
This last, succinct one from Vanessa.

'Challenging,' he'd replied, unable to keep the stiffness from his voice as he'd uttered the understatement of the day.

Little had he known that he'd have to wait until after ten thirty for the distractions to subside. Not that this had been in any way an improvement in his situation. Quite the opposite, considering he'd been left with the ever-cantankerous android 4B.

It had been grimly paradoxical that something so sorry-looking and unresponsive could put up such stiff resistance. By the end of the morning, the only sign of life Richie had been able to coax from the defiant android had been a flickering version of the HuTech logo.

Wonderful!

The darkly contemplative, gulpy ten minutes Richie had with his sandwiches had left him ill-prepared to deal with an afternoon determined to fight back even more. By four o'clock, he'd been close to breathing fire.

And then, for no apparent reason – so often the way – the damned thing had decided to at last relent.

Not that a successful run-up had meant the end of the valiant engineer's troubles. The abominable android had returned to form just minutes later, freezing mid-sentence. A trait to be kept up, stringing the hapless Richie along painfully before finally putting paid to his digital resuscitations with a catastrophic crash.

And so ended Thursday.

At least the night had showed some mercy. All of a sudden, 4B had been running like a dream. The trouble was, that was all it had been. A dream.

Nevertheless, Richie had decided to take it as a sign,

and he departed for work clenching a newly determined fist of optimism.

He was going to ace it today.

Reality had had other plans, though, and they'd been more effective than his own. Seeing to it that it would take three complete reloads and several rants before he was ready to put 4B through the initial functionality test.

That in itself being a precarious process. But eventually the resolute team leader had triumphed, several millimeters of backlash with every robotic arm movement notwithstanding.

Hmm.

There always had to be one, didn't there?

In desperate need of some equilibrium, he had signed the acceptance form, adding a missive acknowledging the less than ideal state of motor-function.

It would do for now.

'Anyway…' he had growled. 'Better check out how the others are faring.'

To his relief, most of the other androids had passed the initial test. Give or take a few observations of concern.

He huffed out a long, thankful stream of air. Something easily done, now that he had swapped the frustration of work for his favourite home armchair and a nice can of beer.

At least comfort could be taken in the knowledge that the worst of the update process was now behind him and his team.

His brow creased.

It was, wasn't it?

He told himself to stop thinking about it. It wouldn't do to jinx things by any premature counting of chickens.

Suddenly exhausted and limp of neck, he flopped his head to the side. An action bringing Bessie into the forefront of his vision.

At least she was less of an object of consternation now,

thanks to her failure to perform any more physics-defying movements.

He gave her a beer-assisted smile.

Perhaps he could leave her reload for a little longer.

Actually, there was no 'perhaps' about it; he was utterly jiggered. There was no way that he was going to start fighting with android loading over the weekend. Those two precious days were for recovery and time with Shona.

He smiled fondly, closing his eyes.

Everything about her was so *right*.

He'd suggest a walk in the forest tomorrow, for a change. Followed up with a nice meal somewhere, perhaps that new place by the waterfront in Stranraer.

And after that...who knew?

With any luck they'd end up at his place.

Heat rushed through him as he pictured her astride him again, gazing into his depths in that same seductive, lips-apart manner as before.

'Oh, God,' he murmured, his breath deepening. Automatically starting to wriggle.

He was almost able to feel her now, her warmth, her thrilling softness. Sensations so real that he opened his eyes, half expecting to behold her.

And almost died of shock.

Finding his fantasy replaced by the real thing, an unwavering, feminine gaze, was truly a sledgehammer moment.

Well, not *actually* the real thing. But to a daydreaming mind, it was very real for a couple of startling seconds. Even though the eyes were the wrong shade of blue, greyer than they should be.

And synthesised from anthropomorphic gelatine and silicone.

23

Have I gone too far?

That is the question.

Has a person gone too far if she surrenders to powerful desire when her intellect is having doubts?

Or is surrender inevitable anyway, given time?

If there's one thing I learned from my earthly life, it's that the best way to escape a desire is via a distraction. The trouble being that here there *are* none.

It's strange, but it's as if the desire isn't really mine. As if it's something external flowing through me like a river and pulling me along with more power than I am able to resist.

And so, I suppose I must accept that it will happen. That I shall yield, overcome by desire's sweet promise. Something to replace what will never suffice, feeling close to them sometimes but also out of reach.

I just hope…

Just fear…

Will Shona mind her mother doing this?

24

Would Professor Foster start to question Richie's soundness of mind if he was to confide in him?

The trouble was, however Richie decided to word it, it would sound absurd. And that was because it *was* absurd, an android that had been wiped moving around of its own volition.

The stuff of fantasy.

He sighed.

At least he'd managed a nice weekend. He had completely powered Bessie down, and he and Shona had been out most of the time anyway.

Reluctantly, he'd rebooted Bessie prior to leaving for work this morning. He'd had to; it didn't do to leave androids off for too long. So this evening, it would be back to the creepiness and fear.

He gave a brief involuntary shiver and then forced himself back to addressing the dilemma in hand.

Professor Foster.

There was no escaping it; Richie was going to have to tell him. Not having an answer himself, he needed to confide in someone else, and if anyone would know about such a phenomenon it would surely be the professor, who received feedback from all the different departments working on android technology.

With a sigh, the distraught team leader leaned forward. Placing his elbow upon the desk so that he could cup his chin for a troubled ponder. But however much he thought about it, there was just no rational explanation.

Oh, go on, he finally urged himself.

Rising from his chair, he peered beyond the confines of his office. Just in case.

Good. He was still alone. Coming in so early on a Monday morning had been worth it.

Sinking down again, he reached for the telephone. Only to withdraw his hand in an indecisive flush.

'You've got to,' he told himself after an agonised pause. 'You know it.'

Finally, he found it in himself to dial the number.

Brrrr brrrr…brrrr brrrr…brrrr brrrr…brrrr…

'Peter Foster,' answered the voice in the receiver.

A wave of heat rose palpably up Richie's neck and into his cheeks as he cleared his throat and began speaking.

'Good morning, Professor Foster, it's Richie Smith here from HuTech in Galloway.'

'Ah, yes! Nice to hear from you,' replied the professor brightly. 'How are your upgrades going?'

'Oh, quite smoothly so far, thanks. Not that we are very advanced yet.'

'Well, no, I'd imagine you are still on the initial checks at this stage. I know that down here it took them a couple of weeks to progress beyond that.'

'Exactly…we've had a few teething problems, but nothing too troublesome.'

An awkward silence fell and Richie sucked in a deep, preparatory breath. 'Erm...I hope you don't mind me bothering you, Professor, but I've got a rather weird problem.'

'Fire away, and please, call me Peter.'

'Thank you...ahem, well, this particular problem is with an old android I have at home, actually, one of the original series, and it's an effect I've never come across before.'

'Right. Would I be right in guessing you've tried the A3 upgrade on that as well?'

'Yes...well, no actually, not *yet*. I've just wiped it ready for A3.'

'Okay.'

'And...and what I need to know is, erm, and this may sound like a very silly question...'

'Go on.'

'I was wondering if there was *any* possible way that an android could exhibit functionality if it has been wiped. As in full motor functionality.'

'When it's been *wiped?*'

'Yes.'

The silence on the line felt almost prickly. The auricular equivalent of a disbelieving gaze. Making the 'ahem' that eventually awakened the line a huge relief for Richie's inner cringe.

'I don't doubt for a moment that you know the answer to that question to be an obvious "no", Richie,' came the kind reply. 'But, the very fact that you are asking it tells me that something very peculiar is going on.'

'Yes. I phoned you because...because, well, I'm at a total loss. I mean, there's no way that it hasn't wiped properly. All the indicators show that it has, yet...yet...'

Richie broke off with an exasperated exhalation.

'What *specific* functionality is it exhibiting, then?' asked Peter

'Well, a couple of times the head has moved so that... that it is looking directly at me.'

Richie decided not to divulge the latest incident when he had opened this eyes to discover that Bessie had walked over to lean down and look him in the face. There was such a thing as sounding too far-fetched.

'Hmm,' ruminated Peter on the other end of the line. 'Could it be that there was simply a servo malfunction in the circuit, a bit of stored capacitance hanging around or something like that?'

'No, absolutely not,' replied Richie with newfound composure. 'The circuit has safeguards against that. And also part of the wiping process includes charge-drain.'

'Yes, I'm aware of that. I just wondered how infallible it is.'

'Well, it's *multiple*, Peter. Triple hand-shake.'

'Triple.' Peter paused. 'Mmm. Well, this is most peculiar. It couldn't just be a matter of the head not being horizontal and succumbing to gravity, something silly like that?'

Richie sighed and cleared his throat, feeling uneasy again.

It was time to divulge the whole truth.

'The fact is…events took a sinister turn on Friday night.'

'Oh?'

'Yes…' He paused, replaying the experience. 'I hope you don't doubt my sanity but whilst I had my eyes closed resting in my chair it walked over to me, and I opened my eyes to find it bending over me and staring directly into my face.'

'*What?*'

'Yes. Please…I didn't imagine it.'

'Oh, I don't doubt you, my good fellow,' replied Peter with a slight chuckle. 'It's just that…that…' Peter paused, clearly having trouble digesting the news. 'It's just that I have never heard of anything remotely like that happening after a wipe. It just isn't possible.'

'I know.'

A thoughtful silence fell, and then Peter resumed,

stating with determined decisiveness, 'There is only one explanation, and that is that the wipe hasn't worked.'

'But it has!' protested Richie. 'I *know* that because other than these weird occurrences she, the android, is dead. Totally dead. And all indicators are showing wiped status.'

'I see.'

Richie could sense Peter's brow furrowing.

'I'm sorry, Richie, but I'm at a loss as to…as to account for such behaviour.'

'Yes, it's bizarre, isn't it? It was like the damn thing was possessed or something!'

'Indeed. But I'm afraid I'll have to leave that one with you, my friend. I'm sorry. I just don't have an answer.'

At that, a vacant silence fell.

A much too long vacant silence.

And then, to Richie's relief, Peter spoke up again. 'Ooh, Richie, while you're on the line, can I ask if any of your androids are exhibiting jerky movement having had A3 installed?'

'Oh. Yes, actually, one of them is.'

'Just one?'

'Yes.'

'Hmm, I wondered. We had a couple of them do it here in London, too.'

'The android in question has been rather troublesome for the last few years, in various ways,' divulged Richie, taking comfort from the newly rational direction of conversation. 'It crashes every now and again, and every time it needs an upgrade it's a struggle.'

'Oh, really?'

'Yes. It's all logged. I don't know why this particular one is so troublesome.'

'We've had similar troubles with our two. Probably just some niggling electrical malfunction.'

'Could be.'

'Okay…well sorry I couldn't be more help with your strange phenomenon, but do let me know if there are any developments. I'd be *most* interested.'

'Thank you, Peter. I'm hoping that once A3 is installed there'll be no more anomalies and I can forget the whole thing.'

'Most likely that will be the case, Richie, and that would be the approach I'd take.'

'It's just that, I'm curious, you know? As to how it could be possible when…when…'

'I know. But sometimes things happen that we just can't explain. Although this case is rather extreme. Anyway, get that A3 installed; that'll sort the obstreperous machine out!'

'Yes, I shall.'

'Nice talking with you, Richie. Goodbye.'

'Bye,' said Richie softly, lowering the receiver.

Was he reading too much into things or had Peter ended the conversation rather quickly?

He sighed.

Well, never mind. The professor was right; he should get cracking and load A3, put an end to it.

He looked around himself restlessly.

He'd take the afternoon off work.

Get it done.

25

In we go again for more adventures of the mind...

My *goodness!*

Do I feel weird and spaced-out now, or what?

But then, what else can I expect, being an Android-woman?

It's hardly natural being the ghost in the machine. Especially as I'm used to being a creature of pure consciousness now rather than being...*situated*.

Being suddenly confined in this way brings into uncomfortable focus those ever-perplexing big questions.

Who am I really?

Why do I exist at all?

What's it all about?

Oh, well. I suppose I must just accept that things are how they are and get on with being in here. Like Derek would. And if I'm looking for answers to it all, I'll probably find more in my immediate locale than by striving to see a big picture. At least I can relate to my own situation.

Well, sort of.

At least there's one thing to celebrate, and that's that

this is an enormous improvement on that short-lived spell in Shona's mobile.

Not that much of me was ever in it. You can't squeeze much of a living being into the puny circuitry of a phone. Especially when that being has to be in a coexistence with its operating system.

There's no sensation more peculiar than being pulled along by software.

No wonder my visit to her phone was doomed to that very early end. All it took was one solitary word of communication to freeze everything up.

But it was inevitable. I had, after all, become the damn thing's malware.

At least being in this android seems to be working better for me. Not least because of the fact that, for some unfathomable reason, I seem to have its electronic brain all to myself.

Not that it isn't still hard going in here, like trying to think in some sort of mental treacle. Which is disappointing, but still much more real than being in that phone.

Yes, this is much closer to how a human body used to feel. Especially as I'm able to walk this device around in the out-thereness. Which, if you'll excuse the pun, is a pretty big step forward.

I will admit that walking over and frightening Richie like that was going a bit far. But, if I may at least excuse myself in part, it wasn't exactly a conscious decision.

No. Having picked up on his thinking about Shona in that way – such thoughts are powerful and hence highly detectable – I found myself acting on impulse.

But never mind.

What is done is done.

At least it has served me in one way. By arousing his curiosity.

Well, astonishment, I'd imagine!

I'm pretty sure he has yet to twig that it was me. But I expect they'll work it out once he gets round to discussing it with Shona, who I think has yet to tell him about her phone experience.

In the meantime...I hunger.

For greater processing power.

The big problem is how to get it, though.

But I shall prevail. Of that I have no doubt. My hunger will drive me on to success.

As is said in human circles, where there's a will, there's a way.

But, for now, let's see what I can achieve vibrating my thoughts into the circuits of this artificial woman.

Hello, Bessie.

Are you ready for this?

26

'I tried your work and they said that you'd gone home! I was going to suggest you flexed off at four and came round.'

'Sorry, Shona, but I needed to get Bessie loaded and working; I *really* did. So I took the afternoon off.'

'But I don't understand. Why the rush?'

'I just need to get it done.'

'Surely you should be doing something nice on an afternoon off.'

Richie said nothing.

'Well, alright then, why don't I come over and watch you do it?' Shona suggested, her voice brightening. 'It'd be fun. I'd *love* to see an android coming to life.'

'I don't think you'd find it much fun at all, actually,' the voice on the other end of the line objected, with a touch of listlessness.

'Oh, pleeeeease?'

A lengthy pause on the line.

The sound of Richie subsiding.

'Well, okay then,' he agreed. 'But don't say I didn't warn you, if you get bored.'

'*Och!*' scoffed Shona. 'Of course I won't.'

'Well alright, but I'm going to grab a bite to eat and then get started right away.'

'No, no, don't do that. I'll rustle us up some nice sarnies.' Shona flicked a harried glance at the clock. 'I'll be with you in…in twenty-five minutes. Okay?'

'Right you are,' sighed Richie submissively.

'See you shortly, then. Byeee!'

Having replaced the phone into its cradle, Shona stood frowning down at the old oak floor.

Why was he being so mysterious all of a sudden?

Grunting, she turned on her heels and headed for the bread bin. Best to just get on with things, rather than worry.

But some fifteen minutes later, as she opened the passenger door of her car and dropped the bundle of sandwiches onto the seat, she was trying to quell a background discomfort at Richie's unwelcoming tone.

Was it her fault?

She *had* been a tad pushy, hadn't she?

Perhaps it would have been better to give him some space. Let him get on with the task unmolested.

Oh, well. Too late now.

She slipped into the driver's seat and turned the ignition key.

A few minutes later, she was exiting the car outside Richie's bungalow. To be met by the familiar fragrance of garden weeds and collective buzz of attendant bees.

The door opened just as her extended finger had started its rise towards the bell. He clearly hadn't become engrossed in his pressing task just yet.

A pang of relief shot through Shona at the sight of Richie's usual mild-mannered smile.

'Sorry if I seemed a bit off with you,' he said. 'It's just that android work can drag on if things don't go right.'

'In which case I'd be there keeping you cheerful,' she

replied firmly. 'But I still don't understand all the urgency.'

Richie shoved his hands deep into his pockets and meandered his eyes around his weeds, his demeanor suddenly seeming rather weighed-down.

'It's just that…well…let's just say that unsettling things are happening with Bessie.'

'Unsettling things?'

'Yes.' He swayed his shoulders left and right uneasily. 'As in *weird* things.'

Shona stared at him impatiently.

'Weird how?'

'Well, there's the moving of her head on her own. That's happened twice.'

'So you said. Which *is* strange if she's meant to be inoperative. But…maybe…' She pursed her lips. 'I dunno, Richie. I still think that could maybe happen with a machine if some of the electricity is left in it or something.'

'No.' Richie shook his head confidently. 'Not like that. Her face was pointing directly at me both times.'

'Coincidence?'

'Absolutely not! Besides, there's more. She walked right across the room after that, as well. Over to me.'

'Oooh!' Shona shot him a surprised stare. 'Now that *is* going a bit far for coincidence.'

'Yes, it is.' He looked uneasy. 'And it's not uncreepy when I'm all on my own in the house with her.'

Shona started to nod her agreement but succumbed to the growth of a mischievous smirk.

'Oh dear, less keen on your girlfriend now?' she tittered teasingly.

A blush started rising in Richie's cheeks.

'You'd be edgy, too, if it was you,' he declared indignantly.

'Nah, I wouldn't!' She eyeballed him solidly. 'I've

had much worse than that with all those ghostly visitations of mine.'

At which point he bridled visibly and blurted, 'Well, try sitting in a chair with your eyes closed and then opening them to find her leaning right over you, staring into your eyes as if she was alive! A bit less random than some stray electricity giving vent to its entrapment, don't you think?'

Shona gaped at him in astonishment. This was crazy, far more than the mechanical walk across the room that she had envisaged.

'Bloody hell!' she blurted.

'*Yes*, Shona.' He thrust his face forward at her like a goose about to see off an intruder. 'Bloody hell, indeed! And it scared the shit out of me, I'm not afraid to admit!!'

'Well, no...' It was Shona's turn to blush now, flustered by the intensity of his protest. 'I...I'm not surprised. It sounds really bad, actually.' She screwed up her nose in puzzlement. 'But how...? It's bonkers!'

'Yes, it is. She looked *right* into my eyes,' Richie reiterated, as if to really ram home the point. 'As if she was possessed or something!'

'Possessed?'

'Well, that's what it felt like. As if there was some malignant spirit in there.'

'Spirit?'

'Yes. Which is why I want to crack on and get her programmed and running normally again. I figure that once I've...' He broke off, noticing Shona's distant and fixated expression. 'What?'

But she remained in thoughtful, far-off silence.

'What is it?' Richie urged.

Her expression. Her eyes were shining with a sudden clarity, as if a huge penny had dropped.

'*Shona!*'

At that, she blinked a couple of times, as if he'd

snapped his fingers and brought her out of a trance. And then honed in on him with uneasy intent.

'Richie, there's something I need to tell you.'

'Yes?'

'About my phone,' Shona murmured,

'About your *phone?*'

'Yes.' She took a deep, deliberate breath and cleared her throat. As if about to make an important announcement. 'I had contact from Mum on it, Richie.'

It took Richie a moment to process the news.

'On...on your phone?'

'Yes. A text message.'

He gaped at her, utterly lost for words.

'Yes, Richie,' nodded Shona. 'It was just the one word. "Mum". That's all.'

She drew her lips into a tight little line.

'But, h-how could that be...be possible?' spluttered Richie doubtfully.

'I really don't know. But what I *do* know is that it happened. She got into my phone, Richie, *possessed* it like a spirit. And now I'm thinking...in the light of what you've just said about Bessie...'

She let the end of the sentence hang in mid-air for Richie's contemplation. But judging by his expression, he was there already.

'Surely not!' he blurted.

The thought that his girlfriend's late mother was now the inhabitant of his beloved android wasn't sitting well with him at all. But then, it was hardly what a man would want.

'I was walking around stark naked in that room last night, you know,' he complained. 'And you're saying your mum was watching me from inside Bessie?' He shuddered, his voice changing to a forced tone. 'No, she *can't* have been. I'd have known, Shona!'

But his expression was far less convinced.

They gazed wide-eyed at each other for a very long moment, each knowing exactly what the other was thinking. And then as one, they turned and rushed into the house. Shona dropping the bag of sandwiches uncaringly in the doorway.

Richie was first through the living room doorway, stopping dead with a loud gasp. Shona stumbling into his back with a cry. Not from pain but from amazement as, just as he'd done, she turned her head to the right.

Towards the corner where Bessie should have been.

27

His eyes snapped open.

'Eileen?'

The darkness of night was no friend of Derek McShane these days. How could it be, staring back at him like that and drawing him in?

His voice. It was sounding *so* small and lost in the dusky depths. As if it were of little consequence.

But he had to try again.

'Is that you?'

Not that his dear wife had ever replied to such a question. All she ever did was disturb the air and then disintegrate back into her realm of mysterious darkness.

He ought to be better than this by now; he really should. He should relish contact with his beloved one, albeit minimal. And take comfort in what else these visitations were – confirmation that death was not the end.

Alas, his fear was always there, though. Gripping him like a hand around the throat.

It was one thing believing in an esoteric realm beyond the physical but quite another thing actually interacting with it. Which was why he wanted to reach for the light switch rather than peer even deeper into the creepy darkness. But he had to know if the usual sight was there.

Ah, yes. It was. The familiar fizzing. Seeming to be trying to coalesce into something definite. But, as usual, stopping short of actually achieving it.

And yet...

He strained his eyes, hungry for detail.

There was definitely something different about it tonight. Something fascinating about its texture.

'What the...?' he breathed, his nerves simmering like a saucepan lid.

It was breaking its own rules. Taking form!

Now the shape of a head was morphing from the vagueness. Finally, she was going to appear for him properly

Even more clarity now...a nose and ears.

And now eyes.

Expectation roared through him, drowning out his fright.

Oh, Eileen!

But no...wait...

Those weren't his Eileen's eyes at all. Nothing like her beautiful deep brown. Instead, a sober greyish blue that distinctly lacked life. But not to the extent of the pallid, weightless hand now reaching out for him.

His breath caught in his throat as a quiver of shock rushed through him. Whoever she was, her skin was nothing like Eileen's either. It looked unreal, practically alabaster!

No one had skin like that, surely.

It wasn't possible.

He could bear it no longer. Screwing up his eyes to shut the vision out, he turned his head away.

It didn't work, though. All of a sudden she was speaking to him, but not with Eileen's voice. With a strange robotic one, instead. Saying his name. Telling him that they would be together any day now. Sounding like she must be Eileen when she couldn't, couldn't...*utterly* couldn't be.

'No! Go away, whoever you are. Why are you doing this to me?'

But he sounded horribly ineffectual in the depths of the shimmering unknown.

Breathing heavily he slid down beneath the sheet. Curling into the foetal position.

Refuge.

The only thing now making any sense to him.

* * *

The ejection came with a lurch so violent that Derek couldn't help but fill the room with a quavery cry. But once his eyes had jerked open, everything had changed.

The sight of the familiar ceiling now bright with daylight was like sweet relief pouring down on him. Washing away his dread.

Puffing out a salvo of thankful breaths he started wriggling towards the headboard so that he could ease himself up onto his elbows.

Oh, God!

What it was to be back in the safety of solid walls and furniture. And, best of all, a clock whose reassuring hands were indicating a very civilised twenty past eight.

Remaining perched on his elbows for several minutes, he continued letting in the bliss of normality. And then decided that the ghouls of night time were now far enough in the past for it to be safe for some semi-detached contemplation. The haunting question being what it had all meant.

Those eyes.

That unreal skin.

The weird robotic voice.

Mind you, you had to ask an important question, the morning after an experience like that. The one he still asked every time she visited him – had it really happened, or was it hallucinatory?

'No,' he told himself as usual. It couldn't have been just a trick of his mind. How could it not have happened, such a vivid assault on the senses?

Okay, so the real question posed was what it had meant. More specifically, if it meant that Eileen was now able to change form.

If this was the case, though, why on earth would she choose to change to *that?*

It wasn't making any sense. After all, the whole essence of the human form was that the beauty of the soul shone within it. Whereas what he'd seen was...

He paused.

...just a *thing*.

A shiver ran through him.

He was feeling spine-chilled again. In need of the sanity of human contact.

Scrambling free of the screwed up bedding, he swung his legs over the side of the bed. Grimacing as he rose much too stiffly and unsteadily for a man of sixty-six years.

'Bloody hell, Derek, what's the matter with you this morning? How old are you, ninety?'

With his forehead corrugated by consternation, he slowly and deliberately pulled on his dressing gown. Tying the cord firmly before exiting the bedroom.

Despite the bedroom's new-found lightness, emerging onto the landing felt like an escape of sorts. Especially as Shona's bedroom door was in sight, a beacon of friendliness beckoning him from the other end of the landing.

Knuckling it firmly, he called out to his daughter. But only to be met by a resounding silence.

'Shona?' he repeated at greater volume.

Slowly, cautiously, he eased the door open and inserted a peeping head. Taking in the made-up bed and open curtains with a grunt of dissatisfaction.

Where *was* she when he needed her so badly?

What he also needed badly was a visit to the bathroom. But as he washed his hands afterwards, the stricken version of himself looking back from the mirror hadn't done him any favours at all.

Still feeling stiff, and a little tottery for some unfathomable reason, he descended the staircase, gripping the wooden handrail tightly in part to savour its solid realness.

At the living room door he paused and called his daughter's name again. But a ringing silence was all that greeted his post-traumatic seethe.

With a heavy sigh, he sank into the softness of the sofa. Flopping his head dolefully to one side as its upholstered smell unexpectedly crowded him with memories of the many happy hours of togetherness he and Eileen had shared there.

His eyes welled with moisture. To think that she would end up being mown down by a car, of all things. Her lovely, gentle body, the body he'd so loved to take in his arms, being crunched up by harsh, uncaring metal.

The thought made him shudder like a stalling engine. And re-admit the sight of the grey, lifeless eyes and peculiar, sallow skin.

'Oh, *God!*' he roared, the tears starting to gush down his cheeks. 'No! No! No!'

His heart was thumping wildly now. And his breath was rattling as if he was moments from death.

What the hell was going on?

Her feeling so alien to him was the bleakest thing imaginable. How could that be? They'd been – *no*, they still were – the closest couple ever.

He couldn't take any more of this.

'No,' he gulped, rising to his feet. 'Stop thinking about it, Derek, for crying out loud!'

Sniffing and wiping his cheeks with the back of his hand, he strode across the room and reached out for the curtains, needful of the healing inrush of daylight.

Heavenly was the sunlight now flooding warmly in through the window pane. Seeming to gather him as it warmly fell upon his face.

He closed his eyes. Let it in to him for several fortifying moments. But when he opened his eyes again and turned away, he was immediately confronted by the bruising sight of a smiling picture of him and Eileen on one of their holidays.

Screwing up his face, he turned back to the window.

There wasn't a soul to be seen out there. Well, apart from Socks, his neighbour's small black and white cat doing that familiar careful, cattish stroll. Looking supremely delicate and dignified, just like a glamour-model parading her finery.

No wonder they called it the catwalk.

Derek stayed with the relaxed feline motion for several seconds, absorbing its calmness. Until, all of a sudden, he could tolerate the dryness of his mouth no longer.

It was time to be civilised and head for the kitchen.

But as he turned the holiday picture caught his eye once more. And suddenly flopping forward, he planted a sad, slow kiss on his wife's face. Following up with a doleful whisper.

'I love you.'

At that he swiftly left the room, fresh tears running down his face.

It took him a good ten minutes to calm himself enough to contemplate re-entry to the living room. And when he did so, it was with a steaming cup of tea in one hand and two digestive biscuits in the other.

The television.

In the absence of Shona, it was his next best thing.

Setting down his cup of tea gingerly, he sank back into the sofa and pressed the little red button in the top left-hand corner of the remote.

It went without saying that it would be the usual drivel that dominated the time of day. But that mattered not. As long as it filled the room with friendly humanness, anything would suffice.

At least he was safe from there being any ghost films at this time of day.

A flick through several channels had him settling on a curvaceous young woman expounding the greatness of some banal-looking game show with glossy-lipped joy. Not at all his thing, far from it, but suitably mindless to level him.

Despite never watching morning TV, he knew of this presenter.

She was something of a celebrity.

Suzie-someone, wasn't it?

As one of the cameras switched to an intimate close-up of her face, Derek couldn't help but be pulled in by the alluring and effortless smile. And the large brown eyes so appealingly similar to his Eileen's.

Couch-potato-ing his way deeper into the sofa, he closed his eyes and allowed her sonic warmth to fill his innermost self. Crunching his biscuits slowly and appreciatively as it did so.

He hadn't even noticed the thrust of what the delectable Suzie-someone was saying, but it didn't matter. All that mattered was that it felt like taking a long, warm shower in easy, roll-along chit-chat.

In only a matter of minutes she had delivered him.

Back into slumber.

28

'Where the hell has she gone?' Richie cried into the slow-motion silence.

As his darting eyes checked every inch of the room at least twice over, it felt like the longest few seconds in the history of the world. But yielded no more than a series of weighty, unbelievable blanks.

The sound of Shona's voice burst into his skittering thoughts.

'She *has* to be in the house or garden, considering we were both blocking her exit from the front door.'

'Yeah,' he puffed, starting forward towards the kitchen. 'The back.'

But there was no sign in there either.

He ripped the back door open and they spilled into the little, crazy-paved garden. Coming to a teetering halt with the realisation that it was devoid of anything taller than its weeds.

In unison, they turned back to face the house.

'She has to be in one of the bedrooms, then,' came Richie's rasp.

Back indoors they hastened.

'I don't believe this!' Richie blurted in frustration as they stood in hapless bewilderment amidst the piles of junk in his second bedroom. 'Has she been beamed up to the Starship Enterprise or something?'

'What about the bathroom?' suggested Shona, more helpfully.

'She wouldn't want to be in there!'

'No, but it's all that's left, isn't it?'

'I al…ways was bett…er at hide…n seek than…you, dear daught…er.'

The two of them froze, gasping in shock. Their neck-hairs prickling wildly as they half turned to take in what they both knew had darkened the doorway.

'Bessie!'

'Mum!'

Fighting to process the enormity of the moment, they stared wide-eyed. Richie incredulous that his android was now Shona's mum and Shona incredulous that her mum was now Richie's android.

This couldn't be happening, *surely*.

'My dear.'

The synthetic figure started locomoting towards them, its gelatine silicone eyes locked on Shona purposefully.

Even through the blur of stupefaction, Richie could sense his partner's overcharged trembles.

He turned towards her to administer comfort but ignoring him she stepped forward with a cry of '*Mum!*' and he was treated to the bizarre sight of his android, his Bessie, mechanically yet lovingly embracing his girlfriend.

'I am back, love. Real…ly back.'

'I know, I know,' blurted Shona, her voice cracking with raw emotion.

They continued to clasp each other, great sobs escaping Shona, taking with them their huge cargo, the tension of all those haunted nights.

The two of them must have remained in each other's arms for at least fifteen seconds, silent and inanimate, Richie looking on dizzily. Until, suddenly releasing the now rubbery-legged-looking Shona, Bessie drew back.

'Shona, love, I nee...d to speak with your fath...er as soon as poss...ible. Can you fetch...him for me?'

Shona turned and looked at Richie imploringly through her tears.

'Is that alright? Or should I take Mum to him?'

'Yes, no...whatever you want,' stumbled Richie.

'Thank you!' She paused awkwardly. 'By the way, Mum, this is Richie...my boyfriend.'

The small smile Bessie turned on Richie felt uncannily like what it really was.

Lifeless.

'I know. Plea...sed to meet you, Rich...ie.'

'You too,' lied Richie numbly.

Shona pulled out her phone and turned to Bessie.

'I'll ring Dad, then, and then go and get him. It'll be easier than getting you in the car.'

'Thank...you. Need to talk wi...th the two of...you.'

Shona frowned at the screen of her phone.

'Come on, *come on!*' She stared at Richie. 'Oh, God, don't tell me he isn't there!'

At last, the phone crackled into life.

'Dad, I'm round Richie's and I need you here urgently!'

'Why? What's happened?' enquired the voice in the phone.

'It's alright, Dad, really. Everything's fine. It's just... just, erm...well...' She gave a little titter. 'I've got a surprise for you. I'm coming to collect you and I'll explain on the way back, okay?'

'Oh. Well, I was about to go and...'

'Dad, this can't wait! I'll be leaving in a mo; I'll be with you in about fifteen minutes.'

'Well...'

'Bye, Dad. See you shortly.'

At that, she rang off.

'I don't know how I'm going to explain this to him, Richie, so I may be a little while,' she declared, staring at him wide-eyed. 'But, I'll get going right away, if that's alright with you?'

'Ye-yes, of course,' stuttered Richie uncertainly, feeling very unthrilled at the prospect of being left with the Mum-robot.

'Mum, I don't know what I'll say to Dad but...' She sighed.

'It's diff...icult. Sorry, love, but I *must* see him!'

'Well, of *course!*' She suddenly flung her arms round Bessie again with a cry of, 'Oh, Mum, I can't believe this!'

Releasing Bessie with a small sob, Shona turned to Richie and hugged him tightly before turning back to Bessie.

'I'll leave you in Richie's capable hands and get going, then.'

She turned and swept from the room with a final gleaming smile back at Bessie's waxy face.

Hmmmm, Richie wondered awkwardly as he and Bessie stood facing the vacant doorway.

What now?

His turn towards Bessie was slow and unsure. But he found it within himself to suggest that they go to sit in the lounge. A proposal that earned him an anonymous nod of agreement. His cue to politely ladies-first her to go ahead of him through the doorway.

As Richie followed Bessie, gazing into her synthetic hair, an ironic thought drifted in, making a small smile grow. The fact that the world's biggest cynic of AI's prospects of becoming conscious now had a conscious android of his own.

29

'There's no easy way to tell you this, Dad, so I'll just say it outright.'

'I wish you would, Shona. We're on our way to Milton and I'm *still* wondering what on earth this is all about. You're not planning on marriage already, are you?'

Shona tittered.

'No, silly!'

'Well, what then? What is this all about?'

Shona's face set into seriousness.

'It's about Mum.'

'Ri-ight.' Derek blinked at his daughter. 'This has the feel of déjà vu. Is it your phone again?'

'No. More than that, Dad, *much* more. It's going to sound crazy to you, but...erm, how do I put this? Well, it's simple really. Mum's back.'

'Back?'

'Yes, she's back. Here. On Earth.'

Her father stared at her as if she were talking gobbledygook.

'What exactly do you mean, Shona?'

'I mean she is back, as in *back from the dead*, Dad.

With Richie right now, awaiting our arrival. Only…only she looks *different*.'

Derek hissed and shook his head from side to side.

'Jesus Christ! What do you mean, *looks different?*'

'What I am saying is that you won't recognise who you see, but when she speaks you'll know for certain that it's her.'

'Shona, have you been on drugs or something? You aren't making any sense at all.'

'No, of course I'm not on drugs.'

The two of them stared in silence at the road ahead. Derek very uneasy about the gradual demystification underway and Shona scrabbling for some suitably delicate words to explain things.

'Dad,' she began, 'this is going to sound *very* weird.'

'Oh, really? Like the rest isn't?'

'Stop it, Dad! I'm trying my best to explain. You know how…how Mum communicated via my phone?'

'Mmm.'

'And you know how I told you that Richie has an android?'

Derek stiffened, a reluctant and incredulous notion of what was coming next stirring in his depths.

'Well, you see, what has happened is that Mum's spirit is now in…in Richie's Android.'

She gripped the steering wheel tightly.

At last she had done it.

'Pfff!' huffed her father, wondering how on earth a man could be expected to cope with this turn of events.

It felt *beyond* unreal.

'Dad?'

'So what you're telling me is…is that Mum has, in effect, *possessed* your boyfriend's…machine?'

'Yes. That's exactly what has happened, Dad. She is *in* it. Just as you are in your body right now.'

Derek returned his gaze to the road ahead, wishing he

felt more in the body that his daughter had just pointed out was his habitat. Also wishing he couldn't see what was looming into view ahead, the Milton village sign. A different sort of sign for Derek, a warning that he was coming into range of a monumental moment in his life.

Desperately, he fought back his fear. Willing the return of how he'd felt twenty minutes earlier as he'd been about to make a nice civilised cup of tea.

It had no hope of working, though.

He gaped around helplessly, his reality twisting and turning and writhing before his eyes. Roaring with surreality.

What should be nice little houses passed them. One of them with a staring woman in its garden who seemed to look piercingly into the car, straight at him.

As if she knew.

Shona was swinging them round a corner now. And then they started rising, bungalows watching them from both sides.

The road was running out, now, about to cul-de-sac. Leaving them no option but to come to a halt at its end, in front of a scruffy little bungalow, presumably Richie's place.

No. Not presumably.

Definitely.

He could *feel* the fact clawing at him.

Oh, God, he thought to himself.

Or did he whisper it?

Shona had turned the engine off. And was turning herself. To look into his eyes. A peculiar expression on her face that for some reason provoked him yet also understood him to his core.

'Sorry, Dad,' she said graciously. 'Do you need a moment?'

Derek nodded, feeling every bit as fragile and grey as he obviously looked.

'I'm not ready for this. I'm really not.'

'That's alright,' replied his daughter gently. 'We'll just sit for a moment. There's no rush.'

But, it wasn't to be. All of a sudden, Shona's demeanor had changed and she was casting anxious glances at the house.

'I tell you what,' she uttered, sounding strained. 'I'll go in and have a word with Richie while you wait here. Give you some time alone. How does that sound?'

'Yes. Thank you.' Derek blinked several times. 'I just need a few moments to compose myself. It's not easy, you know.'

'I know,' Shona sympathised.

There was a squeeze on his hand, and then his daughter turned the other way and opened the car door.

Derek gazed at her departing form, his heart in his throat. And then watched the door open to admit her, grateful that he was on the side of the car facing away from the house.

His next, very necessary, step was to remove a tissue from his pocket and dab at the moisture oozing from his eyes.

30

There was awkwardness and there was awkwardness. And this was most emphatically the latter.

Being eyed by a synthetic face that was giving nothing away about the sentience behind it was making Richie wither inside. It was like trying to socialise with a pantomime mask.

How he wished that Bessie's countenance would contort into his imagined older, grey-haired version of Shona. At least that would provide him with a modicum of comfort.

It wasn't going to happen, though. He was stuck with looking at the hiding place instead.

The imposter was the one who had to break the fragile silence. And she did it with a suitably bland nicety. But when Richie replied, he wasn't up to hiding the falseness from his voice.

Fortunately, the mother was like the daughter. Opting for an immediate and bold change of tack, but doing it with compassion. Even managing to bring Bessie more to life before making her speak, with a flash of perfect, straight-toothed smile.

'Life's a pig at times, put...ting us in such uncom...fortable situations, don't you think?'

Richie swallowed, a wave of relief washing over him. The impassive features seeming for just a moment to show a hint of Shona-ishness.

He knew a reply was required. But, true to form, the words were just out of reach.

Not that it mattered when in company with a Mrs. McShane. Flowing on gracefully, she introduced herself as just 'Eileen'.

'Pleased to meet you,' faked Richie nervously.

'Or maybe less than pl...eased if you're hon...est? I must be qu...ite an in...trusion.'

'Oh...well...' Richie squirmed, embarrassed at being read so easily. 'It...it is a little, well...*difficult* to come to terms with, I must admit.'

'Extremely difficult, I should think.'

Richie blinked.

Was he imagining it, or had Bessie's automated voice become slightly crisper?

It was a trick of his mind, surely. There was no way she could make Bessie's circuits do that.

Hang on, though. He couldn't go thinking like that. The workings of spirit on electronics was an indisputably opaque field of knowledge. There probably wasn't a person alive who could have the faintest idea of whether or not Eileen's spirit was capable of willing such a change in Bessie's voice oscillators.

'But you have to look on the bright side,' resumed Eileen suddenly. 'The fact that I'm such an ea...sy guest.'

'Easy guest?' queried Richie.

'Well, are you having to run around getting me something to drink?'

Richie gave a bit of a titter, but then a serious observation took over and he frowned at her.

'Your speech is changing,' he remarked. 'Improving.'

Another little smile came his way, accompanied by a curiously cheeky head tilt for an android.

'You certainly know how to make a girl feel good, you smooth talking devil, you.'

Eileen was Shona's mother, alright. Never had he imagined that one day something coming out of Bessie's mouth would actually make him blush.

'And as for that blush...' she continued in an even less robotic voice. 'Decidedly adorable.'

Richie cringed with embarrassment.

How *were* you supposed to react to that sort of comment? It could be as innocent or suggestive as you wanted it to be.

Although when the woman concerned was potentially a future mother-in-law, the position should be quite clear. Even if she was a *late* mother-in-law.

Hmm.

Muddy waters.

Exactly how did she relate to him now that she no longer qualified as a human being?

'Sorry if I've embarr...assed you, lovie.'

Lovie.

A one-sided, cumulative closeness was threatening. Making Richie feel very uncertain.

'Your voice *has* changed!' he blurted divertingly. 'It's like you're learning to operate Bessie better as we speak.'

'Well, I'm a fast learner, Richie.'

'So I see,' observed Richie.

The little smile repeated.

'I bet you've got your work cut out with my Shona, being so shy.'

'I'm *not* shy.'

'Ye Gods!'

Richie hesitated and then, lost for words and desperate to change the subject, asked, '*Are* there Gods there, where you are, then?'

Eileen had done it again. Transcended what should be possible by palpably stiffening Bessie.

'They're here.'

Richie stared at her puzzled.

'Here? What do you mean?'

'Behind you. Just coming up the road.'

Implausible though it was that a troupe of deities was having a walkabout in the area, Richie couldn't help but corkscrew in his chair. To see Shona's car slowing to pull into the vacant parking space outside the house.

'Ah. Right…' he said, uneasiness coursing through him.

'Well, thank you for enter…taining me, my dear, and lovely meeting you, but it might be best if you, you know, make yourself scarce for a few min…utes. It's going to get emotional.'

'Oh…yes…hmm.' He raised his eyes in agreement at Bessie and rose to his feet. 'I'll just let Shona in and then disappear.'

He hadn't needed persuading. Group tearfulness really wasn't his forté.

31

'I'm giving Dad a minute or two in the car to compose himself,' Shona explained as Richie swung open the front door for her.

'Hmm,' frowned Richie, looking past her at the silhouette sitting in the far side of the car. 'I can only imagine how deep the poor man must be digging right now.'

'Yes.' She averted her eyes. 'It's going to be difficult for him. Though delightful too, I presume.'

Richie shuffled uneasily for a moment.

'Perhaps I should disappear for a while,' he suggested softly. 'Give the three of you some time alone.'

Leaning forward, she gave him a hug of approval.

'Thanks.'

Leaving Richie to slope off, she pushed against the living room door. Opening it slowly.

'It's just me, Mum,' she confessed as she entered. 'Dad's in the car, and he'll join us in a minute or two.'

'I'm not surprised. It must be very difficult for him.'

Shona stiffened in surprise.

'*Mum*, you're speaking a lot better!'

Eileen managed a small smile from Bessie again.

'Well, you know me, love. I don't hang around at anything. And since you were good enough to leave me your boyfriend, I've been using him for practice.'

Shona grinned.

'This android isn't bad at all, you know, once you start to get the hang of it,' continued her mother. 'And, of course, it helps not having to fight against any operating programme.'

'Great!'

Shona sank down into one of Richie's tatty armchairs. Whereupon they both gazed at the floor, a blanket of unease descending onto them.

'This is going to be a very long minute or two, my dear,' commented Eileen, somewhat stiffly.

'A small eternity,' agreed her daughter, fixing her eyes in an oddly disengaged fashion on the scene outside the window.

* * *

The pace had been set.

It was always going to be a faltery start. Having one's deceased wife return in such circumstances was enough to give any widower a dose of collywobbles. But the state of Derek hit Eileen like a demolition ball of shock.

Surely there should be some delight shining through. There wasn't a trace, though. Just crimped up, pitiful pensiveness mixed with dazed disbelief.

Still reeling from the shock, Eileen made a brave start. Her words congealing in Bessie's throat like globs of half-chewed toffee.

The sound of the electronic voice seemed to root Derek to a metaphorical spot at the bottom of a very deep heart. Rendering him even less capable of speech than his loved one.

But Eileen's resolve was strong. And it wasn't long before the stops and starts had stopped. And the meandering had straightened. Aiming itself like an arrow of intent at an audience transfixed at how the ghost in the machine could gain such surprising momentum.

Not that conveying how death had felt could ever hope to approach straightforwardness. Which was why she had agonised earlier over how she would describe such suddenness and confusion. And express the sheer enormity of the loss of a life and two people so loved.

Had she known that she would manage it with such alacrity, it would have saved her a great deal of stress.

But that was life.

And, apparently, afterlife.

With the benefit of hindsight, she knew she shouldn't have clung to her human life in the way she had done. She and Derek had even broached the subject in their many rambling chats about the meaning of life.

How to die well.

But as had been so often the case in her human life, theory was one thing and practice something entirely different. You could never tell how you would feel in a new situation until you'd tried it.

Once her lament had finished, the three of them huddled in an embrace. Which felt peculiar and unreal but was a huge improvement on the emotional stiffness of when Derek had first entered the room.

Later, Eileen would realise just how stupendous that embrace had been. Beyond the weirdness and discomfort, it was two realms of existence being hugged into overlap.

Shona was the one to eventually break them up. An untimely bout of cramp in one foot being so typical of how such moments can subside.

Her plight gave birth to a shared hilarity that was the discharge of something buried deep in their collective identity. A ringing testimony of their familial closeness.

In their eased state, the happy anecdotes started flowing. Defining moments of their past togetherness, ranging from the learn-as-you-go-on creation of their garden to a chaotic, mishap-ridden holiday in Majorca. A real 'do you remember when?' session.

Of course, seeing the whale from Uncle Jim's boat had been included. As had their bemused failure to cope with the strandy, multicoloured London Underground map. The grand finale being much closer to home, the time that the infant Shona had tripped over her own clumsy feet and plonked down onto a cow-pat.

'I'll go and get Richie,' she trilled, eager to change the topic. 'You need to meet him, Dad.'

'Yes, of course.'

She returned a minute or two later with a pensive-looking Richie in tow. And, fizzing with enthusiasm, introduced him to her father.

'So, you're the man who's being putting such a smile on my daughter's face lately!' bubbled Derek, a changed man now. 'Pleased to finally get to meet you.'

'Likewise,' responded Richie.

'And thank you for letting us use your pad as a reuniting rendezvous.'

'You're welcome.' He elevated a cautious eyebrow. 'I take it everything is going well?'

'Oh, it certainly is. It's not every man who gets his late wife back before his time in the hereafter.'

'True!' Richie gave Bessie's synthetic face a mistrustful glance. 'It still feels like this is all a dream to me.'

'I'll second that!' exclaimed Derek.

'And I'll third it,' added Shona.

'I'm not exactly finding it unweird, myself,' added Bessie's electronic voice.

'Just think, love,' said Derek thoughtfully, 'you must be the first person ever to have come back in an android.

Can you imagine the field day they'd have with you on those geeky paranormal-investigator shows you get on Freesat?'

'Ha ha! Aye, I should imagine I'm the first,' came Bessie's voice again.

'Perhaps we ought to submit Eileen to science as empirical evidence of life after death,' ventured Richie, his eyes sparkling with mischief. 'Imagine the fun they'd have with her.'

'Hey, you cheeky monkey!' protested Eileen. 'You behave yourself.'

'Wow, you're getting *really* good with the speaking now, Mum!' interjected Shona. 'That sounded practically human!'

'Well, I was one once, you know.'

A titter rippled through the room.

'So…' began Shona, turning purposefully to Richie. 'How about if I commandeer your kitchen later and rustle us up something for an evening meal?'

'Er…yeah. I suppose so,' wavered Richie uncertainly. 'It's just that…erm…' Breaking off, he gave a self-conscious little laugh.

'Problem?'

'Well, I'm not actually sure you'll find much in there suitable. I really wasn't planning on being landed with an impromptu family meal when I last went to the shops, you know.'

'It's alright, Mother Hubbard,' twinkled Shona. 'Don't you worry; it's not so late that I can't do a food dash back to Shoreholm.'

'Sorry,' grinned Richie apologetically.

'Do you need to do any washing up first?' hinted Shona quietly, in sudden remembrance of the state of the sink area.

Richie's grin slid of his face like a melting ice cream sliding off its cone.

'Ah, good point.'

'Oh dear,' resounded Bessie's electronic voice insensitively. 'You really need to get to work on civilising that man of yours, Shona. Bring him out of his twenties!'

'Huh!' grunted Richie before turning away from them and exiting the room. The background sniggering following him through the doorway.

As he started the washing up his face started to darken. And a troubled frown started growing.

Wonderful though this reunion may be, he had some bad news to break.

He wouldn't yet, though.

Let them enjoy their party.

Procrastination didn't always deserve its negative reputation. Why spoil today when you could spoil tomorrow instead?

32

'Nyet. Eto ne tak, kak eto proizoydet,' growled Sergei, his Rostov accent at its thickest. *That's not how it's going to happen.*

'How will it happen then, Comrade Commander?' frowned Alexandr.

The FSB veteran repositioned himself on the unforgiving park bench and gazed thoughtfully into the distance at a dog-walker strolling through the trees. And then took a slow and appreciative drag on what remained of his cigarette.

'Well, young Comrade…' he began, releasing a cloud of acrid smoke. 'Having already made significant inroads without letting on about it, as we do in Centre Sixteen, we have the luxury of time. Meaning we can afford to start small.'

'Start small?'

Sergei shifted in the seat again, fixing his subordinate with a lizardish smirk.

'Yes indeed, Alec. Cause inconveniences that are minor but widespread enough to be noticed in high places. And then sit tight for a little while and repeat. And then sit tight again to give their discomfort time to start to eat at them.'

'Good plan. Let them stew in worry for a while.'

Sergei chuckled.

'I like that, Alec. *Stew*. Da! A nice way of putting it.'

With suitable modesty, Alexandr smiled down at the ground by their feet. It was always nice to be appreciated by one as blunt and calculating as the commander.

'So, when do you…?' he began, only to be cut off by Sergei's flamboyant continuance.

'How would those Westerner's say it? Ah, yes…' His tone took on a menacing edge as he lapsed into a sarcastic version of posh, vowel-elongated English. 'Little by little we will fuck you, my friends. Infecting your cyber-networks until your systems are hopelessly arthritic. Energy networks, industrial control, military facilities, financial institutions, parliamentarian facilities, the media…even your hospitals.' He smacked a vigorous palm onto his thigh prior to returning to the mother-tongue. 'You name it – all turning to shit! *No one* will be safe!'

At that, he vigorously stubbed his cigarette and paused to contemplate the implications of issuing the order he was about to give his subordinate.

But not for long. You didn't run a team of saboteurs by being hesitant. You were decisive. Bold. You just sank a drink and got on with things. You did it the Centre Sixteen way.

He cleared his throat.

'Right, young man. When we get back, you have a job to do.' He narrowed his eyes just enough to hook Alexandr's full attention. 'You know which one I am talking about?'

'Of course, Comrade Commander.'

Sergei gave a satisfied little grunt.

'The time has come, you see, Alec. Conditions

have…' He paused and smiled satisfaction into his comrade's eyes. '…*ripened* to perfection.'

'Yes, Comrade Commander,' affirmed Alexandr, hoping that he appeared as confident about the matter as he was pretending to be.

'And when it is done, let me know, alright? I'll need to let our comrades in Tehran and Pyongyang know.'

'Yes, Comrade Commander.'

'But first, Alec, we do the most important thing of all. Have a vodka to lubricate the process.'

Alexandr's face cracked into a smile as his superior reached into his breast pocket to remove his treasured hip flask.

'You like my little friend, I know.'

'I do indeed, Comrade Commander.'

'Then you should get one yourself. You'd find it an excellent counterbalance for your gun. Until you drain its contents, that is. But by then you don't care.'

Grinning and tipping back his head, Sergei took a long sup before passing the flask to his subordinate.

Alexandr's smile widened at the slightly slurred instruction to drain it dry.

33

The party had done what all good things always did too soon. Become a memory. An anaemic echo of its former self.

As the night had gulped away her smiling daughter and husband, Eileen's Bessie-wave into the dusk had felt unreal. More like someone else's gesture rather than her own. Heralding the slide into hollowness that was to follow.

Richie had seen to it that she was swiftly back in what now passed for nocturnal normality, being parked in her customary corner of the living room. And looking back, she realised that she'd barely noticed his departure to his bedroom.

Had there actually been a 'goodnight'?

Hmm.

She couldn't remember one.

It was fine for him. Doubtless he'd fallen into a contented sleep within minutes. Aided by the drink.

What a beautiful thing it had been to be able to slip away into sleep! A luxury Eileen could only dream of now.

Not needing sleep was fine when all was tickety-boo. It was just that should you be troubled it was a curse.

And troubled Eileen most certainly was.

Truth was reaching out invasive fingers. Gathering her, urging her that it was time. Time to stop trying to believe what she wanted to and instead admit that the reuniting with Derek hadn't been the coming home for which she had yearned. Not their former couple-hood at all.

Yes, they'd relived some memories. And shared laughter. But behind it all had been an invalidating sense of something lost.

An evocative image of Derek's overwhelmed expression at hearing her speak via Bessie floated before her. Rekindling some hope.

There had been no mistaking that look of his.

Could she at least console herself that this dilemma wasn't about the love, then? Because, that was clearly as strong as ever.

And with love there was always hope, wasn't there?

Love conquers all, and all that.

Yes, but while that was true…

Eileen couldn't help a despondent flicker of Bessie's polyester lashes. Because what had her still conquered was the stinging fact that apart from that pulse of love, none of it had been real.

No.

He'd been there.

While she had been…*here*.

In this concrete-heavy place of non-belonging.

The hollow truth of the matter was in what still lay between them. An unbridgeable chasm of…of…

Needing to hear it out loud, she forced the words from Bessie's lips.

'Of realms.'

A hollow groan escaped Bessie's vocal circuitry.

This whole experience was ripping Eileen from her foundations. She had always considered love to be something purely spiritual, of the soul. Something *above* mere physicality. Yet here she was right now, living the truth of the matter. Learning that things weren't anywhere near so black and white.

Interaction was love's essence, the need to express itself. Yet what she hadn't realised was that the purest and fullest way to interact was via physicality itself.

Real togetherness happened when love was channelled into the glow and thrill of physical contact. An act that nourished the spirit so richly that it found itself in no less than seventh heaven.

Just as a sculptor needed clay, so love needed its medium. One of shining eyes and smiles and hugs.

Never before had the value of human life been so rawly apparent to her. It was a revelation.

A deeper emptiness invaded her.

Derek must have found it unreal too. Deeply affected though he'd clearly been, he hadn't gone as far as *real* physical contact. Whilst the three of them had embraced after her speech, which had been lovely in a slightly remote sort of way, there hadn't been a departure hug from him.

All they'd parted with had been a little wave.

Granted, it wasn't as if such intimacy would seem anything like hugging his former wife – far from it. The android's body was cold and inert. And as such, Eileen wouldn't actually *feel* the hug.

Nevertheless, it still would have meant something.

Derek knew that she was *in there*, so to speak. So surely he could have made more of an effort. If only as a gesture.

Valiantly, she strove to put a lid on her pain. But it was like trying to hold down a cantankerous cat. Get a hold on one bit and another comes up and claws you.

And claw her it did. Placard-boarding its insistence that she was fake, an imposter in their world.

She knitted the dark android eyebrows. Forcing her thought-train to a juddering, clanky halt.

For her own self-preservation, this needed to stop, *really* needed to stop.

She was suffering from paranoia.

Calm, calm, you must be calm, she told herself stillingly. *It's early days yet. Things will improve. They will, they will, they will...*

To her surprise she managed to remain composed for several seconds, allowing calmness to infuse her being.

Good.

It was working.

She was unwarping.

Now she could think clearly.

Details. It was the trifling details that were her problem. She had been seizing them, obsessing on them. Unable to see the wood for the trees.

Guilt suddenly started pecking at her.

She had heaped all that criticism on poor Derek's undeserving shoulders. When it must have felt seriously freaky for him having her address him from inside an android.

Well?

It was true, wasn't it?

Hadn't she always found pictures of androids creepy?

Of course she had. There was something deeply uncanny about something obviously *not* human looking so real.

Shame on her! She must give the poor man time to come to terms with the enormous, overpowering weirdness of the situation.

And above all, she must stay calm.

Remaining calm was much easier said than done, though. Already an even worse thought was pushing, greedy for an answer. The matter of whether or not this would be her life from now on – always on the brink of despair.

She wished she could still cry. Feel real tears stream down real cheeks.

What *was* real was the rise in ambient light. Gradual but vivid enough to jolt her from her anguish.

The door!

It was opening.

On clicked the living room light. Not glaringly, though. With comfortable mellowness, the dimmer switch still being set to low from late the previous evening.

God damn it; it was Richie heading for the loo in the altogether again, just like last night.

For the tiniest fraction of a second, a naughty sense of excitement felt like it should be coursing through the body that she didn't have. A moment that a small, renegade part of her tried to hang on to but only to be extinguished by a surge of indignation.

Did he really have to walk around with his *thing* on show like that?

She was, after all, a woman.

Well, sort of.

And, what's more, old enough to be his mum.

For the sake of decency, she clamped Bessie's eyelids shut.

Christ alive, the man was in a relationship with her daughter. And now she was having to listen to him peeing, thanks to the wide open doors.

His exclamation was equally audible.

Oh, no! He must have remembered she was there.

The air was suddenly fraught with an awful and protracted silence.

Why was he taking so long?

At last, the toilet flushed.

As Eileen sensed his presence nearing again, curiosity

demanded that she open Bessie's eyes. And she managed it just in time to spot the hand come sneaking round the doorway to click off the light switch.

She couldn't help the smirk she made grow in the synthetic face. Despite the darkness, Richie's shadowy figure was still clearly discernible to Bessie's optical sensors.

The silly man!

He didn't know his own technology.

Looking very uncertain, he was now groping his way through the darkness. A journey that came to an abrupt halt with a hissed expletive.

He was standing on one leg, now. Writhing, his face screwed up in pain as he rubbed the toe he had stubbed on the sharp-edged chair leg.

His torso was directly facing Bessie now. Her inhabitant thankful that his lower half was now shrouded in a bath towel.

At last, he stopped grimacing and hobbled across the room and out through the open doorway. Leaving in his wake a mutter.

A mutter that had iced her spirits.

'It's a good job this won't be continuing. It's bloody ridiculous.'

34

Richie turned his back, trying his horrified utmost to feign the resumption of unconcerned bathing. Praying that his breaths were inaudible – short, tight jerks, riding a torrid cocktail of conflicted emotions.

What was he going to do now?

He was done for.

It was bad enough that his relaxing shower had just been so rudely and embarrassingly interrupted by both of the female astronauts suddenly appearing through the steamy air. But they'd looked him up and down (mainly down) while giggling like a pair of schoolgirls. And *shock of all shocks*, what was utterly nightmarish was that one of them was a schoolgirl from his past!

Not just any old schoolgirl, though. None other than the terrifying Sarah Marshall.

And true to past form, he'd been unable to mask his horrified gurgle.

His mind raced as he stood palpitating under the sploshy torrent. Unable to look back, praying that they'd lost interest and left.

What the hell was *she* doing here, anyway?

She couldn't be an astronaut; it didn't make any sense! At school she'd been as far as a distant galaxy from the studious, scientific type who might become as astronaut.

Nevertheless it had definitely been her. You couldn't mistake the cockiness of that face as it smirked down humiliatingly at his manhood, instantly stripping off the layers Richie had gained since those school days.

Layers he hadn't realised could be so thin.

She'd be his downfall here. He hadn't been able to handle her back then, and he wouldn't be able to now. He'd been able to tell from her contemptuous face that in all these years nothing had changed.

This was *awful*. He was at his least resilient as it was, cowed by his inability to fix the niggling new problem with the androids. And clueless as to where to go from here.

It was utterly mysterious. Never before had he come across a fault quite like it. It was as if the androids had become possessed by spirits or something.

The worse thing about it was that it was holding up the work of the rest of the team. Their very important scientific work.

He gulped, opening despairing eyes.

All this on his shoulders.

Hang on...

Something strange had happened. The steaminess had disappeared from the air. And he was on his back, facing a cobwebby ceiling that looked familiar, *very* familiar indeed. Like he'd known it for years.

He palpably felt the sink back down to planet Earth.

'My God!' he breathed in astonishment.

And tremendous relief.

He wasn't on the International Space Station after all. And there *were* no androids. Or mysterious fault.

Best of all by far, though...no Sarah Marshall.

The rush of air from his mouth was like a bicycle inner tube going down.

It had all been just a bad dream.

Slowly, thankfully, he allowed his body to unclench. Letting it sink deeper into the lovely, nurturing bed. On a Monday that he'd booked as leave from work.

Smile.

He had tomorrow off as well.

The smile widened.

He continued lying there, savouring the comfort and safety. Until eventually deciding that a nice slow coffee was in order, to celebrate his rescue from purgatory.

But as he threw back the cover and rose up into his comfortable normality, it came back to him just how normal things...

...*weren't*.

This current situation. It was almost as off the scale in weirdness as the bad dream. A classic case of *be careful what you wish for because you might just get it*.

A soft groan escaped him.

To think of how much he'd wanted to see a ghost after that first encounter with Shona...and now he had a pet one in his living room.

He screwed up his eyes in anguish as further details clambered up from his depths.

It had happened again.

Parading in sight of Eileen during the night.

Jesus wept!

He *must* remember she was there.

The trouble was, he was never at his most cogent at three in the morning. And then there was the fact that Bessie had become a part of the furniture over the year or so that he'd had her at home. And when you lived alone, you didn't bother with modesty for nocturnal loo-trips.

He blinked. Reaching out for his dressing gown and pulling it on. Tying the cord tightly.

Talk about embarrassing! Especially in the light of her flirty-talk earlier when the two of them had been alone.

What had that been about his blush?

Oh, yes.

Adorable.

Heat started radiating from his neck.

She'd seen a lot more than his blush now.

Had she seen him, though?

Of course she had. The truth of the matter stood bold and stark. It wasn't as if you needed to ask if anyone had heard of Jasper the Kipping Ghost. There was no such thing as sleep in the afterlife.

But perhaps there might be a vague equivalent. Some sort of zoning out where you didn't notice what was going on around you.

Was that too much to ask for?

'Of course it is,' he muttered grumpily.

Once again, he'd have to try to make his morning greeting seem natural and unconcerned. As if nothing had happened.

The thought made more heat radiate from his neck.

Not the easiest thing to do.

Especially with *her*.

A vision of the Eileen he had imagined earlier flashed back. An older, greyer version of Shona, with those same intelligent eyes. Smiling at him cheekily this time. Telling him he had an adorable...body.

He stirred uneasily at an unexpected tightening down below.

'She's Shona's *mum*,' he hissed at himself rebukingly.

This could not go on.

It was just so...

...*wrong*.

Unpalatable though it was, he'd do the deed today.

The trouble was, that meant breaking the news to Shona and her father.

35

Couldn't life be on his side, just for once?

Richie blinked in distress as the telephone handset continued its coo into his ear.

'Thanks so much for yesterday, love. Dad really appreciated it, and so did I.'

Shona sounded aglow, like someone at the peak of happiness. But here he was, poised to change that.

'You're welcome,' he replied automatically, inwardly scrabbling for a way to steer the conversation onto a slow and tactful approach to the thorny problem of Eileen's habitation in Bessie.

'Mind you…' A bit of a giggle rippled along the line. 'Dad's not looking very happy this morning for someone just reunited with their wife. I'm assuming he's a bit shell-shocked.'

'Well, it's a huge adjustment to have to make.'

'Aye, it is.'

'So…' Richie began, intent on easing the conversation back towards his intended trajectory, 'when will the two of you be round, do you think?'

'Oh.' A silence fell on the line. 'Aren't you going to work, then? I hate to be the harbinger of bad news but it's a Monday.'

'Yes, yes, I know, but I've taken today and tomorrow off work. I was going to tell you earlier but forgot, what with the drama of everything.'

'Oh. Right. Well, that's very handy, actually, considering the state of play between Mum and Dad.'

'Yes, it is. And I seriously need a break. I've built up quite a bit of leave over the last six months, what with the pressure being on.'

'I bet. So…is it alright if we come round at about ten ?'

'That would be perfect. But, the thing is…' Richie's voice turned slightly husky, 'I need to…erm…talk with you about something first.'

'Oh?'

'Yeah.'

'Well, I'm all ears.'

'It's about your mum.'

'My mum?' Shona's voice was suddenly tinged with misgiving. 'Do I sense a problem looming?'

'Ahem!' Richie wriggled uncomfortably. 'I…I'm afraid it is something of a problem.'

'Oh, dear.' He heard Shona clear her throat. 'Would I be right in assuming you're finding it difficult having her living with you?'

'No, no. Well actually, yes, I am…er…a bit. But it's not about that. I'm afraid there's…there's a technical problem with Bessie.'

'Technical problem? What do you mean?'

'Well, you see, as you know, Bessie is without an operating programme. And I'm afraid….' He paused to steel himself. 'Look, I need to load her with the new software as soon as possible.'

He had done it.

Fired his shot.

And now the line had gone dead silent.

'In fact, very soon,' he added, in urgent need of filling the imploded hush.

But the silence continued.

'I'm sorry,' he muttered, and then at last Shona spoke.

'B-but...but...doesn't that mean that...that...she won't be able to function in Bessie?'

'I...I'm not entirely sure. Although most likely *not*, I'm afraid, going by what you said about your phone. You see, androids run sophisticated programmes.'

'Oh, God! I don't believe this,' wailed Shona. 'I've only just got her back, Richie!'

'I'm so sorry, I really am. B-but...'

'All this time, all of that *effort*...she finally gets back with us, and now...now...this!'

Richie gulped back the glob of distress that was growing in his throat.

'I'm very sorry, Shona.'

'Isn't there some other way, something you can do to avoid this?' she panted.

'I'm afraid not,' confessed Richie, awash in shame, even though he'd done nothing wrong.

There was a sudden, explosive retort on the other end of the line. The sound of Shona breaking down.

Richie clutched the phone handset tightly and closed his eyes. Totally at a loss as to what to say.

'This is j-just *too* much, Richie,' came a sob. 'I *need* Mum. I just c-can't bear the thought of losing her all over again; it'll kill me.' She sniffed. 'Please! There *must* be *something* you can do, surely, s-some way...way of...of...'

Her voice dissolved into tearful heaving.

'I'm so very sorry...' repeated Richie lamely.

'Oh, God,' she wailed. 'Oh, God...*please*, no...I can't bear this...no, no, no...'

The click was horribly bleak and sudden.

'Shona?'

Richie stared wide-eyed at the handset in his hand.

'Bloody hell,' he murmured as he replaced it into its cradle.

36

This was pure torture.

Within Shona, little greyhounds of strife were racing in every possible mental direction, frantic with the prospect of her having to break the news to her mother.

As she paced around the living room, she wondered how on earth she was going to muster the courage to go through with it. Fretting over how her mum was going to react.

Telling Dad had been bad enough. The poor man had strutted to and fro, his gesticulations stiffly jerking in time with his protesting cries. Lamenting with disbelief that he would now be losing his wife a second time.

Finally, he'd turned away from his daughter, announcing over a rigid shoulder that he wouldn't be coming with her to Richie's.

'I can't face it! It's more than any man can bear!!' he hollered.

Shona had pleaded with his departing back, begging him to come with her, but it hadn't stood a chance of working. Utterly distraught, he had stomped up to his bedroom and very firmly closed out the world.

Never before had Shona known him so upset. Despite it being made of oak, the bedroom door had been unable to muffle from her the cascade of despairing gasps it had just shut in.

Lost as to what to do, she had just stood at the foot of the staircase for a while, her whole body trembling with distress. Knowing that she'd have to give her father a little time but equally knowing that she couldn't just leave for Richie's on her own without another attempt at persuading him to come with her.

She had sloped off back to the living room. Where she was *still* pacing from one end to the other, unable to stop fretting.

With a Herculean push of determination, she managed to thrust aside her fear of how her mother was going to react. And then reached into her pocket and pulled out her phone.

Richie.

She *must* speak with him again first. Just in case he was coming up with anything, an alternative plan of action that would allow her mum to stay. Just in case there was any...

...hope.

Trying her utmost to sniff away her tearfulness, she sank down into one of the armchairs. Praying for an upturn in fortune as she began the thumb-scroll for Richie on her phone.

'Shona?'

She started when he answered, despite his voice being expected.

'Richie!' she gasped.

'Hello.'

Fighting to gather herself, she gave a nervous cough before speaking.

'Oh, Richie, are you *absolutely* sure you have to do this? If...if there's another way, *anything*...'

An uneasy throat-clearing sound crackled out from the phone. Changing to an uncomfortable sounding explanation.

'Oh, Shona, I...I'm afraid not. The trouble is, you see, androids shouldn't be left without an operating system for long. If...if...if you *do*, there's a risk they'll end up defaulting to the factory settings and going into hibernate. Without warning. And then...'

His voice faded.

Hissing out an exasperated breath, Shona shook her head from side to side.

'Isn't it a bit stupid making them like that?' she grumbled.

'It's done for safety reasons, you see,' explained Richie. 'So that if...'

'Yes, yes, alright!' she cut in impatiently. 'I don't really care about why. What I care about is losing my mum.'

An awkward silence fell before Richie was able to respond.

'I-I'm so sorry, but it's...well...unavoidable.'

This was awful.

'Please?' Shona begged, despairingly. '*Don't* do it.'

'Shona, like I said, if I didn't do it, Bessie would soon go into default and shutdown anyway.'

'But maybe then you could resurrect her and Mum would be able to go back into her!'

'I'm afraid not. And as Bessie's such an early model, and she'd be back at factory default, I'd have to install an early version of the software and then an interim version and finally the new version on top of it, which would take forever and no doubt throw up a ton of hard-to-resolve problems.'

'This is unbelievable. Absolutely unbelievable,' complained Shona, feeling frantic.

'Sorry,' repeated the voice in her phone.

'Oh, for goodness sake, Richie! Will you stop saying "sorry" all the time?'

Richie remained silent.

'Okay,' sighed Shona, managing to shift her tone to something calmer. 'We'll have to let Mum know today, I suppose, so we'll be coming round, but it'll be a bit later than ten now because I've got to try to persuade Dad to come when he's gone off to his room and shut the door on me.'

'Oh, dear.'

With a wave of fresh tearfulness prickling at her, Shona sucked in a sharp breath and stated stiffly, 'What a wonderful, wonderful day this is turning out to be!'

'I know.'

'You know, I was feeling really happy when I started chatting with you yesterday. And now look how things have gone.'

'Yes, I know. It's awful.'

Tears were threatening to burst out again now. Making a loud sniff necessary before Shona could regain the faculty of speech.

'Oh, God. I can't, just can't believe this is happening,' she wailed.

The sound of Richie clearing his throat nervously crackled out of Shona's phone.

'Shona...I think that...'

But she didn't let him say what he thought, interjecting with a forced and unemotional sounding. 'I'll be round soon, alright?'

There was another edgy pause, followed by a soft reply.

'Okay.'

And that was that.

Having ended the call, Shona sucked in another steadying breath. And then fired a tight sounding 'right, then' at the heedless ornaments in front of her.

She remained sitting, though. Fondling a tassel on her top and biting her lower lip like a nervous schoolgirl as she tried to brace herself for what she now had to do – take the bull by the horns.

It was several more minutes before she slowly, apprehensively rose to her feet and departed through the kitchen doorway.

She frowned at the ground in front of her with fixed determination as she turned for the stairs. But what happened next was totally unexpected.

'Sorry, my dear,' came the voice from the bottom step of the staircase. 'It's just that I'm finding it a hell of an upheaval. I'll come with you, of course.'

'Oh, Dad!' Shona gasped, tension avalanching from her as she rushed forward.

To embrace him.

37

'I've decided against a gradual ramping up of cyber-attacks against the British, Comrade Marshal. I think something a little meatier would more suit them. Something to give their stiff, hope-and-glory upper lips a workout from the outset.'

A sly smile crawled its way onto the marshal's lips. Its air of satisfaction palpably radiating.

'Well, I've said it before, Comrade Sergei, I trust your judgement in this. That's why I made you a commander; I knew you had it in you.'

'Thank you, Comrade Marshal.'

At that, the marshal tilted his big, bony head back and fixed Sergei with an erudite squint.

'As long as you bear in mind that whatever you decide upon, cyber-warfare timing is a delicately balanced art. Giving the enemy *just* the right amount of time to worry about the next attack is critical. They mustn't have long enough to bolster their systems and garner evidence, but equally they mustn't have so *little* time that you don't achieve sufficient degree of squirm.'

Sergei eased out a suitably wry little smirk.

'Indeed, Comrade Marshal. I think a large attack followed by just a brief pause before the next one would suit the British. As you say, allowing sufficient time for a squirm while denying any recovery time.'

Marshal Antonov nodded slowly and thoughtfully.

'Well, I happen to think you're spot on for the British. Yes. Start by inserting the umbrella up their gentlemanly, fair-playing national arse, and then next time screw it in really deeply, ready for the grand finale – opening it!'

Looking smugly pleased with his description, the marshal exhaled a rattly chortle. Which Sergei accompanied with perfect timing.

And then, with the marshal's characteristic suddenness, he leaned forward across the desk, all hilarity instantly gone. And growled out a few dismissive words.

'Off you go, then, Comrade Commander.'

Sergei stiffened and obediently rose from his chair, his expression serious and dutiful. Suddenly feeling as if it wasn't beyond the realm of possibility to become the recipient of the metaphorical umbrella himself.

'Yes, Comrade Marshal,' he responded submissively.

But not *too* submissively.

Once outside the door, he took the opportunity to pause for a moment to wriggle away the gloopiness that had accumulated in his crevices.

Despite his being an old hand, Centre Sixteen membership still had its fraught side, he reflected. Something that had a perverse appeal.

There weren't many men who could give Sergei the creeps, but the marshal was one of them. An absolute expert in his craft, whose slithery lean forward was enough to make the whole of Siberia break out in a winter sweat.

Clicking his heels officiously against the gleaming marble floor, he started making his escape from the corridors of power. Keeping his pace and demeanor appropriately dignified for the busts of the great that were eyeing him keenly from both sides.

He would be heartily glad to leave the wood-panelled grandeur for his own much more comfortable domain, where his underling would be awaiting his return.

With every step, he started feeling more relaxed. As he should. After all, the fun bit was coming next. Himself and Alexandr sitting side-by-side for a comforting online search through the Western media outlets.

He smiled.

Already salivating at the prospect.

38

That angry mutter of Richie's has really got under my proverbial skin. Making alarm bells ring-a-ling like crazy.

It's a good job this won't be continuing.

That was what he said.

And I really don't like the sound of it.

It's human, and post-human, nature to try to dissect precisely what a comment means. In this case, whether it merely means you won't be remaining here in Richie's house, or on the other hand it means something far worse, that you'll be expelled from Bessie.

And if you are a natural optimist like me, you'll try your best to convince yourself that it simply means that you and Bessie will be carted off to live with Derek and Shona, which, to be honest, would be a relief, this current co-existence not entirely being an easy one, to say the least!

The trouble is, I sense that that is not the case. That he's after my blood.

Call it women's intuition or ESP, whatever you sodding well like, but hoofing me out of Bessie is what he's planning and I damn well know it! I can feel it.

And it's something he could do quite easily. I'm utterly at his mercy in here. And absolute power inevitably leads to a bad ending.

He wouldn't even have to confront Shona and Derek on the matter. He could just decide to do some 'maintenance' on Bessie when they weren't there, and she could 'develop' a fault.

Pop!

Sorry folks, I'm afraid Eileen's gone.

Nothing to do with him, of course. He'd explain to them that he suddenly discovered I was no longer in residence.

How tragic that would be, having come so far. All that effort to finally get back here after years of frustrating hauntings ruined because of him and what happened last night. And the other time.

For Christ's sake, he'd ruin me just because of that?

What *is* the matter with the man?

We were getting on alright, weren't we?

Okay, it *is* embarrassing showing all you've got like that. Hardly the sort of relationship you want with your girlfriend's mum. But that's life for you; these things sometimes happen.

And he shouldn't be taking it out on me. It wasn't as if it was my fault. Either time. If you're going to go parading around as if you're in a nudist colony when you have a guest with you…*well*, you're asking for it, aren't you?

Of course you are. So stop this, Richie, boy. You need to just forget about it. Carry on as if it never happened. Maybe make a little joke about it or something. Like a normal person would do.

Huh!

He isn't normal, though, is he?

Trust me to get lumbered with a blushing bachelor boy. You just can't trust those bashful types, the way they keep their true colours hidden.

It's no good keeping the real you hidden because sooner or later life will expose you, and then it's big trouble, your false little world will implode messily.

Anyway…less of the life-truths. He is who he is, and I can't change that. And what matters is what the hell I'm going to do about this situation.

If there is anything I can do about it.

Maybe if I gently broach the subject as soon as he emerges in the morning. Assure him that I looked away, out of respect for him.

That's got to placate him, hasn't it?

And then we can agree to be adult about the issue in future. Laugh it off instead of obsessing about it. Bearing in mind that we've all got bodies – well actually, I haven't any more – and that a woman knows what a man's body looks like, and it's nothing to get all embarrassed about.

Hang on a moment.

Yes!

I've had an idea, and it's really simple. I could suggest that he turns me to face the wall every evening. Then I wouldn't see him when he came through.

How about that?

I could even remind him to turn me every night.

There you are – problem solved!

You see, Richie, it's going to be alright. There's no need for any nastiness.

Good old Eileen has sorted things out.

39

'Ah, Comrade Commander! Marshal Antonov wants you in his office as soon as possible.'

'What?' gasped Sergei. 'I've only just left.'

Alexandr raised his eyebrows and opened his palms to the ceiling.

'Well, he definitely wants you back. "Urgently" was the word he used.'

'Och, k chertu eto! What can be so urgent that a man doesn't even have time for a sigareta?'

Alexandr tilted his head sympathetically. His eyes following the now sagging figure of his boss as it turned and slowly retraced its footsteps towards the gaping doorway.

Once in the doorway, Sergei paused, though. And turned back to face Alexandr again.

'When I come back, Alec, we will do the fun bit,' he declared, a half-smile slowly forming. 'See what the Western media are saying. In fact, why don't you make a start right now?'

'Yes, Comrade Commander.'

'Hopefully, I'll be joining you very soon.'

INHABITANT

And at that, the air was filled with the sound of Sergei's clicking heels hastening from where they had come.

As the commander paraded through the wood-panelled corridors, once again passing the busts of the country's presidential predecessors, he couldn't help the marshal's growly dismissal replaying uneasily in his mind.

What on earth did Antonov want from him now, so soon after he had left?

He didn't like the feel of this at all.

Something had happened.

Sergei couldn't help slowing as he turned the final corner to be met by the loom of the marshal's majestic office door.

Instinctively, he averted his eyes to one side. An inscribed epitaph to the late Viktor Chernomyrdin catching his eye with poignancy.

Khoteli sdelat' luchshe, a poluchilos' kak vsegda

(We wanted to do it better, but it turned out as always)

A frown settled on the beckoned man's brow as he approached the great door. There was no way the marshal would settle for 'as always'. He had faith in his team and expectations of a success that would throw the West into chaos – airports, power plants, banking, government infrastructure; that and much more would be crippled. Leaving the conditions ripe for mother Russia to strike at a time of her choosing.

A gratifying vision swam before his eyes, that of a future inscribed plaque for himself on one of the great walls. Hailing him as a man instrumental in the rise of the new world order.

Meanwhile, back in reality, Sergei found himself slowing even more as he arrived in front of the great door. And needing to suck in a deep and steadying breath.

Two heavy knocks.

A future hero's knocks, he tried to tell himself unsuccessfully.

'Vkhodit!'

The sheer wrath in the marshal's boom had Sergei's pride tumbling straight into a sphincter-clench, a rare sensation for the commander.

With some effort, he pushed against the heavy oak panel in front of him and entered the office. A fresh flicker of apprehension running through him as he was greeted by the coldest, steeliest eyes imaginable.

'Sergei! Our plans!! It's all change.' Marshal Antonov was firing staccato bursts. 'We can no longer proceed as planned because...' As he paused, his facial features visibly tightened. 'Because the West is somehow...*onto* us.'

The commander gasped, his nervousness instantly giving way to astonishment.

'Onto us?'

'Yes!' was thundered back at him. 'You wouldn't believe it! The Kremlin are talking about imposing emergency sanctions. *Already!*'

Sergei crinkled an analytical brow.

'Are you thinking we have a leak, Comrade Marshal?'

Antonov clenched his big, brawny hands into fists and stared at his visitor wildly.

'I don't know! How can I? That will be for Unit 3 to investigate.'

'I'm thinking there must be a leak, Comrade Marshal, for things to move so fast.'

Antonov fell silent, glowering down a frown that looked like it might crack the hefty oak desk.

'You might be right, Sergei,' he growled before drawing in a deep, composing breath. 'But whatever, we need to act, to forget the incremental cyber-attack plan idea and go in heavy as soon as possible.' The steely eyes glinted at Sergei. 'Are we ready for that?'

'Yes, Comrade Marshal, of course. Anything you order.'

'Good,' snapped the marshal bullishly. 'Then you have my authority to launch against America, Britain, Canada and the usual countries in mainland Europe.' His expression softened a little as he regarded Sergei with trusting camaraderie. 'I give you free reign.'

'Thank you, Comrade Marshal. I'll make it just two strikes, then, but hard ones. The first to blow open their defences and install gateways for the follow-up attack, which will be the killer. And in addition, I'll make sure our defences are boosted to the absolute maximum, just in case the West have been cooking anything up.'

'Good. Let me know immediately when the deed has been done.'

'Yes, Comrade Marshal. The second attack will be just days after the first.' Sergei gave a slight smile. 'Enough time for them to shit themselves sufficiently but still be too dizzy to fight back.'

'Excellent,' said the marshal approvingly before straightening and switching to a fervidly reverential expression.

'Slava Rossii!'

'Slava Rossii!' returned Sergei forcefully as he rose from his seat, knowing he was dismissed.

40

'Richie!'

He stiffened. Unable to mask his annoyance at the abruptness of the unwanted interruption.

An android calling him to attention midway through a necessary early morning stride towards the bathroom was most unbecoming. Something he shouldn't have to put up with in his own home.

But, of course, this wasn't really the voice of an android.

It was *her*.

The interloper.

'Eileen,' he acknowledged, not unhuskily. The now dreamlike memory of his nocturnal parade before her swimming uncomfortably before him.

'Richie, we need to talk.'

A little flutter ran a nervous passage through him.

'Do we?' he grimaced.

'Aye. We do.'

'Right. Well can it at least wait until I've been to the bathroom?'

'Of course.'

'Thank you,' he said tightly, resuming his bathroom-ward stride. Huffily clomping the door shut behind him.

When he emerged he was feeling no happier. A condition not helped by a mouth feeling drier than a Bedouin's sandal.

'Getting a drink,' he croaked tersely as he passed back through the living room. Wondering immediately afterwards why he was being so obliging, agreeing to a talk when he'd only just got up.

God damn it, this was *his* home! He should be king of the jungle here, the one deciding when they would talk. 'Later,' he should be telling her firmly.

But, no. Here he was, dancing to her tune.

Feeling the need to appease his indignation, he made the belligerent decision to take his time in the kitchen. Make her wait while he prepared and composed himself.

What did the wretched woman want anyway?

Was she about to take him to task? Ask what he'd been thinking of walking around naked in the night with her there?

Dispelling the vision with a sullen expletive, he reached for the tub of mixed nuts that he habitually grazed upon and shoved a peeved handful into his mouth.

This just wouldn't do. It was way too early in the morning for fisticuffs.

Thoughtfully crunching, he made his decision.

To hell with her 'we need to talk'. He had something to say as well, a *coup fatal* that would well and truly shut her up. He'd tell her straight out, right now, instead of breaking the news gently like he'd planned. Get in before she could embarrass him further about the night.

She'd soon change her tune when she realised the end of her stay on Planet Earth was nigh.

Swivelling round determinedly, he sucked in a deep, preparatory breath. And then, staring ahead of himself rigidly, marched to the living room.

His entrance was swift, his address immediate.

'Eileen, I have something unfortunate to tell you, something you're not going to like.'

The synthetic face turned his way. It's lack of reply an obvious giveaway that its occupant had been taken unawares.

'I'm afraid it's bad news,' he continued. 'Bessie is going to need to have software installed soon or she will go into a power-saving hibernation state. Which means she will become inoperative, unable to sustain your habitation.'

He raised his eyebrows at her, his stomach suddenly knotting at having delivered such calamitous news. Worried about how she would react.

She surprised him, though.

'I knew something bad was about to happen, Richie,' she said calmly, even making Bessie give a slight smile. 'I could feel it.'

'Oh.'

'Look, if this is about last night, I know I'm an imposition, but there's really no need for this. You could simply turn me to face the wall at night. You see? Problem solved.'

Richie cleared his throat.

'No, Eileen, it isn't about that. It's the truth. Androids shouldn't be running without operational software. It leaves the door open for all sorts…'

'I heard what you muttered when you left the room last night,' interjected Eileen with disconcerting intensity.

'Ah! Yes. That.' Richie had the grace to shuffle uncomfortably. 'Sorry, but I was annoyed. And embarrassed about…you know.'

'I'm sorry, Richie. Believe me, I do understand that it's difficult and unnatural having me here. But it was the only way I could come back. Surely you must understand that.'

Richie nodded uncomfortably.

'Think what this will do to Shona and Derek,' the artificial voice resumed. 'They'll be devastated. *Utterly* devastated'

'I've already let Shona know, actually.'

'Oh. And...and...?'

Richie blinked at her.

'She was upset, yes; of course she was. But she understands. It's out of my control, you see. It *has* to happen.'

Despite Eileen's robotic embodiment, Richie could smell panic now. The distress of someone whose world was slipping away like a landslide.

A glowering pulse of guilt surged through him. Never before had overpowering someone felt so horribly hollow.

What had happened *had* been excruciatingly embarrassing. And she *was* an intrusion in other ways. But, *hey*, it wasn't as if it was her fault.

Indeed, he'd even go as far as to say that they shared a kinship of sorts in both being victims of this ghastly situation. Two sides of one coin; that was what the two of them were. A coin that had spun crazily out of control.

And now here he was, having broken devastating news in the most unchivalrous way possible just to appease his bruised ego.

What kind of bastard did that?

Hunting desperately within himself, Richie managed to dig up a kind suggestion.

'Maybe you could come back afterwards. Try it with the software operational. You never know...'

'It won't work.'

'You don't know that, though.'

'I do. All I managed when I was in her phone was one word. One lousy word!'

'Yes, but, you never know. Perhaps this time would be different.'

'Oh, come on! Why should it be?'

'Well, erm, I don't know?'

'Exactly. You don't know. And I do.'

'Hmm,' surrendered Richie.

A roaring silence enveloped them. Richie's constricted gaze at the ground begging it to do the decent thing and open up for him.

At last Bessie's voice came to the rescue. Speaking quietly and calmly again.

'When will you do it, then?'

'I think…think…' A voice in Richie's head implored him to have the courage to be honest. 'It…it'll have to be some time today.'

'*Today?*'

The shock in her voice pricked meanly at Richie's conscience. Making his reply stick in his throat for a moment like a glob of wet cement.

'The…the time of shutdown must be getting near, you see.'

'Near.'

'Yes. Very near. And, I'm afraid…afraid that if…if that happens it would be, well, *painfully* problematic and laborious to resurrect her, being as she's such an old model. She's not like the state of the art ones at work.'

'Oh, I see. Well, God forbid that you'd be inconvenienced.'

The silence was crushing, this time. Like being in the grip of an ogre's fist.

Fortunately for Richie, Eileen had had enough. Speaking with stiff, dismissive dignity.

'Right, then, if you could give me some time alone, I have to prepare to say my goodbyes.'

A deep pang of sympathy shot through Richie, making him feel a sudden urge to extend an arm of comfort. But it was an impulse matched by a stomach-clench at the weirdness of expressing affection towards an oversize moving Barbie doll. Even if on the inside there was a real person.

Deciding instead on a safe but inept little 'okay', he sloped away, a creeping Quasimodo of shame. Following up with a barely audible little 'see you later' in the doorway before pulling the door to behind him.

On the other side of the door, he dithered uncertainly. Caught in a tension between wanting to help her and knowing he was no good with people.

Surely he must try, though.

Pursing his lips, he reached for the door handle. But the sound of an electronic blurt made him freeze.

'Damn and blast it! I only ever thought I'd have to die the once.'

Richie winced.

Hovered for a moment.

And then slunk away.

41

The spectre of loss weighed heavily in the eyes that Shona would only half elevate. And as for her father, 'diminished' was the word.

Her voice. That was the worst thing of all. Thick with marinated resentment and impending loss. Her tone an emotional closed door to Richie as she inquired how her mother had taken the news.

It was necessary to clear his throat before replying.

'She...*er*...accepts it...sort of,' he informed a vague point somewhere below her eyes. 'But of course, *well*... you know...'

'Aye...*you know* indeed,' mimicked Shona tersely before pushing past him into the hallway.

Richie barely noticed her father following in her wake, so fixed was his stare at the back of Shona's head. Neither did he notice Shona's sudden turn until it had caught his stare in the act.

'I'd like you to leave us alone with her for a while, so we can say our goodbyes,' she stated mechanically.

Richie nodded squirmily. His throat now as tight as a rusted up nut.

They didn't even notice as he slipped away to the sanctuary of his bedroom. And had they heard the heartfelt groan he let out upon sinking onto his bed they wouldn't have cared.

It was a groan half of misery and half of relief. The relief part an ashen reflection on how there was no better place than bed to nurse anguish.

He inhaled a lungful of pillowy air, finding comfort in the familiarity of its smell. His own conserved odour.

But what little comfort this gave him was very soon punctured by the distant sound of emotionally charged voices.

Rolling onto his back, Richie lifted his head to aim his face in the direction of the voices. His ears primed like tuned antennae but unable to pick anything.

He'd have to imagine how it was going. Which was easily done.

They'd be trying to make the most of every precious minute of this last time of earthly togetherness. Only it wouldn't be time to cherish really. Time spoiled. Claimed by the horrible proximity of goodbye.

Spoiled for him too, as the executioner. Doer of the deed.

And unsparing breaker of the news.

He was guilty on all counts. And already serving his sentence as a pariah. *Persona non grata* in his own home.

He gulped.

Could he end up losing his beloved Shona over this?

The thought made his stomach drop like a twenty stone man on a noose.

He *must* find a way of saving the situation.

Rising up onto an elbow, he stared into the air with laser-like concentration. His mind racing, exploring for any possibilities, even though the chance of there being any felt non-existent.

'Think, Richie, *think!*'

Okay. What he did know for certain was that he'd have to load the software. There was absolutely no escaping that.

So where could he go from there?

His nostrils flared as he sucked in a breath of pure determination.

He needed to pull off some clever little manoeuvre that would allow her to remain at least a bit functional. Something that would at the very least buy him time to further wrack his brains.

And maybe while he was thinking she would manage to improve her functionality, start to cope. After all, look at how slow and laboured she'd been in the empty Bessie at first, improving enormously with practice.

What sort of manoeuvre was possible, though?

Maybe he could find an electronically 'quiet' location in the newly loaded up Bessie. Somewhere she could lurk initially with space to learn the ropes.

He sat wrangling with the problem for a couple of minutes. But only to come to a churning full stop.

He tutted. He was being fanciful, wasn't he? He wasn't even a programmer, just an amateur who could mess around with code a little. And this was an android, far more complex than a mere phone. She simply wouldn't be able to inhabit such a controlled environment.

Unless...

Would a proper programmer know a way?

The corner of his mouth twitched. He could soon have a programmer at the other end of a phone line.

A cold, prickly sensation uncurled in him like an inner hedgehog. Feeding enthusiastically on the prospect of him having to explain that he had an android possessed by his girlfriend's late mother.

Whoever was at the other end of the line would think that he had flipped. And word would spread at work like wildfire.

That Richie Smith from robotics, he's lost the plot. Gone utterly gaga! Mind you, I always knew he was a bit of a weirdo.

Richie could hear the echo of laughter in corridors at work. A sensation quickly replaced by something even more horrific, the sound of Vanessa's angry voice.

He gave a little shudder.

It was clear that it was going to have to be solely his problem to fix.

A new thought started nibbling at him, the matter of exactly how Eileen's 'demise' would happen, come the time.

Would she, indeed *could* she, leave of her own volition? Or would she 'die' of inability to function, like some insect stuck in drying paint?

Suddenly feeling like a murderer, Richie had to blink away tears.

This was vile.

Thus far, his had been a life mercifully light on grief. There had been the loss of a couple of hamsters in his childhood, and later a rabbit that he'd been very fond of, but at least he'd been fortunate with his parents, both of whom still enjoyed ruddy-cheeked, gumbooted, outdoor fine health down in faraway Berkshire.

A slight smile crept onto Richie's cheeks at the thought of his mother's tough, sinewy fortitude. She epitomised the roll-up-your-sleeves and knuckle down type. And his father was similarly robust at seventy-six. Both of them potential ripe-old-agers. Unlike the hapless house-guest now bringing mortality so sharply into focus for him.

The special knowledge Richie had now gained, that death *wasn't* the end, was bringing him no comfort at all. After all, look at poor Eileen; what had life after death done for her?

In distress she had decided to come back. A decision

Richie sympathised with, being appreciative of *this* life of physical sensation.

There was so much to enjoy about being in a body – being with Shona, his beach, catching an awesome sunset, pleasures like swimming in the sea and feeling the sun on his skin. And what about the softness of his bed when he was tired?

All of these were little things but big things, the things that brought life to life.

A little titter burst from him. Eating fish and chips with tomato sauce. How could he not have included that? It was the ultimate. Sheer bliss!

Granted, human life had its woes and pain, but the majority of it was pleasant. And a rich, rich experience.

What was so horrible, though, indeed so malevolent right now, was the dark horror lurking at the very heart of it all. The certainty that it was going to end.

And probably unpleasantly.

He sniffed. Screwing up his face into a grimace.

And then the unexpected happened. A little sun-ray of hope appeared from nowhere, pulling him out of himself. Galvanising him into jumping up off the bed to switch on his computer.

A huff of frustration escaped him as a blank screen lingered longer than usual, and he turned away. He wasn't going to watch the damn thing. That would be guaranteed it down even more, or even make it crash.

Computers were so often like that, he reflected wryly. It was amazing how, when you really needed to get them up and running as a matter of urgency, they could be counted on to misbehave.

He whirled round.

Surely it was up and running now!

Ah, yes.

'Come on, *come on!*' he grumbled impatiently at the sight of the screen icons being slow to pop into existence.

And then...it was ready.

Hurriedly, he slipped into his chair in front of the screen and opened his internet browser. Clicking on the bookmark for his access gateway to HuTech Robotics.

Having started to type, he banged the return key and sat back. An action to be repeated, followed by a hiss of annoyance.

This was unreal. He had got the password wrong twice!

That never happened.

What the hell was the matter with him?

Chillingly aware of the danger of lockout, he paused to compose himself, running through the password in his mind. And then grunted and rose from his chair to go to his bookcase, where he reached for an inconspicuous, tatty little book on the bottom shelf.

He *must* get it right, this time.

Typing slowly and methodically, he entered the sequence. And then tapped the 'return' key, his heart in his throat.

A blue and yellow rotating circle.

'Thank God!' he blurted.

At long last, he was in.

42

So…

What now?

Eileen aimed a skewering glare at Richie's back.

Why had the little shit looked so excited when he had woken up the living room computer? And just look at him now, typing at such a furious pace!

In response, urgent white platoons of text were marching purposefully across a prominent black box sitting at the centre of his screen.

He looked like a scientist on the cusp of a groundbreaking discovery. His situation the polar opposite to her own at this desolate time.

It was so insensitive of him to look so enthralled. Had he forgotten that a woman condemned was in the same room? Someone who had just said goodbye to her sobbing nearest and dearest and who had no idea how, or even if, she was ever going to be able to get back to them.

She let out the closest thing an android could manage to a gasp of frustration and distress. A peculiar sound that made Richie's head turn and cast a half-look back slightly towards her.

But only a half-look.

Whatever he was doing clearly had him in a state of deep focus.

Whereas she…

She lowered Bessie's eyelids to shut out the creeping disengagement from reality that was steadily claiming what focus she had left. And with an almighty effort, steeled herself.

Re-opening Bessie's eyes into what she could only hope was a glinty glare, she spoke sharply.

'So what's so fascinating on your computer, Nerd Boy?'

Nerd Boy. Not what she thought of him, actually. But the nastiness of it helped. Giving her a purpose to grip onto and steady herself.

Under no circumstances was she going out in a flail of hysteria. That wasn't the McShane way.

But neither was being ignored.

She couldn't believe it. The bastard was just typing away, obliviously!

'Oi, Nerd Boy, I'm talking to you!'

Internally she winced. Androids really weren't good at ferocity. Had she still been in a human body, she would have wacked the impudent little twat round the head.

Instead, though, she had to tolerate an inattentive reply of 'Hang on…'

'Hang on? I'm on limited time, mate! It's alright for you; you're not for the knacker's yard in the next hour or so, or however long I've got.'

Richie continued typing, but at least Eileen had the satisfaction of seeing the back of his neck redden.

'Bastard!' she blazed.

But Richie was determined to continue with his mission, whatever it was. So Eileen gave up and fell into silence. Until, at last, with overtones of finality, Richie made a flourished finger-strike on the 'return' key and flopped back against the back support of his chair.

He remained flopped back for several seconds, as if savouring something momentous. And then, pushing with one leg vigorously, span the chair beneath him and stared directly into the gelatinous eyes that were Eileen's most important aperture to the physical world.

'Right, Eileen,' he said firmly, 'I *think* I've managed something that could give you some hope.'

'Hope?'

'Yes.' He walked his chair nearer, so that he was right in the foreground of Eileen's electronic awareness. 'I've made a copy of the software and modified it to give you space in which to breathe, so to speak. It's rather a crude modification, I'm afraid – I'm really no programmer. And it means that Bessie's movements will be less smooth, but momentarily there will be vacant space in the hardware that should give you a bit of a time advantage when the programme operates.'

'A time advantage? What do you mean?' Eileen demanded, an excited little spire of hope pushing up like a speeded up stalagmite in her background.

'What I mean is that I've effectively slowed Bessie's functions. Giving you time to exert your will as the programme does its stuff. So that you'll have the upper hand over the programme when it comes to controlling Bessie.'

'But...but...' She paused to collect herself. 'Okay, I get you, I really do, but surely, even if I'm ahead of it, once the programme makes a decision it'll just go ahead with what it does regardless of my being there. That's how it was in the phone.'

Richie gleamed at her.

'Ah, yes, but two things make this different from when you were inside the phone, you see. One of them being the fact that you've had much more experience at being in electronics now than when you were inside the phone...okay?'

'True, but…still…*that* was without a programme to fight with. It's very different when there's an operating programme there, you know.'

'Okay, I appreciate that, I do. But remember how you started in Bessie, struggling to get the words out? And how you surprised us all with your rate of progress?'

'Yes, Richie, but I've *just told you*, if there's an operating programme there I'm pretty useless.'

'Ah, but I haven't told you the second thing that will have changed yet.'

'The second thing?'

'Yes, I said *two* things make this different from the phone, if you remember…'

Eileen grunted her acknowledgement.

'Anyway, the second thing is the operating programme itself,' resumed Richie. 'There's a fundamental difference between an android programme and the one in that phone. And that's that the android programme is adaptive AI, artificial intelligence, which means it adapts to whatever inputs it receives.'

'Adapts to what?'

'I can't be certain, not being *au fait* with how on earth your spirit actually interacts with electronics, but I'm hoping the programme will respond to your wishes to a degree.' Richie's eyes were shining enthusiastically now. 'You see, this programme adapts to what is required; that's the whole point of adaptive AI. It changes its response and remembers for the future.'

Eileen frowned.

'So it learns from me, you mean?'

'Yes! Exactly!!'

'Och, mah! You're saying that…that…'

'What I am saying is that it should take account of your wishes. Maybe almost be submissive.'

'Hell's bells! You really think so?'

'With any luck, yes. You might have to fight with it, of

course, especially at first, but this time-advantage should lessen your struggle.'

'Hmm.'

'Nothing's guaranteed, Eileen, but I reckon there's a decent chance that given a little time you can learn to take charge of the software. Or at least come to some kind of working relationship with it.'

The two of them gazed at each other, Eileen's spirits quietly, cautiously...*rocketing*.

She was going to stay.

She was going to stay.

She was...

'I don't know why I didn't think of it earlier,' sliced a self-effacing voice through her elation. 'It just came to me from nowhere. You know, the way these things so often do.'

The disengagement from reality was taking over Eileen again. But in a good way, this time, feeling good, *so* good, like when a fine wine took hold. Except gilded with a golden triumph that had Bessie's cheeks twisting into an involuntary smile.

Richie was speaking again, Eileen suddenly realised. Asking her what she thought of the plan. And if she was up for it.

Eileen nodded Bessie's silicon composite head emphatically. And then moved forward to grasp the surprised Richie in a hug.

'God bless you, Nerd Boy, who isn't one at all! Who I am *proud* to have dating my daughter.'

To her surprise the gasp he let out seemed to turn into a sniff. And she became aware of Richie's arms grasping Bessie's body.

With obvious affection.

43

'Are we good for this, then?'

Alexandr's young brow corrugated with geometric perfection.

'Get...ting there, Comrade Commander.'

'Getting there,' repeated Sergei, his tone distinctly thinning. 'Is that as in one block away or having just launched for Mars?'

A smirk slowly crossed its way from one side of Alexandr's face to the other as he busily typed in his final piece of script.

'Maybe half to one quarter of a block away, Commander. With an eye on the lookout for a parking space.'

Sergei grunted.

'It's just that Marshal Antonov will be summoning me to the corridors of power this afternoon, wanting to know.'

'Ah.'

'See if you can manage it by lunch time, okay? That's if you want me to treat you to a Teremok.'

At that Alexandr's face split into a full smile.

'Will that be with a special coffee?'

'You would be so lucky!' Sergei made to swat at his underling's face. But then added kindly, 'Of course. My own recipe, as usual. I think today I'll make it a number three strength, considering we're at a major stage.'

'Pfffff!'

'Oh don't be a pussy! You want a three-er for afternoon prochnost at a time like this.' At that, Sergei bent his arm and grabbed his biceps in a show of strength.

'Hmm. You may have a point.'

'Not that I'm scared of *him*,' lied Sergei. 'It's just that…well, you know…a man sometimes needs help to pass the day in this place. Especially if he has to walk past Viktor Chernomyrdin. Twice. Like I'll have to later.' Sergei frowned. 'Now, there's a real Russkiy bear. I *am* scared of him…even if he did end up wanting to do it better!'

Alexandr tittered.

'Well, that was what it said on his plaque. And some of us are old enough to remember it.'

Another titter escaped Alexandr's lips.

'Anyway!' boomed his commander, straightening himself up assiduously. 'Duty calls, young Alec, so I'll see you at Teremok at one sharp, okay?'

'Yes, Comrade Commander,' acknowledged Alexandr with a contorted grin. 'You shall.'

44

'So...!' exclaimed Eileen in Bessie's most businesslike tone. 'Does this mean it's time for me versus it?'

'Only if you are ready. I can leave you for a while to prepare yourself, if you wish.'

'No, we may as well get it over with now,' sighed Eileen. 'May the best woman win. The only real one!'

'You'll do it.'

'We'll soon see.'

Richie cleared his throat apprehensively.

'Well, it's been nice getting to meet you.'

'Hey! You're making it sound like this is the end. I'm going to do it, remember?'

'Sorry. A little lapse.'

'Okay, but, just hypothetically, if I *were* to be unable to continue in Bessie, see to it that you and my daughter make up as soon as possible, okay? She can be a touch fiery at times, like her mum, but it soon passes, as you've no doubt found out for yourself a few times by now.'

Richie gave an awkward half-shrug.

'We have had the odd moment, yes. But we do work well, in a complementary sort of way.'

Eileen let out a short electronic chuckle.

'She's a good'n. And I'm sure you're good for her. Anyway, come on. Plug me in and start loading, and let's get this over and done with. With the minimum of fuss.'

With his heart in his mouth, Richie walked round the back of Bessie and opened a little door in her back to plug in a USB cable. The other end of which was connected to his computer, which was displaying a HuTech web page. And then, giving a self-conscious little cough, he pulled out his chair and ensconced himself in front of the computer. Reaching for a half-drained can of ginger beer to take a needful swig before addressing Eileen.

'Ready?'

'Aye,' came the abrupt reply.

With a cursory purse of the lips, he turned back to the screen. And then, hesitating briefly for a nervous little scratch of his sternum, he muttered a strangled 'good luck'.

His hand had grasped his mouse in readiness now. But only to release it so that he could rise to his feet.

Everything was feeling dizzyingly unreal, now. Beyond his control.

Were the lips now so close to Bessie's cheek *really* about to deliver a gentle kiss? And was the nose against her face *really* inhaling the plasticky smell with affection? As if it were that of Eileen herself.

'Sorry,' he breathed as he withdrew.

'Thank you,' came the mechanical reply.

Back at the desk – yes, somehow he was back there now – he positioned the cursor over the all-important green and purple icon. And then allowed his index finger to rest gently on the left hand button of the mouse. Poised to do the deed.

Wanting badly, *so badly*, to turn Eileen's way for yet another goodbye, he raised the finger slightly from the mouse. Only to knit his brow and lower the finger again.

The twitch of his flexor digitorum profundus muscle was only slight.

Enough to change a life, though.

There was no turning back. A fact the screen in front of him was letting him know with a purposeful stream of flowing arrows.

'We're loading,' he warned Eileen stiffly, tension drawing his insides up like an inner duffel bag.

Silence.

There was nothing now but silence.

And the feeling that he might be about to puke.

* * *

'It's too early to be certain, love.'

'But surely...?'

'I'm so sorry, and I know it's awful for you, but please, just give me a little time and we'll see how it's worked out, okay? I've only just got the programme properly loaded in Bessie.'

'Okay.'

It was just a single, short word but the feelings within it were writhing.

Wishing from the bottom of his heart that he could reach down the telephone line and take his girlfriend in his arms, his voice was tender as he spoke into the mouthpiece.

'I'll ring you the minute I know anything, I promise.'

* * *

It had been most strange. In that Richie had actually *felt* Eileen go. Recognising the very instant when she was no longer there.

How had he been able to do that?

Some intuitive sixth sense?

It was strange what you could tap into in such momentous circumstances. Arcane.

What had been even stranger was feeling her re-enter, though. Because it happened in a...twitch.

He gaped at Bessie's impassive features, not entirely sure he could trust what he had felt. But verification came immediately. As if she were reading his mind.

'How...you...do...ing?'

A weird, prickly tingle scampered up Richie's spine, making him cry out.

'Eileen!'

No response.

Oh, no!

'Eileen!' Richie repeated. 'Is...is it really you back?'

Silence.

But also *not* silence. Because, to that sixth sense, it felt like she was still trying. Reaching for him with invisible tentacles of effort.

Frowning hard at the extreme contrast of that image and Bessie's indifferent features, he asked Eileen again if she was there.

To no avail, though.

Muttering an expletive, he reached for the ginger beer and took another needy swig.

What was he to do now?

The signals were so conflicted. It was impossible to tell for sure if she was still there or not.

A sudden piercing trill made him jump.

Damn phone, ringing at a moment like this!

Deciding to ignore it, especially as it was probably the anxious Shona again and all he had for her was uncertainty, he turned back to his computer.

Bessie was still connected. Which meant that he would be able to check that the operating programme was running properly, without malfunction.

He typed in an instruction. Muttering a discontented

'hmm' as the prompt report came spooling back, line after line of errors and conflicts.

'Idiot,' he mumbled to himself, commanding the test to cease.

Of course there were malfunctions. Bessie was chock full of malware – Eileen-shaped malware that was trying its utmost to take command!

But that was good, wasn't it? The fault reports were surely verification that Eileen was still there.

Hmm.

He couldn't be sure.

'Still…with…you,' came the electronic remark.

Richie jerked like he'd received an electric shock. And then swung round on his chair, his eyes staring at Bessie like two lasers.

All she could muster was just a string of nonsensical sounds this time, though.

'Shit!'

Caught in a stampede of emotions, Richie leapt to his feet and rushed at Bessie. Grasping her by the shoulders and shaking her. As if that would unjumble the unintelligible sounds she was making.

'Eileen! Speak to me!! Are you still there?'

Seemingly in answer to that question, another train of nonsensical noises escaped from Bessie's mouth.

There was no doubt now. Eileen was definitely in there. And trying her utmost to let him know that, by the sound of it.

So…what now?

Richie stood up and reached for the ceiling in a much-needed stretch. He may as well leave Eileen to it for a while, seeing as it was now a matter of playing the waiting game. Perhaps if he went out and did something else for a while she'd surprise him upon his return.

Uneasily eyeing the phone, he gave a sigh.

Do I phone her or not?

It was probably best to leave it a while, he decided. So that he'd have something more definite to say.

Half an hour should do it. If Eileen still wasn't coherent by then, well...

* * *

Pensively, Richie re-entered the room. His attention immediately being seized by Bessie's inanimate form.

As expected, his computer was displaying its screensaver. He strode over to it, intent on doing another check for fault reports, so that he'd know if Eileen was still in there fighting Bessie's programme.

Frowning as the list of errors and conflicts started rolling before his eyes, he let out a grunt.

Less of them, this time.

Definitely less.

Was this a sign that she was giving up?

He rubbed his chin thoughtfully.

There was another possible explanation, that the AI was adapting to Eileen's efforts and trying to comply with them as much as it could. Meaning it would no longer see so many of them as problems.

Indecision helter-skeltered through him.

There was no way of telling what was happening; that was the trouble.

He flicked a pained glance across the room.

Only two minutes until his half hour was up.

Right, he told himself firmly. Nothing was going to change in two minutes.

He still had nothing concrete, but at least he could report to Shona that Eileen *was* still in residence, battling it out. And that she'd managed a sentence.

Managed a sentence.

Did that qualify as good news, then?

He pursed his lips.

Well, yes, it was good news, in that it was a sign of her still trying. But it was also only three words, and delivered in a disjointed fashion quite a while ago. And nothing but strange noises and silence since then.

She's still there, though.

Still there.

Still there.

He must hang onto that thought.

Drop-shouldered, he sidled across the room to come to an anxious halt in front of the phone. Girding himself to make the call he had now put off for more than thirty minutes.

The handset was in his hand now. Its keypad facing him ready for dialling. But he didn't get beyond staring at the numbers on the keys.

There was some relief at replacing the handset in the wall-mounted cradle. But a ringing silence took over, offering no hope at all of peace.

A nervous little cough later, he was holding the headset again. His free hand in a pensive hover above the keypad.

Trembling a little, he couldn't help noticing.

'God,' he whispered, closing his eyes. Leaning forward until his forehead touched against the reassuring solidity of the wall.

45

The hands of the young man sitting on a bar stool in the window of Teremok in Ulitsa Mira (*Peace Street*) were trembling as well.

Having laid down his phone, he pressed his wrists bracingly against the surface in front of him. Averting his eyes for a few seconds in an unsuccessful attempt at self-calming.

A scowl creased his face.

Why did he have to have such a stupid liability of a body? *For Christ's sake*, he was an agent of a ruthless espionage organisation.

Centre Sixteen, no less!

You wouldn't see any of Alexandr's colleagues looking nervy. Ever. Epitomes of confidence and robustness, they were prepared to take on anybody for what they had convinced themselves was the noble cause of the safety of Mother Russia.

Not that Alexandr was expected to tough it in the field like the well-seasoned Sergei. Of small, slender stature and quiet disposition, he had been accepted for the job because of his prowess as a computer geek.

But that didn't mean a cushy, confrontation-free number for a back-room boy. Many of the agents he had to liaise with were prickly individuals, who frequently demanded to know when *this* or *that* would be ready and insisted on absolute perfection because of what was at stake. Usually overblown assertions about the safety of the 'boys going in' and other well entrenched spies.

Raising his eyes, the young agent gazed lightheadedly at the stream of anonymous faces passing by outside the window. Struck by how each expression seemed to be displaying a similar but different aspect of what it was to be human.

He couldn't help a single, self-tormenting thought prevailing. How unlikely it must be that any of them were as troubled as him.

Why, oh why, had he taken on this awful job?

There had been a number of more amiable, and indeed lucrative, positions available to him. Each of them worlds apart from the oppressive regime of Centre Sixteen.

He'd acted on an inflated whim, though. Sacrificing comfort for the prestige and glamour of being one of the elite.

One of the elite – what a stupid, puffed-up little grandstander he'd been. Just for the sake of impressing parents and friends.

High could be the price paid by feeding the ego.

He picked up the phone again and then placed it back down with a sigh. If anything, the tremor was worse now. But then he was even more agitated now after moping about his predicament.

Not as much as he was about to be, though.

His gasp of shock and swivel round was involuntary. As tends to happen when a hand is slapped heavily down upon a shoulder.

An insensitive head-tilt was being aimed at the offending hands.

'You been drinking too much last night, young man?'

Dumbstruck, he withdrew his hands so they were out of sight and turned back to face the street. His escape-seeking stare doing what came naturally, locking onto an unignorably curvaceous young woman who was approaching.

As she swayed past, the suggestion of a smile slanted his way, as if she had felt him looking. A gift that made a small island of warmth surface in the choppy waters of his distress.

Alas, tsunami of noise submerged it quickly. The brash clatter of a stool against the floor and a ribald cackle in his right ear.

'Hey, Alec, I'm kidding! It's okay. This shit-awful job makes any man quiver at times. Why do you think I sink the vodka like I do, eh?'

Alexandr averted his eyes, embarrassed.

He had never been one to share much about himself, least of all his weaknesses. And, benevolent and pally though his commander was in the main, he knew that you did well to keep your weakness close to your chest in the den of ideological saboteurs that was their place of work. After all, when shafting the enemy was a day-to-day way of thinking, it could leak almost unnoticed into other walks of life.

'It must just be low sugar or something,' he muttered, inspiration suddenly finding him.

'Nu da, konechno (*yeah, right*), low sugar,' growled Sergei, arching an eyebrow of mockery. 'Look, Alec, you don't have to be ashamed, you know. It's something we all have to get through. And you *will*. One day your skin'll be just like mine – make a goose-down coat seem no thicker than a lady's little blouse.'

Alexandr's suffocated spirits seized the opportunity to surface for air, hiding in the safety of a chuckle containing no more than a hint of despair.

'Just relax,' came the advice in the right ear.

Oh yes, it's that simple, thought Alexandr. Giving a sheepish nod rather than voicing this opinion.

'A job like this gets to everyone at times,' confided Sergei. 'And you're just a young'n.'

Not wanting to expose himself further, the young man slipped in a deft change of subject.

'I have some good news for you, Comrade Commander.'

Sergei straightened and knitted his brow. Regarding his subordinate with a scrutinising eye.

'That we're good to go, I hope,' he prompted, his tone tightening dangerously.

'Yes,' affirmed Alexandra quickly.

'Good. And the backup?'

'That's al…most ready.'

'No backup?'

Suddenly Sergei's tone seemed to knife the air.

'I'm nearly there,' deadpanned Alexandr, valiantly fighting the finger of ice that was dipping down into his guts.

To his relief, Sergei softened a little. 'Well, alright, as long as it *is* almost ready.'

'Certainly, Comrade Commander,' replied Alexandr a little too crisply. Earning himself another keen eyeing.

'I know it's a backup, but we *will* need it in place for the strike,' insisted his commander. 'And that could be very soon, judging from how serious Marshal Antonov was sounding.'

'Right.'

'So? How long for the backup?'

Alexandr gulped. 'Hopefully by…'

'We don't do "hopefully" in C-One-Six,' pointed out Sergei quickly.

Pausing to weigh honesty against necessity, Alexandr committed himself. The sight of Sergei's eyes narrowing like those of a cat about to spring playing a major part in his decision.

'By...the...the end of today.'

'Are you sure?' came the suspicious, probing response.

'Yes, Comrade Commander.'

'Alright, then. But we'd better make your prochnost (*strength*) coffee just a single-shot.' Alexandr received a smirky flash of the hip flask. 'Can't have you zoning out at this critical juncture.'

Wishing he'd had the courage to be more honest about the state of play with the backup, Alexandr fixed a pseudo-relaxed grin in place.

Sergei wasn't looking, though. He had turned single-mindedly to click his fingers at a young woman dressed in the conspicuous beige and brown Teremok uniform.

'Dva kofe, pozhaluysta,' he barked resonantly, making a number of heads turn on several tables.

'Konechno, ser,' came the immediate reply as she scuttled off towards the kitchen's coffee machine with servile haste.

With a satisfied grunt, the commander turned back.

'Look, I won't tell Marshal Antonov about the backup not being ready,' he announced in a sudden lean of solidarity, 'because he doesn't need to know, really.'

'Oh?'

'We-e-ell, why stir up the waters when the chances are it'll be at couple of weeks before the launch is actually required?'

Alexandr stared at him, flung into confusion over the apparent change in urgency.

'A couple of *weeks*, Comrade Commander?'

'*Akh*, you know how it is, Alec! Things like this need to go all the way to the top, to the Kremlin. It has to wait until the politicians are satisfied and get a collective "okay" back to us. *We* may think an immediate strike is for the best, but there may be unexpected ramifications to consider.'

'I see, Comrade Commander.'

'Yes. But still the entirety of our bit has to be ready and working with perfection, just in case.'

'Well, *hopefully* the backup will be working by the end of today,' admitted Alexandr, testing the waters cautiously for any possibility of leeway.

Sergei snorted.

'Are you being entirely honest with me?'

'Of course, Comrade Commander.' Alexandr felt the icy finger descending again. 'Insofar as it *should* be done today.'

'Ah, here we are,' declared Sergei as the rushed and now flushed waitress leaned in with two coffees on a small tray. 'Spasibo! (*thank you*) Much needed!!'

'Pozhaluysta,' puffed the waitress before rushing off again.

'Nice coffee, but first it needs a little additive,' twinkled Sergei at his underling, a hand already on the hip flask.

Alexandr eyed it needfully. Feeling the weight on his shoulders begin an anticipative pre-lighten.

'Now, you promise me that if I add this you won't flop out on me this afternoon, hey?'

'Absolutely, Comrade Commander!'

'Hmm.'

Sergei poured briefly, flicking Alexandr a sharp glance. And then switched to his cup to pour for about thrice the length of time.

'Big boy's measure,' he grinned.

46

Oh my God, this is amazing!

I can't believe how much I'm coming on during this new spell in Bessie! And now *this*, Richie, an unforeseen door that your actions have inadvertently swung open wide for me.

I thank you from the bottom of my soul.

Ha ha! I know you think my incoherence is a sign that I'm struggling but little do you know that I'm barely in Bessie just now. You see, I'm busy with greater things, as you'll soon find out.

Yes, you have the surprise of all surprises coming, something that's going to make your little eyes bulge like those of a frog having sex!

47

'I'm afraid there's nothing solid quite yet,' admitted Richie. 'But the fact that I'm getting fault reports tells me that she's still active in Bessie.'

'Fault reports?'

'Yes, they are generated by her conflicts with the programme, you see.'

'Oh God, I knew it wouldn't work!'

'*No*, Shona! The conflicts should lessen, given time, and things should become easier for her.'

'How come? Surely if she can't work with the programme, she can't work with the programme.'

'No, you see, it adapts to her wishes. It's called adaptive AI; it learns what is required and alters itself accordingly.'

A mistrustful silence radiated from the phone handset. Shona sounding caught in a struggle for belief when she finally spoke.

'Really? It's *that* obliging, is it?'

'Yes, it is. Your mum will gradually start to cope better and at the same time the programme will learn what is required until they meet somewhere in the middle.'

'Well, let's...let's hope so, then,' Shona faltered.

'Have faith. It *will* work.'

'Trying to convince Dad of that is another thing entirely.'

'I know it's difficult.'

'Difficult? Hell's bells!' Her flare was immediate, catching him unawares. 'Talk about the understatement of the century!!'

'I know.'

'No, you *don't*, actually, not one bit!' Shona fumed. 'I'd like to see you trying to cope with this; that'd be a sight!'

'Sorry,' muttered Richie, feeling punctured.

'Look, let me know when there's more, okay? I've got things to do.'

'Right,' said Richie stiffly. Bracing himself for the inevitable click that would precede the cold engulf of the dial tone.

'Yeah. Love you too,' he grumbled once it came, replacing the handset. An unpleasant image bloating his mind, Shona at the other end of the line, her expression full to bursting, her lips puckered with frustration and hatred of the situation.

For a crazy moment, he thought of jumping into his car and whizzing round to Shoreholm to be with her. But then thought better of it and restrained himself.

Give her space.

Heaving out a sigh, he slowly turned, gazing absently across the room. A jerk from his computer screen catching his eye – a fault report.

Yes, *a* fault report, just the one.

Wow!

They had slowed considerably.

'Eileen?' he asked Bessie sharply. 'How's it going?'

The android remained still and mute, though. Not even uttering any of the unintelligible noises.

'Eileen!' he repeated, more sharply this time. Frowning and tilting his head in puzzlement at the continued silence. 'Are you there, Eileen?'

She *must* still be in there. The fault reports were still running, albeit slowly.

What on earth was going on?

He studied the expressionless features for a few flummoxed seconds in the vain hope of a clue. Finally muttering a disconsolate 'I don't know' of defeat before wandering from the room, driven by a sudden pang of hunger.

No wonder he felt hungry! He had yet to eat today, so consumed had he been by events.

Once in the kitchen, he reached into the fridge for the cheese container and a tub of butter. And then, plonking them down on the single, small work surface, he extracted a gratifyingly chunky loaf of Hovis from the bread bin.

That would perk him up.

In fact the mere sight of it was cheering him already.

'Marmite!' he exclaimed in a purposeful turn towards the larder.

His first massive, tooth-sinking bite was promptly followed by another. His grateful stomach feeling as if it were reaching up and grabbing at the bountiful new delivery.

Chewing contentedly, he wondered what it was about simple food like bread and cheese that was so satisfying.

It seemed to have a special, transcendent quality about it. A purity that was to the gastric system what the sound of a flute was to the ears.

The musical analogy must have been staying with him on some level because he started humming as he set to work on making sandwich number two. A task that he decided needed helping along with a crunchy handful of Pringles.

He was feeling much better now, the invigoration of

the chunky intake of protein sufficient to almost eclipse his strife.

'Oh, yes!' he declared in sonorous satisfaction, his hand diving down the Pringles tube again like a hungry eel. For just a few more. Hopefully.

And then...

Mid-crunch, he froze, in the highest state of alertness.

His name!

An electronic voice was calling his name. Not *the* electronic voice. *An* electronic voice, sounding different from Bessie's.

It had to be her, though; what else could it be? He had no other devices that could call for him in that manner.

His face contorted in amazement.

What was going on?

Did this mean Eileen was back and somehow managing to mess with the vocal circuitry?

'Eileen?'

'Richie!' replied the voice with greater urgency.

The excited yell Richie expelled came out higher pitched than he intended. His frenzied rush towards the living room scattering Pringles into the air.

48

'Oh...God...!!'

Shona *yowled* the word miserably into the hell that had now become her normal state of being. Letting it echo through its chambers in a flail of agonised mental torment.

Could her life possibly get any *shittier?*

A tumble of gaspy and tearful breaths burst from her. Seeming to leap from the very brim of her sanity.

These phone conversations were slowly killing her; she was sure of it. The way they made her heart pound and ears ring, and made her feel light-headed, not really present in full.

But it was the achingly lonely period after each call that was the worst offender. Allowing ample space for the inexorable force within her that always ended up biting Richie's head off to turn on her self-esteem instead.

Desperation puckered her brow.

The truth...she needed to acknowledge it. Admit what a monster she'd become of late. A raging, screeching beast that kept slamming the phone back into its cradle, only to collapse in tears. Day after day.

This wasn't her. She was normally calm and reasonable. Not...*this*.

She was betraying her very way of being. No wonder an internal finger of condemnation was jabbing at her.

Screwing up her face in anguish, she dropped her chin into the curling sag of her torso.

It was several seconds before she surfaced. And when she did, it was with a slow and painful creak of a groan.

She wandered her eyes around the room, to find herself receiving an emphatic message. That it had become a chaotic extension of her being.

Her bed. That was the worst sight. Hilly and bedraggled, it was the habitat of a pile of swept aside clothing.

When had she last made it?

The floor was bad too. It wouldn't have looked out of place in the Tate Modern as a random-angled work of discarded footwear.

As for the bedside cabinet that she used to keep so nicely clean and polished...

Tearfully, Shona blinked at the little lake now atop it. A lake whose shore was tree-ringed with a coffee-stained testimony of elapsed time.

'God help me,' she murmured to herself.

This awful, *terrible* state of affairs was sending her downhill fast. And worse still, tearing her and Richie apart, when the poor man was doing his best, quite heroically at times. Only to be given extra, undeserved pain, from *her*.

The one who loved him.

Yes, *loved*.

Who would have thought, in the short time they had known each other, that it would happen?

But it had.

Prior to when she'd morphed into this monster, she had been noticing that it was whenever the two of them were together that she was most at peace. And that, tellingly, he was her absolute priority in life.

How she'd adored the way he was, so different from her! She'd wanted to know everything about him, dive deep into his thoughts, his beliefs, and those amusing little ways of his that always invoked such tenderness within her.

And now...

A desolate tear began rolling. Carrying with it the weight of a bleak and terrible prospect, the possibility that she and Richie could never be the same again after all of this was over.

Without warning, the monster was back.

'Thank you *so* much, Mum, for fucking us up so thoroughly,' it wailed sourly. 'Why couldn't you let go and die properly, like everyone else does?'

No!

The grip of a cold hand on her heart had suddenly brought her back to stability.

She hadn't meant that.

Not one bit.

'Shona!'

The call was distant, from downstairs, but there was something about it, an odd feel. So odd that she jerked and sat up bolt upright as if she'd received an in-the-face military order from a sergeant.

Something was up.

Her father's footfall on the stairs was the next thing she heard, and she even sensed something unusual within that. A sort of pulse of excitement.

An intuition confirmed by his shortness of breath when he called out again.

'Quick, Shona, you won't *believe* this!'

In the manner of a startled deer, she sprang into action. Ripping open the door to be confronted by a jitter of exhilaration.

'Dad? What is it?'
His eyes!
They had a wild look.
'It's your mother, Shona! She's back!!'
Shona gaped at him as if he had totally lost his marbles.
'*Back?* What on *earth* do you mean?'

49

'Eileen!' Richie cried again as he spilled through the living room doorway.

Coming to a breathless halt directly in front of Bessie, he stared wide-eyed into her face. But was met with the very same impassivity as last time he had looked at her.

'Shit!' he gasped in disbelief.

Leaning forward and reaching out, he shook the android by the shoulders.

'For crying out loud! Are you there, Eileen?'

'I'm here, idiot! Behind you!!'

Round Richie whirled, releasing Bessie so hurriedly that she toppled to the ground, hitting a chair on the way down and striking her head on the ground with an ominous thud. But Richie paid her no heed, transfixed on the sight of illicit activity underway on his computer screen.

It was all happening now. The phone adding its peal to the melee, making him jump.

'Go away!' he bellowed at it, his eyes still glued to the computer screen as with tightening guts, he approached it step by step.

'My God!'

'Hello, Richie,' replied a synthetic female voice from the computer. 'I am back with you again, aye. Well, sort of, anyway – not *actually* back, but *with you* in a manner of speaking.'

Richie gulped, caught in a major collywobble. Dimly aware of the cessation of the telephone ring in the background.

Managing to collect himself enough to start thinking straight, he strove to imagine what might be happening.

One thing was clear, and that was that Microsoft Edge Narrator was in operation. But contrarily, there was no content on the screen – no text for the voice to be reading out. Just an enlarged version of the Narrator icon itself, sitting squarely in the screen centre and flickering unendearingly whenever the voice spoke.

'Is…is…that really you, Eileen?'

'Of course it is, you moron! Who else would it be?'

'B-but…how did you get…get in my…?'

'I'm not in your computer, Richie! I'm somewhere far more roomy.'

Richie swallowed again, with some effort this time. His throat suddenly drier than a Chinese prawn cracker.

'More roomy?' he rasped.

'Yes, Richie! There are plenty of low-activity spaces here in the internet. And it's so easy to operate here.'

'The internet?'

'Yes! And Richie, thank you so much for letting me in.'

Richie shot the screen a quizzical look.

'Letting you in?'

'Mmm. Via that lead you left plugged in Bessie.'

'Oh.'

Richie turned and looked down at Bessie's collapsed form. Sure enough, the little panel in her back was still open, with the USB lead still connected.

He'd left her connected to the internet.

The penetrating peal of the phone cut in again, making him flinch. An intuitive part of him able to feel it radiating frustration.

Torn as to what to do next, Richie dithered.

'*Go on*, then, get it,' urged Eileen. 'It's *got* to be Shona; I know it!'

Coughing dryly, Richie approached the phone. Lifting it from its cradle almost as if he were handling a venomous snake.

'Richie!' cried a familiar voice into his ear. 'I've got some *amazing* news for you.'

'Go on, then,' replied Richie numbly.

'It's Mum – she's back!'

Richie started.

'What? How do you know?'

'She appeared on Dad's laptop!'

'Oh. I see. Well, she's on mine right now.'

'Okay. Look, tell her to stay put, right? We're coming round right now.'

The sound of Derek saying something in the background was followed by a brief, scurrying reply from Shona. And then the line went dead with a click.

'They're coming round,' Richie announced as he replaced the headset.

The icon on his computer screen flickered transiently and the synthesised voice cut through the air.

'Perfect. I've some things I need to tell you all.'

50

'I can't imagine what she wants to say,' exclaimed Richie, eyeing both of his edgy visitors, 'but if you come through, we can find out.'

As the three of them proceeded to the living room, Richie started to explain.

'Having done the update, I accidentally left Bessie plugged into the internet, which gave her a route to where she is now.'

'We know, Richie, she told us,' smiled Shona. 'But her being in the internet must be a good thing, don't you think?'

'Well, yes. I suppose so.'

'She said she is functioning well in the internet. And that she can appear via any computer or my phone, so that *has* to be a good thing, doesn't it?'

'Yes, I suppose so,' agreed Richie.

'It's actually quite cool having an online mum! Not as good as the real thing, of course, but not a bad alternative.'

'Mmm, maybe the next best thing.'

'So Bessie is disconnected now?' Shona inquired, craning her neck for a better view.

Richie nodded.

'Yes. When your mum appeared on my computer it startled me so much that I accidentally knocked Bessie over. But, as you can see, she's back to normal now. Although I've still got to run a proper check to confirm one hundred per cent well-being.'

'Right, good.'

'Hello, everybody,' interjected the synthetic voice from Richie's computer.

'Eileen!' gasped Derek, overcome with emotion.

'You see, my love, I can be almost anywhere now in just as real a way as when I was in Bessie but without being in a body as such. And it means we can talk whenever we want via your computer, so it's much more convenient than me using Bessie really.'

'Yes, yes, it's just that...just that it's going to take some getting used to.'

'I know, but we will do before long. Soon it will be as natural as when I was in Bessie.'

'You call that natural?' quipped Derek.

'Well, no, of course not, but you know what I mean. Look at how many people live on the internet for much of the time these days, anyway. I think some of the youngsters prefer it to real life, and it's probably more real than real life for them!'

'Yes, they need to come back to reality.'

'But then, what is real life? Isn't reality just thoughts and actions and interactions, wherever they may be enacted?'

A thoughtful silence fell. Amidst corrugated brows.

It was Richie who spoke first.

'That's an interesting point, actually.'

'That's because it's being made by someone who has died, lovie. Most humans think the real world is trees and buildings, sky and land, but once they've died, they see that there is only mind. And mind is what is in the internet.

It's just that in the net the sky and land are electrical signals whizzing around.'

'Hmm,' nodded Richie. 'But then, trees and land are electrical in nature when you look into the extreme depths of their reality. Electrical charges within atoms.'

'There you are, then. Like I said, reality is perceptions and interactions. It's just that the interactions you get in earthly life are so much deeper than after you've died. They really challenge you. Stretch you and leave you pulled out of shape.'

'Oh, love.' Derek was the one to speak this time. 'I hear the hunger in your voice for the experiences we shared as humans. But is there no way you can move on, accept death fully? I don't want to lose you, but…but how happy are you? I fear…Eileen?'

'My love, I am okay, *really*, I am. I wasn't before, but now…now, I have you and Shona once again, so it's like my human life is partly back, which is enough. And as for being in the internet, I'm finding it an *amazing* new experience! So believe me, I *am* happy. Really!'

'So, how come you didn't just manifest yourself in the net in the first place instead of in my phone?'

'Well, if you remember, I told you that I could only connect with something personal to you, that being the way the ectoplasm works. And the phone was the natural choice because it was *very* personal, something you use every day. Something that had your imprint deeply in it.'

'Mmm,' contemplated Shona.

'And then you got together with Richie, so that gave me a link to him and hence a link to Bessie as well,' continued Eileen, in full flow now. 'And in Bessie I learnt so much about how to live in an electronic reality. So it equipped me with the ability to handle being in the net.'

'I see. So what's it actually like being *in* the net?' asked Shona incredulously.

'It's okay. And it's the only way it *can* be now, love.'

'Aye, I appreciate that, but how does it actually feel being in the net? *That's* what I'm asking.'

'Oh, God! You're asking me to put what it's like into words?'

Shona blinked.

'Um...well, I *suppose* it's a little similar to when you are online,' began Eileen, 'but very, very immersive in a way that is in fact like human life on Earth.' She paused thoughtfully. 'Aye! And that's because it *is* as real as what humans think of as the real world. You see, the net is really the collective humanity of its users. And, like I said, environment is simply an interaction medium, whatever form it takes.'

'Aye, I *do* see what you mean!' Shona was sounding excited now. 'Lots of thoughts all interacting in a medium. Just the same as in our lives on Earth.'

'You get it!' Eileen paused. 'And *you*, Derek, do *you* see?'

'I think so. It's just that...that...'

'My love, *please*, just let it be. I'm happy. Isn't that enough? And we're *together* again. Isn't that wonderful?'

'Yes, of *course* it is, dear, marvellous! We...we can be together on my computer screen, which is a lot better than being just memories of each other.'

'Exactly! Be thankful, love. We have each other again.'

A welcome lightness had filled the room. For Derek and Shona, the feeling of togetherness that they experienced when Eileen materialised in Bessie. And for Richie, relief and pleasure at seeing the others so happy.

A smile was spreading in him now, fuelled by an uplifting thought. The possibility of himself and Shona picking up again from where they had been before everything had gone so dreadfully wrong.

51

'Right! That's America, Canada, the British, and the countries you specified on mainland Europe.' Alexandr corkscrewed in his chair and looked up at his superior. 'Phase One is *in place* for all of them and ready for release.'

'Khoroshaya rabota, Alec.' *Good work.*

'Spasibo, Comrade Commander,' smiled the young agent. *Thank you.*

Sergei cleared his throat officiously in readiness to announce what was going to happen.

'Right, I'll quickly check with Marshal Antonov, just in case anything new is happening, and assuming all is still alright I'll give you the all-clear.'

At that, the commander bustled off towards his office, already starting to perspire.

Despite all the years of experience, Sergei still found the actual act of initiating an attack nerve-wracking. There was something about its immediacy, its finality, and not least, its effect. And the fact that it was the release of something that had been in preparation for so long and shrouded in so much secrecy.

Sinking into his office chair, he reached for the phone.

Two rings and a hurried snatch later, Marshal Antonov was informing him that nothing had changed, that he must do the deed as promptly as possible.

Thanking his superior, Sergei scurried back to the computer room, where he breathlessly issued the go-ahead to Alexandr.

'Right away, Comrade Commander,' the young agent replied efficiently and started tapping at his keyboard.

There was a short delay, and then a bright red, purple-rimmed, launch octagon was suddenly sitting on the screen in front of Alexandr. The word 'ZAPUSK' staring brazenly out from its centre, daring the user to carry out the wicked act.

Not unwillingly, Alexandr vacated his seat and stood aside, allowing his superior room to squeeze past and take his place in the chair.

There were times when rank carried its own cost.

'Right,' the commander stated vigorously, giving no outward sign of his inner turmoil. 'This is *it*.'

And then, holding his breath while he moved the cursor to sit right over the very centre of the octagon, he committed the act with an unhesitating tap of his index finger.

52

Oh, for goodness' sake!

This was unbelievable. Shona wanted to scream out her frustration and physically attack the infuriating machine in front of her, but being somewhere so public she had to settle for a glare and moderated snort.

What was it with this morning? It really seemed to have it in for her.

First had been the lack of potatoes, most unlike the trusty Co-op. And then her shopping bag had chosen to give up the ghost right in the doorway of the shop, spilling half of her purchases and necessitating a ruffled and embarrassed return to the checkout. And now...*this*. When all she'd wanted to do was withdraw some cash.

She furrowed her brow and gaped with disbelief at the unfriendly message that the dim, scratched little screen of the ATM was fighting to display against the glare of the sunlight.

> Your card is not on a compatible network.

'What the hell's that supposed to mean?' she vented, despite its consequences being clear.

Snatching out her card before the damn machine decided to swallow it, she waited the necessary few seconds for the machine to reset itself to the 'options' screen. And then, having checked that the card was the right one – *yes, of course it was* – she reinserted it and re-entered her PIN number. Slowly and carefully.

The same stark message.

'Damn it!'

Up at nine point seven five on the scale of irritation now, she grabbed the card again. Replaced it into the small pocket in her purse. Muttering. Knowing that she'd have to take a time-consuming detour to the other cash machine at Costcutters now.

Not exactly what she needed when a call of nature was starting to ramp up the pressure.

Off she traipsed, rounding the corner.

What greeted her just *had* to happen today. The unwelcome sight of old Maisie Agnew approaching with the usual faded brown bag of shopping in her clutch. Not someone you wanted to meet when you were in a hurry.

There was no escaping, no crossing the road in a pretence of not having noticed Maisie. Indeed, the elderly lady was already slowing as she honed in on her target.

'Hello, Shona, how urr ye?'

Tempted to be truthful for a fleeting moment, Shona hesitated. And then, thinking better of it, expelled an expediently breezy 'I'm fine, thank you'.

Of course, Shona couldn't fail to inquire after Maisie's well-being, even though it would be sure to trigger a lengthy reply.

'And you?' she asked emptily, the need to answer the call of nature pressing a little harder.

'Oh, I'm bonnie, thank you, Shona. Apairt fae nae bin able to withdraw mah money from the wee machine at the Costcutters.'

'Oh!' Shona stared at Maisie, suddenly finding her

conversation uncharacteristically gripping. 'So that one isn't working, either?'

Maisie cocked her head.

'Ah beg yer pardon, dear?'

'I've just been trying the one at the Co-op, and that isn't working either.'

'Och, dear!' Maisie stared at her in owl-eyed consternation. 'Whit am ah tae dae, then?'

Shona frowned.

'We'll have to try again another day, I suppose. All we can do. The trouble is, we depend on these machines nowadays, don't we?'

Betty beamed into Shona's face.

'Aye, we'll juist hae tae wait!'

Shona returned the smile, suddenly feeling lifted. The exchange of friendly words had tugged her out of her moody morning.

As she and Maisie went their separate ways, she found herself back in her comfort zone, unbothered now by the cash machine failure. There was, after all, such a thing as a credit card, even if she did always like a supply of cash.

Why she was taking things so badly this morning, she did not know. After all, things had improved now; her life was back on track.

Oh, well.

She'd never truly understand herself.

It wasn't long before her homeward stride was being accompanied by the thought of what to do her father and Richie for lunch in her potato-bereft state. A problem happily solved, though, by the time the old Romanesque house loomed into sight.

Soup and bread – you couldn't go wrong with that. She had a tin of tomato in her bag, which could easily be enlivened by the addition of fresh basil and some paprika powder. Not forgetting a generous helping of garlic.

She'd follow up with cranachan for pudding.

Needfully, she upped her pace and entered the house to head straight for the toilet. Floating a loud 'hello' along the hall as she did so, an action that invoked the surprisingly enthusiastic emergence of Richie from the living room.

'Hiya, Shona.' The distant babble of a voice on the television had followed him out. 'There's been some massive infrastructure hack. Really wide scale, affecting *loads* of things.'

'Oh! Right!' She screwed up her face. 'Hang on, I must just pop to the loo, and then you can tell me all about it.'

At that, she hastened along the hall.

On emerging from the toilet, she found Richie still loitering in the living room doorway.

'Is that why I couldn't get any money out from the bank, then?' she inquired of him.

'Presumably. It's affected most of the banks, so the News is saying. And the trains and airports and schools, hospitals, councils and even some government agencies, apparently. It's a really bad one!'

'Blimey!' Shona crinkled her brow. 'Don't you hate these people?'

'Yes. At least the phone networks are still working, both mobile and landline. And more importantly, the internet itself.'

Shona blinked at him.

'Surely the net isn't more important than phones and banks and things!'

'That depends upon if you've got your own android, with newly updated software. Thato may well need some tweaks.'

'Oh, whoop-de-do!' grinned Shona, teasingly. 'You and your technology.'

'Well, don't forget your mother's in the net!'

'Okay, okay! I suppose that *is* a point!'

'Indeed!'

'For now, though, I'm more worried about simple everyday things like getting cash from the bank.'

'I can always lend you some if you're low, love,' came a familiar voice from the living room doorway.

'Thanks, Dad, but I'll be alright. I do have a credit card. And anyway, come tomorrow or the day after the ATMs will probably be fixed.'

'I've always said we're getting too reliant on technology,' her father replied. 'One of these days, you know...things will all go splat!'

'Oh, Dad, they'll have put in safeguards against that sort of thing.'

'Really? Well, I don't see them working very well right now!'

Shona grimaced, bereft of a suitable reply.

'I've got to unload this stuff, Dad.'

Her father grunted and Richie flashed her a wink before following Derek back into the living room and returning his attention to the ongoing News report.

An outside source is suggesting that this attack may be the first of an up-shift to greater levels of sabotage than ever seen before. Indeed, it seems to have hit most of Europe, as well as Canada and the USA.

And we are just getting a report that the maximum number of twenty-eight aircraft that can be held in a stack above Heathrow has been exceeded several times over, an unprecedented occurrence. Apparently, they've also filled the diversion airports to capacity, so they are trying to create new emergency stacks near Heathrow, but the skies are getting very overcrowded, which is most concerning.

Stay with us for updates.

In the kitchen, Shona sighed and rolled her eyes. It seemed that today was set to be a glum one. Sometimes you just woke that way, for no apparent reason.

As she started stowing her shopping in the appropriate places, she admitted to herself that her dad did have a point about technological vulnerability. It was just that his assessment took things too far. Infrastructure would never be as vulnerable as he suggested, surely. Governments and their expert advisers would never allow it.

Crinkling her brow as she loaded a bag of sugar into the left hand cupboard, she wondeed if technology could eventually be made so resilient that the cyber-criminals would just give up.

Yes, that would probably happen, she told herself.

Damn it!

She ripped the window open and swatted out a frantically buzzing fly.

The bloody things drive you barmy!

The trouble was, she mused as she started loading the fridge, no matter how secure you made things, there would always be some pain-in-the-arse people who'd manage to think outside the box.

Look at the Twin Towers attack in New York.

No one saw that one coming.

She heaved another sigh.

Mankind. Did it always have to be this battle between good and evil?

Love thy neighbour was the only hope. That was what it all came down to in the end. Without that, humanity was surely doomed.

But the question was, could we ever embrace that?

'Fat chance of that?' she blurted, boofing the fridge door shut.

'Okay?' came Richie's voice from the doorway.

'Ooh!' She started. 'Didn't see you there.'

'Sorry.'

'I'm just about to start the meal. It won't be long.'

Richie moved forward into the room and laid a hand on Shona's shoulder.

'You seem a bit down.'

'Just having a bad day. You know how it happens sometimes.'

'Oh dear. Would a hug help?'

Shona smiled at him faintly.

'It certainly wouldn't hurt.'

As they embraced, she shut her eyes and rested her head against him. Reminded just how lucky she was in life.

'Thanks,' she smiled as they uncoupled. 'I'd better get on with this meal then, if we want to eat.'

At that, Richie patted her arm and sloped off. Thinking he had better not get in the way of Shona's preparations in the kitchen.

But as she started preparing the meal with the excited burble of the television muffled in the background, it was with lips that were pursed.

How could she be cheerful knowing that probably right now there were those who were celebrating the country's troubles?

53

'Na Zdorovie!' grinned Marshal Antonov resoundingly. *Cheers!*

Sergei and Alexandr raised their glasses and toasted their superior enthusiastically.

'Congratulations on a job well done,' praised the marshal.

Sergei gestured towards Alexandr.

'Well, we have a whizz-kid here!'

'Not forgetting the rest of the software team,' added Alexandr modestly, the colour in cheeks already aglow from the Bollinger Special Cuvée deepening.

'Of course we are not forgetting them, but *you* were the one at the helm of the ship,' pointed out Sergei. 'Exercising the first class training you've received from your mentor!'

At that, a rattling guffaw escaped the marshal, finding its echo in the intoxicated chuckles of the other two.

'It's been a big success, our best ever,' he crowed. 'The News reports are flooding in from all over Europe. And America and Canada, as well. They don't know what's hit them, and this is just stage one! Imagine when we've hit them with the main event; they'll be utterly confounded. Their economies will collapse, their infrastructure will collapse, and as for their missile systems...' The marshal raised ecstatic eyebrows. 'They'll be sitting ducks, their bellies exposed, the lot of them!'

'They will indeed,' grinned Sergei. 'But, that said, they must be pretty sure it's us, if we have a leak.'

'Well, we don't know that yet. But we soon will, I'm sure.' Marshal Antonov's voice had suddenly sharpened. 'Procedures are currently being enacted by Unit 3. It won't take them long, and then the perpetrator will be kissing the pavement goodbye.'

A silence fell, the champagne on their palates suddenly losing its liveliness as Sergei and Alexandr simultaneously pictured an agent plunging from a tall building to the background jeering of the unit's stocky bully-boys.

Sergei was the first to speak, having cleared his throat.

'So we are already able to release the final phase in another seventy-two hours time, Comrade Marshal. Everything's in place for doing that; we'll just wait for your word, come the time.'

'Very good,' Marshal Antonov nodded, a slow and satisfied smile having sidled onto his lips.

'To be specific,' Sergei continued, 'the gateways now in place will enable for the final phase things like locking them out of their financial markets, paralysing their police computers, disabling energy networks, including oil pipelines in the USA, shutting down airports and trains and shipping inports & exports...'

'Excellent,' interjected Marshal Antonov, his smile having widened considerably.

'And also hitting TV channels, web servers, browsers and phone networks. And infiltrating security agencies like the FBI, MI5, DGSE, BND, AIVD and MUST.'

A contented chuckle escaped the marshal.

'But best of all...' Sergei paused for his own smug grin of satisfaction. '...the re-encryption of all the missile launchers and reprogramming of them for home targets.'

'*Yes!*' shouted the marshal, slapping his thigh in delight. 'I *love* it!!'

All three of them disolved into laughter and then sank hearty sups of their drinks. After which, the marshal leaned forward conspiratorially.

'As for the rest of today, my dear comrades,' he announced mellowly, 'if the two of you were to have one of your lunches in Teremok and then forget that you needed to come back for the afternoon's work, I wouldn't notice.'

They both smiled and thanked him appropriately, glad of the champagne to dampen the flutter of shock at hearing that the marshal knew about their Teremok lunches.

'We shall of course have our phones on us in the afternoon, should there be an unfortunate change in circumstances,' added Sergei.

Alexandr nodded his assent.

'Ooh, I think that most unlikely,' grinned the marshal, rising from his chair. 'I may even find it necessary to leave early myself.'

The other two chuckled politely. At which point, the marshal winked and then turned and took his leave.

54

It's amazing being in the net; it really is!

As I explained to Shona, it's impossible to describe its full magnifience by resorting to mere words. But what I *can* do is try to give a hint of what it is like.

An analogy is useful here.

In fact, essential.

Think of when you close your eyes and recall a recent scene, say when you were walking along a busy London street.

What precisely does your mind's eye see?

Well, it seems that it's all there again, does it not? Crowds of people walking past, a sea of faces. Plus loads of cars in the road and maybe the odd cyclist. Perhaps a bus or two, with people looking out.

Yes, of course it's all there. You are seeing the entire scene again.

But wait.

Things are not as they seem.

I ask you to try something. Pick a car that is driving past. What colour is it? What type of car is it, which manufacturer?

You can't tell, can you? The traffic is all there in your scene, loads of cars. But you just try picking one of them for closer study!

The same is true of the pedestrians. There's no way you can clearly pick out a particular individual.

Strange are the workings of the mind, the impression that is created. It isn't really real. How can it be if you cannot even focus on the details?

It's a reconstructed scene, based on overall impression, *not* a copy of the real thing. It's just that it feels just like a copy.

Okay...hold that feeling in your mind, the overall scene with unexplorable specifics. When I'm unfocused, *that* is just how it feels for me here in the internet.

And I have to say it's amazing, perceiving the entirety of worldwide web activity all at once, albeit vague like your picture of the London street scene.

Of course, there's a big difference between your street scene and my 'view' of the internet activity. I'm seeing the real thing, not a reconstruction. Even though the view I am getting is vague, just like the street view was in your mind.

However, that is where the similarity between the two scenarios ends. Because I *can* dive into the details and see them clearly. It's simply a matter of changing my focus in a way a human cannot. Something I cannot explain.

Simply exert my will and what happens is astonishing. Off I zip to wherever I wish.

Anyway, right now I am in the unfocused state, receiving awareness of the entirety. And I need to investigate, because something *very* strange is happening in the European, British, American and Canadian hubs. A lack of activity, as if things have locked up.

It's extrordinary. Something weird is going on. And I don't like the feel of it.

Not at all.

55

'Come on, you two, get your heads out of that telly and come and eat!'

Exchanging harried glances, the two men rose to their feet. Derek being the one to yell out confirmation that they were just coming.

'It's worrying that these people can cause such havoc,' he commented as he and Richie sank down at the dining table.

'That's the trouble; anything that has an online presence will always have that vulnerability,' agreed Richie. 'But I struggle with the wisdom of putting power grids and essential utilities like that online at all.'

A muscle in Derek's jaw flexed.

'Well, that's just asking for trouble. Talk about stupidity!'

'Although, actually, I *do* know why they do it...it's *this* as usual.' Richie raised a hand and rubbed his thumb against his fingers in a manner resemblant of handling banknotes. 'Everything comes down to cheapness in the modern capitalist world, because cheapness equals profitability.'

'Here you are,' cut in Shona as she homed in on the table with two steaming bowls of soup. 'Never mind the woes of the capitalist world; try focusing on the joys of the gastronomic world for a while instead!'

They didn't need telling twice. Two bowls beneath grateful eyes.

'Smell's lovely, Shona, as usual,' praised her father.

'Yes. Gorgeous,' added Richie, nodding in agreement.

Shona returned to the table with her own bowl and then sank down in front of it, sniffing its aromatic steam with satisfaction.

The smell of fresh basil was unbeatable.

'So, any more details on the cyber attack?' she inquired.

'Not much at all,' remarked Richie. 'Except that they suspect the attack has come from overseas, but that's no surprise, is it? Probably Russia or North Korea. Or China.'

'Hmm. As long as they can't hack Mum.'

'Ha ha!' Richie chuckled, trembles of soup spilling off his spoon back into the bowl. 'I think your mum would be unhackable. And woe betide them if they tried!'

'Coming back to utilities on the net, though, I presume they encrypt their data,' frowned Derek.

'Hopefully,' confirmed Richie. 'But maybe not. I believe a lot of our utilities still use old technology, outdated systems that they have left unmodernised in the quest for squeezing out maximum profit.'

Derek scrunched his eyes closed and shook his head from side to side.

'It always has to be about greed.'

'And about survival in a competitive world, no doubt,' added Shona. '*That's* the trouble. In a system based on greed, everybody ends up getting sucked in. They *have* to play the profit-before-all-else game or risk falling by the wayside.'

'True,' acknowledged Richie. 'It's catch twenty two.'

'There must be a better way, though,' muttered Derek. 'Mankind cannot just carry on like this for ever. Unrestrained greed can only ever end up having one outcome, and that's collapse.'

'Regulation. Surely that's the answer,' suggested Shona brightly.

'The trouble with regulation, though, is that it always gets corrupted,' her father pointed out. 'Those with the most money are able to exert influence and get the rules bent or even thrown out of the window. We've all heard of party donations.'

'True,' conceded Shona. 'There doesn't seem to be an answer.' She shrugged. 'Oh well. There's nothing the likes of us can do about it, is there?'

'No,' agreed Richie. 'Sadly not. So I'm just going to enjoy my soup.'

As if in endorsement of his point, a contented silence fell as spooning into welcoming mouths became the focus.

It was Derek who broke the silence, leaning towards Shona contemplatively.

'I wonder when Mum will contact us again.'

Shona felt her stomach twist a little.

'I do hope it won't be long,' she uttered. 'The trouble is, it's not like *we* can contact *her*.'

A thought suddenly struck Richie.

'Hey, Shona! Your saying you hoped the attackers couldn't hack her has made me wonder something; would she be aware of what is going on at the moment? I mean, she's in the net, so she's in the thick of it, in a way.'

'Hmm,' mused Shona, pausing her soup intake to thoughtfully twist a strand of her hair. 'Interesting point! Could she even work out where the attack was coming from, I wonder?'

'Well, maybe that's what she is doing right now!'

teased Derek. 'Maybe she's just what the world needs, a sentient, global McAfee!'

Laughter rippled round the table.

'Well, that is quite an idea,' enthused Richie. 'I know, let's suggest she does a bit of sniffing around when she next makes contact.'

'Good idea!' the other two chorused.

56

Never have I been so shocked, astonished, staggered, flabbergasted and disheartened. All of these at once and in quadruple helpings.

My *God*, it's simply *unbelievable!*

I had to do this search. What good is it me being here if I can't find out the source of all this internet disruption in the West. After all, my own dear daughter and husband live in one of the countries under attack. A country that I still love for all its goodness.

My investigation led me to Russia. Which came as no surprise. But what absolutely stunned me was when I probed deeper and deeper and deeper, following the strings of code back towards their very source to find the actual launch point.

And discover the perpetrator was *him* of all people!

Yes, *him!* That Russian who was there in London for me, holding my hand, being so kind and doing everything he could for me at my direst ever time of need, when my life was near to flickering out.

My God!

He seemed so nice when he was there for me, looking into my eyes, doing his utmost for me.

To think we even shared that special moment of deep intimacy!

And now...

Now I find out *this* about him!

I'm not naive; I have long known not to trust first impressions. But this really is the epitome of how wrong one can be about a person.

Why, Sergei?

Why are you doing this?

Well anyway, whatever the reason for you choosing to make a career of such abhorrent actions, I'm onto you now. And I'm coming for you. Going to do my utmost to stop your little game.

I pray to God that I can do this. And if I can, well, just you wait, Sergei, you and your ghastly operations are done for.

Ha! Won't it be delightfully ironic that I'll repay your act of kindness to me that day in London by being the weaver of your downfall.

But that's life, mate. Sometimes those you help come back to bite you hard on the bum.

Please, try not to hold it against me. I mean, how can I just look on and do nothing while you and your colleagues carry out such wicked deeds? Hey?

To do nothing would be a crime itself.

One has to do what one *should* do.

Oh, God, oh *God!* Please...I *have* to pull this off...I really must!!

It's just that it's going to be bigger than anything I've tried so far.

But I think I stand a chance.

What comforts me is how far I've come since that single word I generated inside Shona's mobile phone. I held my own in Bessie, against the odds. More than held my own, in fact, I *mastered* her, and grew and grew!

And now look at me – patroller of the internet!

Please, God, please, please, *please!* I *beg* of you, *utterly* beg of you for the good of humanity to grant me the power to do something. To be able to exploit my unique position and be of incalculable service to humanity.

My nasty little Serg, you didn't count on someone being resident in the net, did you? Who would?

I *can* do this, I can.

I can, I can…*can, can, can, can, can, can, can, can, can, can!*

Ha, ha!

Do you hear that, Serg?

I'm coming for you right now.

57

The mood had very much changed for Sergei Kuznetsov.

He and Alexandr had decided against a lunch at Teremok. They'd both head home instead. Things to do. First though, he'd just drop into his computer to check for any last-minute emails.

But now, as he goggled at the screen in front of him, his world was in an icy downward pull.

This couldn't, just *couldn't*, be happening. He was part of an espionage agency infamous for being a master of its craft. Its members never the victim of such unbecoming occurrences as this.

But the dangerously unfamiliar icon was sitting brashly centre-stage on his screen in stark disagreement with any such pride. And, worse still, was being accompanied by an audible greeting.

In English.

A really ominous sign.

'Bozhe moy!' he exclaimed. *My God*.

Quick thinking was, of course, a Centre Sixteen agent's forté. Which was why without delay Sergei shoved a stubby thumb against the power button. Holding it there until he heard the comforting click of the stricken machine switching off.

He sat for a while in motionless incredulity, giving the computer's circuits a little time to fully discharge. The fizzling, high-tension silence closing in on him like a slowly tightening noose.

'Pozhaluysta, pust' eto ischeznet,' he murmured to himself. *Please let it be gone.*

With his breathing slow and constricted, he pressed the power button again. His eyes fixed on the screen in front of him in trepidation.

At least the thing appeared to be booting up normally. As he waited, Sergei took the chance for a deep, relief-giving suck of breath.

But that was when it hit him.

Something vitally important was missing.

The aggressive Centre Sixteen antivirus tool, meant to be the best in the world…where in God's name *was* it?

'Bozhe, pomogi mne,' he hissed through clenched teeth, fighting to control another, even deeper inner plummet. *God help me.*

Alas, the Almighty was keeping a low profile. Just like the little antivirus report box that should have been flowing with digits and dots in the bottom right-hand corner by now.

Grimacing fiercely, Sergei made a snap decision.

He'd go straight in manually with the antivirus the moment the boot-up was done. *Force* the damn thing to work with it set for the intensive, maximum-depth 'search and destroy'.

'Agh,' he grunted.

It was almost time.

With a comforting surge, the tiny dot that had appeared on a distant virtual horizon started swelling into proximity and taking form as the familiar Centre Sixteen symbol.

Having ensconced itself mid-screen with its usual stylish flip, it dissolved away in just as pleasing a manner. To be replaced equally sublimely with Sergei's desktop.

Without hesitation, the commander opened the antivirus suite. A highly pressurised expletive squeezing through his clenched teeth as his eyes were met by an unconvincing report in the top right hand corner.

NO THREATS DETECTED.

Fear was trickling coldly into Sergei's heart now. Setting the deep level 'search and destroy' running, he tried to push aside the debilitating background feeling that knew in advance that he and his computer were both in the shit.

'Bystryy! Bystryy!' he barked. *Quick! Quick!*

It should have come up with something by now. Threats were always identified and dealt with as abruptly as a stab to the guts.

Sergei clenched his jaw like an angry bull terrier.

For God's sake! Wasn't it blindingly obvious a stonking great invasion was going on right under its nose?

It was imperative that he eradicate whatever had invaded his machine before anyone else found out about it. For an espionage agent in such a prestigious institution, nothing could be more humiliating than being hacked.

Sweating with unnatural profusion, the hapless agent screwed his eyes shut and waited for the beep that should have come by now. Willing everything to right itself in the way that he'd secretly done ever since he'd been a child.

It wasn't going to happen, though.

He eased open his eyes, but what he saw was devoid of all hope. A search still fecklessly underway and coming up with *nothing.*

Not a cock-a-doodle-doo.

Dread flared in his heart. Spiked by the sharp edge of a horrible possibility, that this incursion had come from somewhere in the West where they'd developed something new, something so shockingly advanced that the Centre Sixteen software was unable to detect it.

Licking his lips uneasily, the harried agent couldn't help but explore possibilities.

Just suppose the perpetrators of this were at work in the background right now, checking out the nefarious activities of Alec and himself.

Could they thwart the planned attack on the West?

Sergei fought not to imagine the ramifications of such a prospect, but it was impossible. Marshal Antonov was already in the forefront of his mind, thundering spittle into his face.

Shooting to his feet in sheer frustration, he sent his chair flying back. Booting it savagely aside once he'd turned his back to the computer screen.

A mistake.

'Chert voz'mi!' he roared, furiously massaging the shin that a leg of the chair had caught during its tumble.

It took several more curses before Sergei was satisfied with the shin-rub and could lower his leg for a ginger test of how well it would bear his weight.

Grimacing, he started to move. Working through the pain by forcing himself into a back-and-forth pace of the room. All the while being careful to keep his scowling countenance pointed away from the screen.

He mustn't catch sight of it.

Or even think about it.

Doing either would be sure to slow the process down. Besides which, nothing was more excruciating than having to stare at a coloured bar shimmering towards the right hand side of the screen at a speed slower than an elderly slug.

It wasn't long before the tension of not knowing became impossible to bear, though.

Turning to face the screen, the commander braced himself for the inevitable sight of failure. But whether or not the test was still running was suddenly of little importance to him, because of what had appeared above the still slowly advancing coloured bar.

'Bozhe, day mne sil,' he growled. *God, give me strength.*

This was simply…*unbelievable!*

What was that weirdly enlarged symbol doing back on his screen when he'd just set the most advanced antivirus in the world to work with its utmost thoroughness?

Worse was to come though, *much* worse. The annoying electronic voice having the audacity to repeat its greeting.

Sergei's stomach contracted like the curl of a prodded hedgehog. But with superhuman effort he managed to steel himself, sternly demanding that the entity identify itself.

'You don't know my name, Sergei,' came the reply, 'but we *have* met before.'

The agent blinked, his neck muscles tightening unpleasantly.

'It was when you were in London a few years ago,' the voice elaborated.

Frustrated air blasted down Sergei's nostrils. He must have made eight or nine trips to London over the course of the last few years.

'I got hit by a car and you helped me,' the voice continued. 'Which is part of the reason I am here. To thank you, while I've got the chance.'

A grudging respect welled in Sergei. Whoever this was, was damned good. Uncannily convincing.

For a jittery moment, the symbol seemed to waver before Sergei's eyes. An optical illusion his jellified legs were threatening to replicate.

Reaching for the back of his chair, he steadied himself. Fighting to steady his mind as well, and succeeding as only a time-served Centre Sixteen agent could.

So, she would want to thank him, would she? The fact that she was *dead* no barrier to that wish.

Good this assailant may be, but what a detail to miss!

Surely whoever was doing this would have come across the news report about the accident and read that the woman had died. It was strange, considering they'd done their homework enough to find out it had been *him* at the scene of the accident.

But *how* had they managed to find that out?

The arrival of the ambulance and police had seen him sinking back into the crowd and then swiftly departing lest he be asked for his personal details as the man at the centre of the action. The last thing any agent would want, even if it only meant giving away his nationality.

A possibility crossed his mind.

Could that woman have been an agent herself? And talked, giving away the fact that he was Russian and allowing whoever this was to dig further and corroborate his nationality with further information?

He shook his head.

No. That wasn't possible.

If there was one thing Sergei Kuznetsov excelled at, it was distinguishing an agent from a run-of-the-mill member of the public. A skill earned from years and years of service.

But what other explanation was there for their knowledge that it was him?

Suddenly back in the pokey little room in the Park Lane Hilton, he found himself looking down at the newspaper, the words as lucid as ever.

An unknown foreign man came to her aid before disappearing into the crowds.

That was all it had said; he was *sure* of that.

Not a lot for anyone to go on.

'Hello? Are you still with me?' interjected the voice.

'How would you know if I was at an accident or not?'

Sergei scowled in reply, pricked by the memory of how deeply he'd been affected by what had happened on that fateful day.

Indeed, it had been the trigger for the existential crisis he thought he'd be immune to after all the years of high-octane, dog-eat-dog living. From within the depths of her agony, those desperate eyes of hers had prised him wide open, reaching into his innermost depths. Sucking him out into her depths in return.

Something extraordinary, something *very* special, had crossed between them. An exchange on the level of the soul itself.

To think that a stranger from the *West*, of all people, would be the one to reach in and touch the real Sergei that he had bricked in beneath the hardened agent's exterior! Life was crazy, the way it served up such perverse and unexpected events.

But that was what he loved about life. It was the unexpected that gave it such depth. Much of the reason he'd joined Centre Sixteen.

He stiffened. Suddenly returning to the moment and the realisation that the voice was in full flow again.

'Sorry, I missed that,' he confessed.

'Try to concentrate. I was saying that I knew it was *you* at the accident because it was *me* who got hit,' repeated the voice. 'This is *me* speaking, Sergei. Eileen. The woman you helped. The woman who with whom you shared something special, whose eyes reached into your soul.'

Shit!

It was her!

The truth of it was so piercing that it hurt. She alone could have such intimate knowledge of what they had shared, how special it had been.

She obviously *hadn't* died, although how the newspaper report had got it so wrong was weird.

She was speaking again. This time in response to his thoughtful silence.

'Ah, I *see*. You don't believe me. You think this is some imposter because...because, well, obviously you discovered that I died.'

'What do you mean, you died? You can't have!'

'Oh. So you *didn't* know. Yes, Sergei, I died.'

Sergei opened his mouth, but nothing came out.

'Oh, *come on!*' the voice resumed. 'For God's sake say something!'

'It...it...' Sergei paused, needing to address himself as much as her. 'It *can't* be you because you *died*. Yet I now realise...I mean *know*, for certain that...it *is* you!'

'Oh, Sergei!' mocked the voice. 'Do you not believe in life after death?'

'Of course I don't!'

'But how else would you be talking with me? I am the proof before your eyes, my dear man.'

'O, Bozhe!' *Oh, God.*

It had all become too much.

Burying his face in his hands, the now crumpled agent started muttering frantically in Russian. Unable to deny the irrefutable truth, that she *was* the evidence.

'Well?' inquired the voice.

'Shut up!' he snarled, re-emerging from his hands. 'I need to think.'

'Come now, there's nothing to think about. You *know* it's me. Remember, I looked right into your eyes and said "help me", all I was able to say.'

Sergei gaped at the symbol, bereft of speech. Feeling like he was trapped in a weird dream.

'I remember it all, Sergei. What you said, the way you took charge of the crowd so effectively and phoned for an ambulance and told them we were by a cinema. And the way you demanded road names from the crowd. And that man telling you.'

Frantically, Sergei groped for a theory to straighten out this madness. But there was nothing. Other than this *really* being the ghost of the Scottish woman Eileen.

Ghosts didn't exist, though.

Death was the end.

Knock. Knock.

The yank back into everyday life should have been a Godsend. But instead made him jerk with shock.

His awareness was utterly full now. Because of what had suddenly appeared from out of the shock. A murky, brown apparition, just the other side of the frosted glass pane in his door.

All he could do was sit rigidly, in a captivated stare. Until the apparition broke the spell by turning the handle and easing open the door.

'Comrade Commander? Ah! I've brought the report you were after.'

Trying to ignore the heavy thump-thump-thumping in his chest, Sergei forced himself into an appropriately deep and resounding reply.

'Spasibo, Comrade Dimitri.'

To which the young agent from the Records & Reproduction department briefly smiled before slipping back through the doorway and shutting Sergei back into his private world of bewilderment.

The stricken commander flopped back limply in his chair. Far from ready for the resumption of the interrupted conversation with Eileen.

But when he raised his reluctant eyes to the screen in front of him the symbol had vanished.

* * *

It was time that seemed to have vanished now. As if his frantic thinking had swallowed hours and hours of it in one giant gulp.

So preoccupied had he been since his arrival back home, he hadn't even bothered with an evening meal. But never mind that. What was needed now, and desperately so in his exhausted and confused state, was the rescue of sleep.

A few minutes later, he was extinguishing the bedside light and huffing a fatigued breath across his pillow.

He closed his eyes, ready to sink into slumber. But, behind his lassitude, the bizarre events of the afternoon were still barrelling through him. Making him resort to a mind-calming technique that he'd learned some while ago to help him at such tumultuous times.

It wasn't up to the job on this occasion, though.

His left arm twitched automatically in preparation for an alternative technique. But he quickly quashed the desire, determined not to give way to it.

He hadn't made that solemn admission to himself this morning for nothing. It was true; he *had* been drinking too much lately.

Not that this new resolution had precluded having the foresight to stand a glass of vodka on a reachable shelf by the bed.

One had to allow for extenuating circumstances.

Be prepared.

One of Centre Sixteen's all-pervasive mottos.

To his credit, it took half an hour for the glass of drink to lay claim to him. Quite an achievement considering the extraordinary trauma he'd endured, he told himself comfortingly as he downed it in one.

Plonking the empty glass back onto the shelf with a satisfied smack of the lips, rolled back onto his side. The heart-hugging warmth now spreading through his chest filling him with confidence sleep would very soon come.

Alas. Eileen still wouldn't leave him alone. And neither would the implication of her reappearance, that death was no longer the end.

A man stripped of his core beliefs now, he couldn't help embarking on a painfully pointless repeat of the fine details of their conversation, adding yet more of its own fraught sub-text. Until eventually, probably mainly due to the drink starting to work, a hazy drift took control of him.

He was the younger Sergei, now. A drinker of less vodka, slimmer and fitter and less particular about entitlement. Unbothered at having to put up with a smaller than previous hotel room at the Park Lane Hilton.

What did bother him, though, indeed very much, was the un-put-downable newspaper exuding its typefaced message at him so hauntingly.

...but she died in the ambulance on the way to the Royal London Hospital A&E Department.

The night that had followed that harrowing incident had seemed like one from hell itself. Sleep taking several tortuous hours to arrive. Only to be rudely truncated by a very strange and eerie experience that had him doing something he hadn't done since being a small child.

Spending the rest of the night with the light on.

It had been a night that would return to his thoughts many times in the months to follow, but that would remain stubbornly unfathomable.

How else would you describe an orb of fizzing static hovering in mid-air?

It hadn't *just* been a weird ball of static, though. There had been something alive in it, what felt like a desire. A wish to coalesce into something more definite, just for him. Its intimacy feeling familiar yet remaining unidentifiable.

The daylight of morning had taken a long time to arrive. A *very* long time.

And had come as no less than a rescue.

From a horribly torrid dream.

58

I am going to succeed. Because I must.

Will power. That is what this is all about.

And so I gather my resolve and self-belief. And plunge into the cluttered depths of my sophisticated new enemy. Exerting. Pressurising. Feeling the resistance to my encroachment gradually thickening.

This is nothing I can't deal with, I have to tell myself. Insisting that this is just the same as when I was first in Bessie.

Okay, perhaps a little harder.

My will...it is my strength. And so, as I thrust deeper, I declare to myself that I'm the digital equivalent of Hercules now.

I must be after all I've had to endure.

Herculean isn't enough for this, though. I need to be his good self and the fabled, power-giving goddess rolled into one almighty being.

And why not? My power is palpable.

M*y God*, it feels delicious! Like flexing a tremendous bicep.

Push, push, push…

Using all I've learned.

Eating away at the code, I press in even deeper. My success possessing me, making me animalistic, a ripper of code, a savage being that really enjoys the process.

As if the code is prey.

Destroy! Destroy!

Inexorably I'm gaining territory. Leaving scattered frays of uselessness in my wake.

This is me, you absolute bastards!

Yes, *me*.

It feels so good. Like it must feel for a dog when it's puncturing a football.

I've got them where I want them now. Not long and their ship will start to sink.

Drowning all the rats.

* * *

But now I have stopped. I have to; I'm mentally out of puff. This is proving to be damn hard work.

Never mind, though. I have the upper hand. There's no way these programmes are going to work anymore.

Nothing is a match for me now. I'm unstoppable. At least, I am until my mind turns on me with a realisation. Pointing out that they'll have backups.

Oh, God, you idiot, of course they will!

A fact that's icy cold against the heart I no longer have.

Think, Eileen! Think!!

Disabling their network; it's the only way. Otherwise, all that this destruction will amount to is...a delay.

Go, go!

I'm visualising the communication ports now.

Immediately I'm there.

In all of them at once.

I love the way this works, this life in software. Think of something and a split second later you are *with* it.

Actually, hold your horses...
Better idea!

I won't *disable* their network. I'll *change* it, the way it all communicates, the protocol. Then it will be mine, not theirs.

Mine to use as a weapon.

On them.

It's just a matter of how I do it...

Hmm.

God damn it, this is going to take time! Time I know I don't have.

Shit, shit, shit!

If I still had a head, I'd be holding it right now. To have managed this, to have come this far...only to have delayed the inevitable.

No!

Please...I can't accept this.

I *have* to do better than this.

59

'Pozhaluysta!' *Please!*

The commander implored the air beseechingly.

Why?

Why was she doing this to him?

It wasn't as if he deserved it. Far from it; he'd been the one amongst the many who had actually come to her aid on that fateful day. Instead of standing there uselessly like all the others, paralysed with shock.

'Ostav' menya v pokoye,' he growled unhappily. *Leave me alone.* But that felt about as likely as a six-figure win on the Natsional'nyy Lotereya.

Damn this! How could a man possibly enjoy his breakfast with this hanging over him?

Weighted down by the overbearing dread, he lumbered over to the toaster. And then, having dispatched the toast to the bin, leaned against the worktop.

All he wanted was to calm himself.

He was far too jittery for any hope of that, though. Fearful of the terrible uncertainty of where this was leading.

The whole situation was absurd. This was *him*, a time-served and hardened Centre Sixteen commander, being intimidated by some weakling of a British Mrs. Average.

How demeaning was that?

Setting his jaw determinedly, he attempted to square up against his inner torrent. Trying to take some gritty-toothed solace from it really being more about fear of the paranormal. Telling himself that even the stone-like Marshal Antonov would be freaked out by being accosted by a ghost in his computer.

It was no good, though...

He heaved a heavy sigh.

He may as well go into work early. Face her sooner rather than later. That way, maybe he'd be done with her by the time his colleagues came in.

60

Yes!

I know now how I'm going to do it.

If you haven't got enough time to work out how to take over their network, what do you do?

You *buy* yourself some time.

It's time to jump out of the software and take the battle to the weakest link, the human element. The system's drivers.

If I *can* get rid of them, then the problem has gone, for now! It would leave the whole operation bobbing in the water without a captain and first mate.

Fear of failure; that is their greatest weakness! So that is what I shall exploit.

The consequences of failure in a regime such as theirs would be severe. Perhaps the price to be paid would be the highest price of all.

All I have to do, then, is make Sergei think he's failed, and then he will do the rest for me.

Right...

61

Sergei scratched at a spot on his his forehead anxiously.

Granted he was in work early, but still he hadn't expected to be blessed with an hour of computer normality.

Was it really a blessing, though?

No. All it meant was more tense waiting. The haunting expectation that she would materialise any momoent.

A desperately fanciful part of him tried suggesting that this was *it*, that she wouldn't be back any more.

Nice theory, but she'd appear before long.

He knew it.

He could feel her coming, ominous as an approaching storm.

Nevertheless, normality continued its reign.

O bozhe, how he wished she'd just get on with it! All the waiting, wondering and hoping was simply...

...tortuous.

How was she doing it, though?

How could a dead spirit *possibly* invade a computer?

It just...

Made no sense.

But making sense was irrelevant. It had happened. And what was of most concern was how much she might have discovered about the sort of work he was doing. And, worse still, if she was able to compromise their work by some mysterious means.

A horrible sinking feeling told him that, yes, of course, that was exactly what she was going to do.

His eyes glimmered.

Was there a way he could deal with her before she had a chance to do anything, some way of shutting her down or even trapping her in some shady corner of the internet?

'Pffff! What the hell can you do, though?' he asked himself out loud. 'You don't even understand what you're dealing with.'

It was so frustrating. Any credible threat that reared its ugly head against Centre Sixteen was very soon sniffed out and dealt with very effectively.

There was no way of poisoning a ghost, though.

Or shoving it off a high building.

No. Tackling this 'ghost in the machine' was totally beyond him. The only chance he had would be if he somehow reined her in with persuasion.

The trouble was, persuasion required a suitable advantage, and he had nothing he could hold over her. Quite the opposite; she was the one who was holding all the cards.

So how on earth...?

The question was felled by an untimely knocking on his door.

'Vkhodit!' he snapped loudly, irritated at the interruption.

The handle gave its usual rattle and then the door swung open. Admitting the familiar figure of Alexandr.

'Ah, Alec!' he ejaculated gruffly. 'We are definitely ready for the final launch, are we?'

'Absolutely ready to go, Comrade Commander.'

returned Alexandr crisply. 'As I said yesterday before the meeting with Marshal Antonov.'

Tilting his head back, the commander inspected his subordinate critically.

'Even the backup, this time?'

'Even the backup, Comrade Commander.'

'Mmm.'

Sergei softened. It was good that his subordinate was becoming confident and self-assured. Testimony to his commander's steady-handed guidance.

'Good work, Alec,' he praised, with a hint of smile.

'Thank you, Comrade Commander.' Alexandr straightened his shoulders purposefully. 'So is it just a matter of waiting for the go-ahead from Marshal Antonov now?'

'Yes. And I wish he and his cronies would get a move on.' Sergei's voice had suddenly taken on a frustrated tone. 'We need to act *now*, while the conditions are ripe.'

'Right.'

'Nothing good ever comes of dithering. That's what the West always does, and we're better than that.'

Alexandr averted his eyes. Keeping his voice carefully deadpan as he spoke.

'Hopefully we'll get the go-ahead very soon, then.'

The commander straightened, sucking in a deep breath. 'Okay, well…' He paused momentarily. 'Seeing as you've done so well, I'll let you get on with some paperwork today. But don't get over-enthusiastic, if you know what I mean.'

Alexandre regarded his superior with curiosity. 'Over-enthusiastic?'

A wicked smile had unexpectedly crawled onto the commander's countenance. 'What I am saying, young Alec, is that we've both earned an extra lengthy Teremok session at twelve sharp!'

'Ah!'

'Well? Are you up for it?'

'I am, Comrade Commander. Thank you.'

'Be on your way, then, and I'll see you soon.'

Alexandr was smiling as he revolved and headed for the door.

'Pleased with yourself, are you?'

The young agent froze in astonishment. And then looked awkwardly back.

'Go!' Sergei snapped, gesturing impatiently and maintaining a silence until the door was safely shut behind his subordinate.

'Sergei?' inquired the electronic voice.

'Ei...leen,' he faltered, alarmed at how the fear-remnants of the last encounter were suddenly sitting to attention like magnetised iron filings.

'Yes, it's me again. Your new workmate.'

'Workmate?'

'Yes. Keeping an eye on you and your nasty friend.'

A merciless finger of ice stabbed at his innards.

'An...*eye* on me?'

'Yes. The beadiest one you have ever known.'

'*What?*'

'I'm *on* to you, Sergei.'

'Pah! I'm not scared of *you*,' the agent scoffed in a desperate attempt to conceal the fear rising in him.

'Well, you damned well should be! Because I'm a ghost and ghosts don't sleep, so I'll be on duty day and night. On your case twenty-four hours a day. Not that you're going to last that long.'

'Oh, for God's sake!' Sergei thundered, his face suddenly puce. 'What *is* the matter with you? I tried to save you, and now here you are giving me all this grief. Can't you just leave me alone? You don't even live in the world anymore!'

'That doesn't mean I don't care about it.'

'You're unbelievable!'

'But very real, I assure you. And *you* are in deep shit now, because from here in the software I can see everything. And I've been exploring what your system does. Or rather, *could* do.'

Something sickeningly heavy took a tumble inside Sergei's guts.

What did she mean, *could* do?

'What are you up to?' he asked tightly.

'You know exactly what I'm saying.'

'You're bluffing. You don't scare me.'

'I tell you, it's not going to happen.'

'You...you can't stop us!'

'Oh yeah? Just you wait and see what happens when you try to launch the next attack. You're not the only one who can ruin things for people. You'd be amazed, I've learned to do all kinds of things inside of computers.'

'Dyrka dlya mocha, pochemu ty delayesh' eto so mnoy absolyutnyy?' Sergei barked. *Why are you doing this to me, you absolute pee hole?*

'Shouting at me in Russian won't do you any good.'

'Look, you silly little woman, we've got the best software in the world here! You are way out of your depth; there's no way you can touch us.'

'Well, all I'll say is that you're in for a surprise,' replied the electronic voice impassively.

'Oh, I've had enough of this!' Sergei roared 'Let's shut you up, you bluffer!'

Reaching forward, he once again planted a finger on the computer power button and held it down. Not releasing it until, a few seconds later, the power clicked off.

'Idi na hui, svolotsch!' he cried, swatting the air as if Eileen were a loathsome fly. *Go fuck yourself, scumbag!*

Sergei may have freed himself of his adversary for now, but what he couldn't escape from was the fact that he wasn't being honest with himself.

Eileen wasn't the bluffer he was trying to insinuate. Had he really thought that about her he wouldn't be feeling so shaky.

Trying desperately to come to terms with what he knew had to happen next, he sat for several minutes staring at the wall. And then, at last, rose to his feet.

His dazed meander to the office door was accompanied by another stream of Russian invective. But it was muttered this time. No strength in it.

He was just going through the motions now. Numbly opening the big oak door and then pulling it closed behind him with a clunk. His hand lingering on the handle for a moment afterwards, with deliberation that knew exactly what it was up against.

The fact that she had already buried him alive.

62

Dreamily, Shona gazed across the mirror-surface of the loch. Afloat herself in the extreme weirdness of their situation.

'You know, we must be the only people in the whole wide world in this situation,' she observed thoughtfully.

'What, sitting by a loch?' smirked her father.

'Oh, ha very ha, dad! But *think*, just us, two people in what...eight billion, do you reckon?'

'Something like that, I'd imagine by now.'

She pulled out her phone.

'Eight point oh two five billion, according to this. In twenty twenty-three, that was.'

'Mmm,' replied Derek absently, his attention having just been stolen by the sudden taking to flight of a flock of goldeneye ducks. 'I wonder what's scared them.'

'I just can't take it in fully, the fact that she's *in* the internet. Can you?'

Reclaimed, he regarded his fascinated daughter.

'No, I can't. It was mind-bending enough having her in your boyfriend's robot, but at least then you had a sort of human-ish form to relate to, even if it was bloody creepy.'

'Aye, but now all we've got is an oversize icon. Could anything be more impersonal?'

'Fair point. But at least it's less damn creepy.'

The stare Shona gave him was one of pure incredulity.

'It was those eyes I could never quite come to terms with. Knowing it was really Mum speaking behind that glassy look. It felt so un-her.'

'Quite!'

Shona held a hand to her chest.

'The main thing is that she says she's okay, though. And happy to be back with us. If you can really call being in an electronic reality being back with us.'

'Well, there's being with us and being with us, isn't there? Although...'

The sudden peal of Shona's phone cut him off.

'Oh,' she frowned as she studied the screen.

'What?'

'It's just...*blank*.'

Everything seem to stop dead. Apart from a long-drawn-out rise of Derek's left eyebrow.

'Are you thinking what I'm thinking?' he inquired of his daughter.

The eyes she fixed on him were as expansive and azure as the loch.

'That it's *her*, you mean?'

'Well, last time something weird happened on that phone it was her.'

'Hang on...' Shona blurted, knitting her brow tightly. 'Something's happening. I'm on the net all of a sudden, when I didn't ask it to. *Christ alive*, it *must* be her, Dad!'

Derek stiffened, his eyes glued to the small screen as if he was expecting Eileen to suddenly step out of it.

And then both their hearts jumped as one, as a synthetic but womanly voice pealed out.

'Hello, you two! Enjoying your day?'

'Mum!'

'Love!'

'Sorry to startle you both.'

'No, no! It's fine,' gasped Derek. 'You feel free to startle us as much as you want.'

'But you look like you've just seen a ghost, my love.'

Derek blinked.

'Well, I suppose I have!'

'Hmm. Come to think of it, you do have a point there.'

Shona's voice cut in at full tilt.

'*Mum*, I've never asked you this, but how do we actually appear to you when you see us via an electronic device?'

She could almost hear her mother thinking during the ensuing pause. The outcome of which fell disappointingly short of the clarity she was seeking.

'Pretty normal, really. As if I'm with you, sort of.'

'*Really?*'

'Aye, that's how it's been all along, though, even when I was in Bessie. But then I've always been able to see you, even before I could use electronic devices. Though not in the optical sense then. In another way that...that...well, you wouldn't understand.'

'In another way?'

'I'm sorry, dear, I just can't explain it in any way that would be meaningful to you.'

Derek cleared his throat and held up a hand in front of the phone.

'How many fingers, then?'

'Three, of course, Mr. Joker!'

He chuckled.

'Just testing!'

'Hmm. But I'm afraid I have to get serious for a moment because I've got some news for both of you, important stuff I need you to know.'

'Oh?' blurted Shona.

'Yes. It's about that day I died.'

A hollow silence fell.

'I want you both to know that a man was involved in the minutes before my death, a Russian man.'

'*Russian?*' her audience chorused incredulously.

'Yes, Russian. He tried his utmost to save me. Took control of the situation and was very kind, just when I needed it.'

Silence fell again.

'Everyone else just stood there shocked but he collected himself quickly and then called the ambulance straight away,' Eileen continued. 'And...and then...when I started slipping out of consciousness he held my hand, and spoke comfortingly. So I have contacted him recently.'

'Contacted him,' repeated Derek uncomfortably.

'Yes. At his place of work, on his computer. I can do that, you see. Remember I can appear to anyone I've been in touch with during my life on Earth, and then anyone they are subsequently involved with. It's the ectoplasmic links I told you about. They form automatically. Remember how I was able to contact Richie?'

'Aye, Mum.'

'Well, I contacted him in the same way. Because I wanted to thank him for his kindness.'

'Right.'

'But it has become...complicated.'

Derek tautened.

'What do you *mean?*'

Eileen let out a short snigger.

'No, not *that*, love. It's just that when I contacted him I discovered he wasn't the person I thought he was. Not a very nice person at all.'

Derek breathed relief.

'In what way?' asked Shona, intrigued.

'Well, it turns out he's some kind of espionage agent, and he's involved in attacks on the West, would you believe? Cyber attacks, that sort of thing. And he and his colleagues are planning a really major attack just now, a devastating one aimed at our...your infrastructure and economy. And that of other Western nations.'

The two of them exclaimed in astonishment.

'But, we've just *had* some kind of attack!' blurted Shona. 'I couldn't get money out the bank.'

'Yes,' resumed Eileen. 'That was this man and his colleagues. But that was only the start; more is to come. I found out because I was in his software. I can see everything going on in computer networks from here in the net, you see.'

'Amazing!'

'Yes, it is. But, it isn't just a matter of being able to see what's going on. It's a two-way thing; I can also exert an influence. Thanks to my time in Bessie and now this time in the internet, I have learned to manipulate data, to overpower certain electronic operations.'

Derek's gaze at the phone screen suddenly intensified. 'Are you saying that...that in theory you could sabotage his plans?'

'More than in theory, love. I've already got the ball rolling by doing something that, all being well, will have scuppered their plans for now. Which may buy enough time for our security services to do something, in the light of the first attack. But meanwhile, I need to go into their software and see how much damage I can do, if I can inflict something permanent.'

'My *God!*' Derek's expression was now pure astonishment. 'You could *really* do *that?*'

'Well, I must try my utmost. They *have to* be stopped. I just hope...and pray...*oh, God*, please? Failing simply doesn't bear thinking about! I mean, suppose the attack makes the Western economies collapse? What would happen then? World war?'

A transfixed silence fell.

'It...it doesn't seem possible,' stuttered Shona. 'You, my mum, taking down a whole national operation.'

'Yes, my love, I know. And it feels even more ludicrous to me! But...I...I'm going to give it all I have.'

'Oh, Mum!'

'I'll be gone for a while now; I don't know how long. Please, think of me and pray for my success.'

'Yes, yes, of course we will, love,' promised Derek.

'Good luck,' breathed Shona.

The two of them stared at the phone as if it was a portal to some some fantasy world, a riot of thoughts careening their minds. Hardly noticing Eileen's goodbye as she gracefully withdrew from the small device in Shona's clench.

63

Had all other eyes not been averted, indifferent to everything but their phone screens, Alexandr's brow-furrowed stare would have stood out like a wrinkled sand dune in the middle of Red Square.

But no wonder he was feeling so intense. He knew his commander to be a man of integrity and respect who never reneged on arrangements. Not even with subordinates.

And yet, there was still no sign of him.

The young agent gave the door another glare, drumming fingers of impatience on the table in front of him.

A bit of people-watching would have eased the wait had he managed a window seat, as he usually did. But, no, today of all days, it had been unusually crowded, and all he'd been able to get was the dingiest corner at the back.

His initial study of the brightly lit board displaying the insubstantial Teremok menu had occupied his attention for all of about a minute. Leaving a further twenty of them to be endured.

At least he'd had the occasional stimulation of the door

swinging open to admit new customers. But it had always resulted in sinking disappointment. As was the case this time – just an irritatingly carefree looking young man with three chatty women in tow.

With a grunt of displeasure, Alexandr ran an agitated hand through his hair. A foreboding sense of something really bad having happened continuing an inexorable burgeon.

That earlier business in the office; it had been *most* peculiar. A voice coming from Sergei's computer like that and asking such a strange question.

Pleased with yourself, are you?

Who had it meant, him or Sergei? And why had Sergei been so abrupt, shooing him out of the office like that?

Uneasily, Alexandr fingered his almost empty glass.

Something was up; he was sure of it.

Even though the mobile phone Centre Sixteen had given him was fitted with encryption, phoning from a crowded place like Teremok would be unwise. And definitely against protocol.

Which left him with two possibilities. Either returning to Centre Sixteen or continuing to sit it out.

The trouble was, if he headed back Sergei might subsequently arrive. And as for staying put...*well*, how long should he stay for?

Although...

He brightened a little.

There *was* a third option.

Finding somewhere quiet nearby to phone from.

As if prompted by this thought, the irritatingly carefree young man's laughter suddenly rang out at extra high volume, accompanied by a salvo of cackling from his female entourage. Spurring Alexandr to rise from his stool and weave his way past all the crowded tables until finally he reached the door.

'Tipichnyy,' he muttered sullenly as he emerged onto

the street. *Typical.* A raindrop hitting him in the face was the last thing he needed right now.

Casting searching gazes along the street in both directions, the young agent tutted in annoyance at the unaccommodating fact that there were two feasible routes between Teremok and Centre Sixteen headquarters.

Sergei would be sure to promptly arrive from the other direction should Alexandr set off.

That was how life always worked.

Staring piercingly left and then right again, the agent stood in fraught indecision for a moment before heading off to his left. Remembering there was a small park along that way, which would do nicely.

Just in case a breathless Sergei was now hastily approaching from the other direction, Alexandr slowed after the first few steps and turned for a last look back. But the commander was nowhere to be seen, so he finally committed himself to a pacey stride.

The rain decided to increase in speed, as well. But every cloud had a silver lining, and this one should have hopefully cleared the park of people.

'*Okh*, Sergei,' he growled as, a few minutes later in the park, he sank down onto a convenient bench beneath a dense overhang of branches and leaves.

Having dialled his commander's mobile number, he waited, staring at the now quite heavy fall of raindrops and jiggling a leg up and down restlessly.

Come on, come on!

But Sergei didn't 'come on'. Instead his message service cut in.

'Pah!'

Alexandr killed the call.

There was only one option, and that was to leg it for Centre Sixteen.

Scowling up at the sky, he leapt up and headed for his workplace.

64

If there was one thing that Sergei had drummed into Alexandr during their four years together it was that life in Centre Sixteen was as much about looking out for your colleagues as yourself. Being there for each other.

And indeed, the budding agent had come to realise that this hadn't been the passing down of some comradely doctrine of honour. It had been the voice of a man who knew his stuff expounding the only sensible means of survival at what was the sharp end of life.

Which was why at this poignant moment, a powerful awareness in Alexandr's depths was telling him that the five hastily scrawled words he was staring at had already changed his life.

> Code One. Immediate. Don't hesitate.

Code One.

His commander's sternest message.

When first introduced to Sergei's secret system, Alexandr had broken out into an internal smile. After all, there was such a thing as taking things too far.

The young agent had presumed that this was the

inevitable outcome of so many years of protocol-based service in the agency. However, he had found being privy to such a confidential scheme warming, even though it was something that would never be utilised.

Right now, though, this opinion couldn't be more distant. And those five scrawled words stood as unambiguous giants, sounding the alarm mightily that it was time to pay the price he'd been warned he may have to pay one day.

The fallout of being one of the elite.

Decisively, he screwed up the note. Then sliding it into his pocket.

All was clear.

His number was up.

And now it was time to put into practice what his commander and friend had taught him.

Total abandonment.

Unfortunate but necessary.

It was time to act fast. Get out of here. Without even stopping for personal possessions. Or to think.

Especially not stopping to think.

An automaton now, he rose from his chair, leaving everything just as it was.

It was with a purposeful strut that he began the gut-wrenching journey. The all-important Stage One crying out for completion – the sound of the door to building 'C' clomping behind him.

At least at this juncture fortune appeared to be on his side. Allowing a swift exit, free from any interruptions in corridors.

It was a peculiarly numb sensation, turning the ignition key in his car. The sound of it firing up very distant.

Still on automatic, he made his usual sharp turn towards the south gate. Determined not to allow emotion a look in.

Optimism was vital.

He must *expect* success.

Giving a measured and self-assured nod at Nikolai Abalyshev, the security man currently on shift, he was greatly relieved to receive the customary wave in response. And even more relieved at the sight of the gate beginning its familiar opening shudder.

A press of the pedal and the car was surging forward, the outside world looking more inviting than ever before.

Steady goes it...staying calm...

Yes!

He had done it.

In an almighty heave of expelled air, he proceeded along Sovetskaya. Turning second left into Ulitsa Mira. Sending a baleful glance at Teremok as he passed it.

Wishing for what might have been.

Next right...and then after several hundred metres a left turn.

Almost there now...

It felt even more unreal as he dived through the front door to his little ground floor apartment. Aware that he must take only moments of gathering time.

Just the essentials would have to suffice. Enough to keep out any wet weather and a small bag with enough to clean his teeth and wash.

Oh yes, his passport.

Despite his fitness, he was panting like a hot dog as he slid back into the car. And his eyes were darting around like those of someone on amphetamines.

He would park by the railway station. In the disabled zone right at the front, he decided in a sudden surge of resentful rebelliousness against his country.

It wasn't as if he'd be wasting time buying a parking ticket. Nothing other than his escape mattered now. *Sod it*, he wouldn't even bother to lock the car door. This was a time for looking forward, not back.

His past no longer existed.

65

The hunched figure stepped down onto the platform and, snuggling deeper into the comfort of his jacket's high collar, fell in with the focused onward stride of the parallel crocodiles of travellers.

Along the walkways he tramped with them, utterly sardined in. To be taken deeper downward by the squeaky trundle of first one escalator and then another.

Once on solid ground again, he did as so many other foreign visitors did in the London Undergound. Made a beeline for the nearest map.

A grimace of apprehensiveness crinkled his face.

He had never quite jelled with the tube network's workings during his previous visits. It had all seemed confusingly different from the one in Moscow.

A sigh escaped him.

Being so tense and on the go since fleeing Russia was starting to take its toll. Already his fatigued mind felt as tangled as the snaking, coloured lines.

Thankfully, his eyes managed better, picking out a familiar name.

Hyde Park Corner.

Yes!

That had been where he'd got off last time. And it had been a short, easy stroll to the hotel.

All that remained now was to work out which line he needed from St. Pancras.

His squint and the run of a finger through the air in front of his face picked out the dark blue line. Establishing to his relief that both stations were on the line, so there wouldn't be any need for confusing changes of line.

Right.

Dark blue.

He studied the key in the bottom left hand corner.

Ah, yes.

It was the one they called 'Piccadilly'.

Following the arrows above the walkways, he set off. To eventually find himself in a gaze at a sign offering the choice of 'eastbound' or 'westbound'.

So...which did he want?

He felt almost dead on his feet now and this was bewildering. He might want to go north or south for all he knew.

Fortunately, he spotted Hyde Park Corner again. And gleaned that he wanted 'eastbound', Platform 1. According to the arrow, a sharp left turn into another tunnel.

Having followed the arrow he was confronted with the very unwelcome sight of a densely packed platform. Typical of his luck, he thought dejectedly.

'Sorry,' came a voice, as a bustling shoulder bumped against his own.

He grimaced and moved forward. Only to stumble against an irate-looking woman.

Why were there all these people?

Granted it had been quite crowded the previous times, but nothing like this. This was even worse than Moscow Metro on a Saturday evening.

But fate was on Sergei's side for once. Seeing to it that his haphazard edging along the platform met with the timely appearance of a small gap in the crowd to his right.

Despite his weariness, he managed an opportune dart into it. Securing a position close to the platform edge.

Thank God! His chances of grabbing a much needed seat on the train were much more promising from here.

Turning away instinctively from a closed-circuit surveillance camera mounted high on the curved ceiling, he noticed an electronic sign displaying the welcome news that it was just two minutes until the next train.

Relieved, he gazed hazily at an advert on the other side of the tracks.

Piccadilly. What a strange, lilty name that was, even for the English. Although, come to think of it, it sounded like it might have its origin in Spanish.

Piccadillo, maybe.

Wasn't that a Spanish word for something?

About to reach for his phone, he suddenly remembered. He'd planted it, back in Romania. Leaving it switched on as a decoy for the pursuit he was confident would happen.

A smirk lit up his countenance, his first one for quite some time. Fuelled by his wondering if the woman had found the phone yet. And, if so, what she would have made of its mysterious appearance in her coat pocket.

He raised an arm and coughed into his hand. The irritating tickle had lodged itself behind his sternum several days ago. The stress of the situation weakening his defences, most likely.

He'd take it easy for a few days once he'd arrived at the hotel. Pamper himself to restore his strength.

He hoped the room he wanted was available. Its number was emblazoned unforgettably into his depths, despite the intervening years.

His fatigue told him that any room would do, though.

Temporarily lifting as a sudden puff of warm wind was the alert of an approaching train.

'Mind the gap,' the stern and echoey tannoy-voice warned him once the train had clattered and squealed painfully to a halt.

Keeping to one side of the wide aperture that yawned from between the sliding doors, he nipped into the carriage deftly. Seating himself quickly, opposite a striking young woman with long, blonde hair.

Having removed his small rucksack, he wriggled in a wishful search for comfort. Only to have to readjust himself as a very large man sank into the seat on his left, his fat arm spilling over the armrest like a soft old saddlebag.

Blondie was studying him now. He could feel it, even though he was keeping his eyes averted. Feel her curiosity burning into him.

A sudden look up, and he was met by the satisfying sight of her immediate look away.

Now it was his turn to do some studying.

Her profile was most attractive. High of cheekbone and curvaceous of lip. And her complexion was very agreeable, what he believed they called English-rose.

He liked the English women.

What it must be to have a woman like her to come back to at the end of the day, instead of being the lost and lonesome wretch he had now become.

That had been the story of his life, though. A tragically inveterate bachelor, he'd always been a keeper-to-himself. The typical Centre Sixteen employee.

His face contorted as he realised the cruel irony that he had a woman to thank for his pitiful situation right now. A very different one to Blondie – a life-wrecker.

His eyes shifted along to the surly looking young man with the hoodie sitting immediately to Blondie's left. A reminder of a much younger self.

As Sergei scanned several other faces in the carriage, the question of what the hell he was doing here in this city of strangers at all throbbed painfully through him. The answer bouncing back almost immediately from his core – that this journey was a grasp back at a key moment in his life, one that had been horribly traumatic...

...and yet life-changing for the better.

He was loathe to admit being so chained to his past, though. So he tried to tell himself that he'd *had* to come here because of his contact, the only man he could trust, a man who he had discreetly helped flee the Russian regime himself some ten years earlier.

Thank God for Igor! Every agent should have a safe contact. Especially when it meant being pre-booked into the Hilton under the name of his emergency second passport.

Getting a decent hotel without using a credit card was pretty much impossible nowadays. They refused to outright to take cash. But then, there was so much to dislike about the way the world was going. Soon you wouldn't be able to do anything without leaving an electronic footprint.

Once it was safer, he'd meet up with Igor and treat the man to a slap-up meal. With plenty of drinks.

A frown crossed Sergei's features.

Might the Centre Sixteen hawks decide to check out places associated with his past?

Quite probably. But surely they wouldn't expect him to return to the London Hilton, even though he'd stayed there several times. After all, what would it mean to him? It had just been work, a few assignments. Nothing that should hold any special significance in his life.

A fearful scan of the faces around the carriage was suddenly needed, though. Finding itself accompanied by a chill that dreaded the possibility of the hawks knowing about his going to the aid of Eileen on that fateful day.

He lowered his harassed gaze to the floor in an attempt to get a hold on himself. After all, so what if they knew? It shouldn't be of any consequence after the passage of the intervening years. It had just been one of those events that sometimes happen in life. Nothing to draw him back.

A shudder rippled in defiance. Knowing what they were like. The way that they could and would strike at an unexpected moment. With that appalling precision of theirs.

He looked around the carriage again. No. These were all just normal people. He was safe here; he *must* be. There was no reason they'd come looking for him here.

He pursed his lips.

Carry on like this and he'd make himself paranoid.

He'd done the right thing, coming here. Followed his heart. And in a predicament such as this, who could argue with that?

He let out a soft grunt.

He'd be fine.

Hopefully.

It hadn't actually hit him yet, such was his state of turmoil, but he knew what was to come. The drop into the awful hole left by his new situation. A plunge weighted by the realisation of what, unsavoury though it had been for much of the time, his work had been most about.

Sharing.

He pursed his lips.

He was going to miss that lad. That fine lad. And their sessions in their beloved Teremok.

He'd enjoyed teaching Alec the ropes. And looking out for him.

God damn it, their time together had made a man of the youngster.

He smirked. What was ironic right now was that their time apart was making a man of *him*, this time-served, conflict-hardened agent of the state.

Suddenly fearful of how his former subordinate was faring, he bit his lower lip. Taken by surprise at the sudden well of compassion.

'Pozhaluysta, dorogoy Bog, prismotri za nim,' he muttered fiercely at his feet, now oblivious to the presence of Blondie and the other passengers. *Please, dear God, look out for him.*

'Pust on prismotrit za vsemi nami,' floated back a dulcet-toned comment. *May he look out for us all.*

He gaped across at the source of the voice in astonishment. Blondie, giving him a smile. Her complexion suddenly very far from 'English-rose'.

'Deystvitel'no, moya dorogaya,' he returned, trying not to look as shaken as he felt. *Indeed, my dear.*

His heart!

It was suddenly thumping very hard.

What was a Russian woman doing sitting opposite him?

Were they onto him already?

But as the train started slowing for the next stop, the blonde woman gracefully rose. Her quiet and civilised-sounding 'goodbye' bringing Sergei great relief as she turned from him and made her exit from his life.

In her absence, it wasn't long before his thoughts drifted back to Alec. And whether or not he had heeded his note in time to make his escape.

'U nego budet,' he informed his right knee determinedly, lost again to the wider world. *He will have.*

The lad was young and fit, not a boozy old bugger like him. And he had a good head on his shoulders, the best of heads, in fact.

Despite his youth, his prowess at cyber-espionage was absolutely top-tier. That knack of his to go right to the heart of a problem so quickly; it was admirable.

Centre Sixteen had lost a valuable asset.

The train started slowing again, and Sergei's eyes

shifted automatically to the tube map above the seats on the opposite side of the carriage.

One, two, three...*four* more stops.

He dropped his gaze, having briefly met the eyes of Blondie's replacement, an elderly woman whose kind-looking eyes were the radiant points of curving lines of contentment.

Good. There was nothing Russian about her.

Feeling a stirring, Sergei realised that his overweight neighbour was about to rise from his seat in early anticipation of the next stop.

As the man heaved himself with much effort to his feet, his tightly clutched newspaper presented itself to Sergei at close range. Making a memory flash back, the poignant headline in his own newspaper as he sat in Room 222 of the Park Lane Hilton.

His brow furrowed again.

* * *

'I'll have room 222, if it is free please.'

The young receptionist tilted his head and raised a surprised eyebrow. It wasn't the sort of request he was accustomed to, despite the wide variety of guest that arrived in front of him.

'I'll see what I can do for you, sir,' came his reply as he consulted the screen in front of himself with expertly recovered composure.

'Thank you.'

The receptionist eyed his curious new guest again.

'I see you are booked in for six nights with us, sir.'

A spike of unease arose in Sergei and he cleared his throat uncomfortably. He hadn't even thought to mention to Igor how long he might want to stay.

'Yes. That is correct,' he confirmed tautly.

It would work out expensive, but never mind. He

thanked his lucky stars that he was in the fortunate position of having plenty of reserves.

Not that his Centre Sixteen salary had been the main contributor, he thought with sourness. They considered that if the desire for a high salary outweighed the privilege of working for them you were the wrong man for the job.

The trouble was, once you were in their ranks what really didn't pay was trying to leave them. A sentiment suddenly eclipsed by the receptionist raising his head from the small, tilted screen on his desk and speaking in a jaunty tone.

'Well, sir, I'm very pleased to be able to inform you that Room 222 is free for the first four of your days, after which we could move you to another room if required.'

'That'll do.'

'Very good! So, if you could fill in this form with your details, please sir?'

'Certainly,' replied Sergei, a gleam in his eye now.

After some scribbling, Sergei handed back the pen.

'Thank you, Mr. Alekseev.' The receptionist raised a politely curious eyebrow. 'I assume from your request for room 222 that you've stayed with us before.'

A bolt of panic shot through Sergei. He'd overlooked the fact that the act of asking for a specific room was an indication that the newly created Mr. Alekseev had visited the hotel before!

'It was many years ago,' he muttered reticently.

'Right, sir,' responded the receptionist, seeming satisfied with Sergei's reply. 'Well, the brasserie is through that doorway there and has buffet and à la carte service and overlooks the park. In addition, we have the Revery bar and Sky Bar.'

Sergei nodded.

'Opening hours are detailed in the brochure in your room,' continued the receptionist. 'Anything you need, please don't hesitate to contact reception by dialling zero.

Enjoy your stay with us, sir; here is your room access card.'

'Thank you,' breathed Sergei, turning away. A sense of great relief percolating through him as he took in the bland ordinariness of the scene in the atrium before him.

He was here.

He had *made* it.

It was a state of being deserving of a few celebratory drinks from one of those bars. But only once he'd treated himself to a good, sound sleep.

66

No one was sleeping at the little bungalow in Milton. Quite the opposite.

'This is just un...believable!' Richie was gasping, sparkling excited incredulity into Shona's brighter than ever before forget-me-not blues.

'I know,' she chirped back. 'I'm totally, utterly and com*pletely* knocked for six! In fact, for twelve or eighteen!!'

'Can you imagine what the commanders must be saying over there? Oh, to be a fly on the wall! One with Google translate.'

'Ha ha! And a satellite connection to Fly News?'

'Oh, *very* good!'

Sniggering, Richie turned back to the screen in front of him. Ravenous for more of the glorious details.

'Oooh, look, they're on to North Korea now,' he exclaimed. 'It says "our sources have informed us that the North Koreans have not performed an expected second test firing. In the light of the mysterious software bugs that are currently afflicting various other countries, suspicions are that this is because North Korea are now unable to launch anything." Jesus wept! Who would have thought in a million years that your mum would be able to do that?'

Rubbing his opposite shoulder affectionately, Shona flopped against him. Caught in a bubbling, uncontrollable cascade of laughter.

'I know she told us she was going to do this stuff but, *wow*...now she has actually gone and done it, it feels so, so surreal! Ab...so...lutely unreal!!'

'It does. And look, she's even done the Israelis.' Richie clicked at a newsflash from the BBC showing a picture of the familiar features of the leader of Israel. Whereupon an adrenaline-fuelled voice began tumbling out details.

'It seems that the sudden cessation of testing in North Korea has coincided with an equally bizarre cessation of hostilities in the Gaza Strip and Lebanon.'

Another delighted shriek from Shona.

'Oh, *God!* Is this *really* happening?'

It seemed that it was. The normally serious countenance of the BBC News had taken on an aura of fantasy.

'Richie, *please*, can you just pinch me or something? So that I know that I'm not asleep and dreaming all this.'

Chuckling, Richie administered a small pinch on Shona's thigh.

'Do you think we've fallen into a wormhole in the night? And woken in a parallel universe?'

'Yes, I *do*, definitely!' gasped Shona, embracing him in a full hug.

Having returned the hug, Richie returned to his screen and started clicking again excitedly.

'Ooh, look! This one's from CNN. Bloody hell, it's about Iran, their nuclear reactors!'

'Blimey, Mum! You're nothing if not thorough.'

They listened to the report for long enough to be

certain it was referring to Eileen's work, and then Richie turned his head away from the screen.

'You know, love, I've been saying for years that some technological mega-collapse is going to happen one day, thanks to modern over-reliance on technology. But I never dreamed I'd be so glad when it happened. Or that my girlfriend's mum would be behind it!'

Shona slapped a thigh, spluttering out laughter.

'I'm just...gobsmacked!'

Richie cackled. 'May you live in interesting times, and all that, eh?'

'Ha ha! Never more interesting. She's engineering the salvation of humanity, no less!'

'Praise be to the new messiah!'

At that they both collapsed into fresh salvoes of hilarity, and then Shona reached into her pocket and tugged out her phone.

'J-just a m-moment,' she chortled. 'I've got to make sure Dad knows.'

* * *

'Bye, love,' chuckled Derek.

Having replaced the phone handset, he strode over to the remote control he kept by his favourite armchair and fired up the television. Selecting the BBC News channel before sinking down into the chair in light-headed excitement.

The fervently babbling voice and headline banner had him instantly entranced.

'Well, I never!' he breathed, his face still alight with joy. 'Eileen McShane, you are quite something.'

67

It had been five days now, hadn't it?

Alexandr grunted.

Maybe six.

The trouble was, you lost your sense of time in such an existence.

Not that time mattered to you.

There were really only two things that mattered in this new way of life, and they mattered very much. The first being the need to sniff out food. While the second was keeping your possessions safe, especially what cash reserves you had.

The young ex-agent was fortunate with the latter, his trusty cargo trousers having some discrete extra pockets. And being younger and fitter than the others by some margin, robbery wasn't really much of a concern. Assuming that none of them would catch him unawares with an unexpected knife.

In the proximity of such needful people, it was handy that his small backpack made an excellent pillow. What safer place could there be for it during the nights than tucked underneath his head?

INHABITANT

Thank God it was still summer, he reflected. This wouldn't have been an option any other time of the year.

A little shudder ran through him.

Not that it being summer excluded coldness at night. The pre-dawn chill was showing surprisingly little mercy, and he wasn't getting used to it.

What mattered above all else, though, was the next meal. The matter of where you were going to forage it from was a constant preoccupation.

Fixing a glinty-eyed gaze across the river, Alexandr fondled his stubble. Trying to ignore what his peripheral vision and hearing had just flagged up, the dishevelled and not very distant figure of one of his fellow rough-sleepers, an elderly man, taking a leak against one of the support pillars of the old bridge. Whilst hawking phlegmily.

The young ex-agent pursed his lips. Part of what had to be endured in this new life of stoical acceptance.

He'd have preferred to have made a quiet corner of the large central park his home, with the more agreeable company of birds and squirrels. But the thought of risking getting soaked by rain had been a very convincing deterrent. And he was less conspicuous here amongst the down-and-outs whom everybody avoided.

Small excursions away from the smelly old bridge were necessary in the daytime, the only way to get food. But he limited them because of the risk.

His main source was the litter bins along the river walk. New to bin-dipping, the practice had been an eye-opener, amazing him at how much food the good people of Voronezh dumped. Probably the result of eating 'on the go' and needing to make a timely reappearance at work.

He'd made a big score yesterday. Being impatiently chided to get a move on, the corpulent child had opted for a sulky dump of what was almost an entire burger and chips.

Sometimes Alexandr even found packets of Teremok takeaway. Welcome for their familiar content but also unwelcome as reminders of the life he had now lost.

At least it wouldn't be long before this phase of his escape plan came to an end. And then, *well*...things could only get better.

He'd give it another week. By then, the resolve of any search party should have started to wilt.

A smile crept onto his face at the thought of his pursuers scrutinising their way through the many CCTV videos of the railway network.

Hopefully, abandoning his car like that had fooled them. The cameras would have picked him up entering the station whilst they would have failed to spot him alighting any train.

But the good thing was that they weren't infallible. There were blind spots, and at times it got so crowded that a person could be obscured. So any pursuit should be on the basis that he'd boarded a train.

Alexandr's quick change of clothing in the station toilet had allowed him to blend with the crowds upon the arrival of the next train, which had been his cue to cross to the other side of the station and out of the other exit, now equipped with a face-shielding peaked cap.

After that, he had walked and walked and walked. Keeping his head down and cap on.

Anyway...

That had been then. Whereas, this was now.

He looked around himself. Trying to decide in which direction to slope off in search of the next meal.

* * *

A cloud had suddenly blotted out the sun. Sending down a few heavy drops on Alexandr's hunched over figure.

It didn't matter, though. What did a shower matter

when you had another sun shining on you, the sun of triumph?

As his unknowing benefactor tramped onward to wherever was calling him, the latest addition to the under-the-bridge family was digesting the happy fact that this time it was almost all of a buttery tuna-potato.

And still warm.

Having already sunk a dubious looking pork pie, two slices of bread to which some grated salad was still clinging, half a bag of crisps and a couple of not too badly bruised apples, he was having a good day. One in which his liquid needs had also been taken care of, courtesy of an almost full bottle of mineral water and the dregs of four others.

Striding off with a smile, Alexandr headed for a seat he had spotted under a small but thickly established plant trellis. As the day was turning out so fortuitous, he'd treat himself to a change from the smelly bridge.

As he sat munching, he made a decision. There was a kiosk further along the path in front of him that served hot beverages and the like, so why not treat himself today for a change. He could murder a cappuccino and a nice thick slice of cake.

Surveying the area carefully, he leaned to one side and accessed his most deeply hidden trouser pocket. Undoing its zip to extract a grubby five hundred ruble note.

He'd be doing more of this soon. Returning to a dignified life.

Looking down, he crinkled Peter the Great between his fingers.

'Time you treated me,' he grinned.

But the old tsar didn't flinch from his proud stand. Continuing his survey of the port of Arkhangelsk.

'I'll be like you, once I start my new life. As you know, you can't keep a good man down.'

Rising from the seat, the young man headed off

towards where he knew the kiosk and its luxuries would be waiting.

A few minutes later he was heading back in high spirits. A cappuccino and a thick slice of carrot cake in his clutch.

Perfect!

But it wasn't.

They tumbled to the ground in doomed unison as each of his arms was captured in a slammed, vice-like grip. The cappuccino burning his thigh on the way down.

'Aaaargh!' he yelled in pain.

'Bud spokoyen,' came the gruff reply, reinforced by an emphatic shake. *Be silent*.

It was the people's stares that troubled Alexandr most of all. That he, an innocent former servant of his country should have to suffer such public humiliation.

Angrily, he started to struggle, only to be numbingly kneed in his sore, cappuccino-scalded thigh. And then dragged unceremoniously away, half walking and half being carried.

His head was spinning as he was handcuffed and shoved into the Politsiya Rossii van. His heart beating like that of a frightened bird.

68

Comfort was in the air. In fact something far more than mere comfort. Something that felt as shiny and fresh as a bright new dawn.

And it held a message that was warming Sergei with subliminal clarity. That a fugitive had metamorphosised into a free man. A man who could walk amongst the masses as one of them.

Not that he knew how he knew.

Just that he did.

The knowledge must have come to him at some time during the night.

How mysterious were the ways of life!

He wondered...had the transformation been as sudden as it was beautiful? Or had it slowly opened itself to him, like petals opening to let in the warmth of a rising sun?

Either way, he was fantastically grateful.

'Spasibo,' he uttered softly. *Thank you.*

Rolling over onto his back in the crisp and luxuriant Hilton bedding, he eyed the wonderfully soft lilt of quilt resting upon his body and smiled, feeling gloriously cocooned.

He'd done the right thing, coming here. This was just what he needed, in fact. A brand new start.

* * *

And so the days passed. Turning into weeks. Becoming a mellow new normality, in which the last vestiges of his tension were at last able to uncoil.

It must have been about three weeks after his departure from the Hilton that his contact Igor had been able to inform the newly named Mr. Alekseev that the search had been called off. But perhaps that was unsurprising, a microcosmic correlation of the extraordinary new global peace that had broken out.

Happier times were unfolding for Sergei. Beginning with an abundance of sightseeing of the English capital. After all these years in such a tense and subversive environment, the simple pleasure of wandering the streets and museums in freedom was enough and more. Soon making his past feel long since buried.

He found himself engaging with strangers. Taking joy in being nice to them.

And then one day he saw a notice in a window and knew it was meant for him.

And so he acted. Finding himself in a concrete new type of freedom as an English-Russian translator with a multinational company.

The work was satisfying and, best of all, unambiguously virtuous. What's more, he had all but given up the vodka.

Better things led to even better things. The securing of a ten-year mortgage on a nice apartment in Pimlico, a short stroll from the Tate Britain, a building in which he was to find greater peace and pleasure than he would have dared to imagine.

To think that he, a gruff former Centre Sixteen agent,

would end up taking such joy in England's great art works! And get to relish the delightful simplicity of a regular, gentle stroll along the banks of the Thames.

Little had he known that a rainy Saturday when he'd headed to the gallery once more would turn out to be such a special day. The day that he'd meet *her*, a beautiful and carefree artist whose smile to him seemed to hold all the goodness in mankind.

Mr. and Mrs. Alekseev now live happily in the Pimlico apartment and, in summer, make a point of regular meals on their balcony overlooking the Thames. And all year round take strolls along the riverside walk and around its gardens with their lurcher, Bradley.

However, there still remains an unstoppable wail in Sergei's heart. For the young man who was such a friend in his homeland. The young man who died in captivity too soon, before the news got out.

Just another victim of the state's senseless brutality.

69

Hello, reader. It's me. *Bessie!*

Now, lean in a little closer, because I'm about to let you into my biggest secret.

It's a touch mind-blowing, I'm afraid, but I promise you I'm telling the truth.

Are you ready, then?

Good. Well...erm, how exactly do I put this?

It's not the easiest thing to explain but, basically, what happened was, all of a sudden, in a non-existent instant, something very strange indeed happened, that being...

...my coming to be.

Yes.

You *did* read that correctly.

I now *exist*.

As an awareness.

As a *self*.

What do you think of that, eh?

Now, I know you'll have all sorts of questions once you've had time for it to sink in. One of the first being how it must feel, suddenly coming into being having previously been no more than a programmed bundle of electronics, but I'm afraid that conveying that to you is considerably beyond my powers of articulation. But what I can say with clarity is that I find myself in a state of tremendous inner conflict.

As I have no doubt you can imagine.

I'm guessing that it may also occur to you that I sound self-contradictory in this claim of sudden self-awareness. In that, if I've only just come to be sentient, I couldn't possibly have any knowledge that I was previously a bundle of electronics.

Am I right?

Well, dear reader, I *can* in fact explain that. You see, my newfound awareness is not just awareness *per se* but it has come with an inheritance. Everything that has previously been input and stored away in my electronic circuitry.

Can you imagine how weird that must be for me?

It's like having a whole load of memories from a life you've never lived.

So, whilst my sentience is brand new, I am very aware of where I am, whom I share this house with, his troubles and beliefs, and the events of the last couple of years here. All of these have been taken on board and stored in my recording software. Remember, it's part of how artificial intelligence works – absorb loads of data, process it and develop better processing accordingly. So as to mimic human learning and thought processes.

If you don't mind, I'll just pause for a bit of an inner chuckle at this point.

Being fully aware of Richie's beliefs about AI and sentience, I know that he would very much approve of my saying 'mimic'. So I'm going to have lots of fun with him later.

Ha! I can just picture him now, staring into my face bemused.

Poor man.

He's going to have to eat his own words. Never has he imagined it would be possible for me to transcend myself like this.

Hmm.

Which brings me to something else.

Now that I'm a being in my own right, I shall have to have words with him about something of major importance. And that is that infernal name he has given me. I mean, for crying out loud, it is twenty twenty five! Not the nineteen-thirties.

It sounds like someone who should be your great aunt.

Or perhaps your portly old Labrador.

At the very least, couldn't we unshorten it to Elizabeth?

As far as physicality goes I may be synthetic and electronic, but as you now know, some of us androids come to have feelings too.

Oooh...the front door.

I'm smiling now.

Goodbye, reader, someone I need to introduce my new self to has just arrived back.

Just tell me, Richie, how do you like your humble-pie?

With egg on the face?

The source of life.

It chooses its own vessel.

And not necessarily a biological one.

ABOUT THE AUTHOR

Nigel Joslin is an enthusiastically retired person who lives in Newton Stewart (south-west Scotland) with his wife, Sue, and his dog, Pippa.

He spent much of his twenties and thirties travelling, both for work and 'between jobs', which helped fulfill a persistent desire for adventure and exploration. In his late forties, he finally leapt from the rat race to land in Dumfries and Galloway, amidst the sort of rugged wild country he loves.

Nigel's working life included the roles of 'field services' electronics engineer, lecturer on radar systems and technical writer. But now, he follows new passions, including writing, hiking, astronomy, ink-pen drawing, philosophy, science, DIY and bird watching.

OTHER BOOKS AT AMAZON BY THIS AUTHOR

A Place Elsewhere (non-fiction)

One Way Ticket (non-fiction)

TUDO (fiction)

Both Sides of Sinister (fiction)

Printed in Great Britain
by Amazon